Lie By Moonlight

Other books by Jayne Ann Krentz writing as Amanda Quick

Wait Until Midnight
The Paid Companion

Other titles by Jayne Ann Krentz

Light in Shadow
Truth of Dare
Falling Awake

Amanda Quick

Lie By Moonlight

PIATKUS

Copyright © 2005 Jayne Ann Krentz

First published in Great Britain in 2005 by
Piatkus Books Ltd of
5 Windmill Street, London W1T 2JA
email: info@piatkus.co.uk

This edition published 2005

First published in the United States in 2005 by
G.P. Putnam's Sons, a member of Penguin Putnam Inc.

The moral right of the author has been asserted

A catalogue record for this book is available from the British Library

ISBN 0 7499 0722 3 (HB)
ISBN 0 7499 3591 X (TPB)

Printed and bound in Great Britain by
MPG Books, Bodmin, Cornwall

This one is for dedicated teachers everywhere.

You change the future every time you walk into a classroom.

Lie By Moonlight

Midnight in a fog-shrouded graveyard. There could be no darker place on the face of the earth, Annie Petrie thought.

She shivered and clutched her cloak more tightly at her throat. She had never been more frightened in her life. But the rumors regarding the man she was here to meet were very plain. An appointment with him was conducted at the time and place of his choosing or not at all.

She had changed her mind a thousand times that day about whether to come here tonight. Her nerves had nearly failed her altogether that morning when she had awakened to discover the note on her bedside table.

She had picked up the piece of paper with shaking fingers, stunned by the realization that he had entered her lodgings in the middle of the night. Somehow he had gotten past her locked doors and shuttered windows. She had never heard so much as a whisper of sound; never sensed his presence. It was as if she had been visited by a ghost.

When she finally calmed down enough to read the brief message, she discovered that it contained a simple list of instructions. In the end, knowing that she would never be able to rest soundly again until she had some answers, she obeyed each item on the list with great care.

The directions had included turning down the lantern when she came through the gates of the cemetery. Now the lamp cast only a weak glare that reflected off the eerie fog. The dark shapes of the stones, crypts and monuments loomed in the vapor-laced shadows.

It took every ounce of will that she possessed to keep moving forward. She had come this far, she told herself. She would not give up now. It was the least she could do for poor Nellie.

"Good evening, Mrs. Petrie."

The voice was as dark and ominous as the graveyard. It emanated from the doorway of a nearby crypt. She froze, too terrified to scream, let alone flee.

A gentleman's voice, she thought. Somehow that knowledge only made her all the more anxious. She managed to turn slowly, straining to make him out in the shadows. But the limited light of the lantern did not spill into the cold darkness that marked the doorway of the old stone crypt.

"I did everything on the list," she said, aware that her own voice was quivering uncontrollably.

"Excellent. Would it surprise you to know that some who make an appointment with me never keep it?"

"No, sir, it wouldn't astonish me in the least to learn that." She was startled to discover that she had a bit of nerve left, after all. "There's not many who would fancy meeting a stranger with your reputation at this hour in a place like this and that's a fact."

"True." He sounded amused. "But I find that such odd times and locations help to eliminate those who are not entirely determined upon their course of action." He paused. "I only work for clients who are resolved to obtain answers, no matter what the cost, you see."

"I've made up my mind, sir."

"I believe you. Now then, why don't we get down to business? I assume this concerns your sister's death two days ago?"

That comment rattled her. "You know about Nellie?"

"When I got word that you wished to meet with me I was naturally curious about your purpose. I made a few inquiries and learned that you had recently lost your sister in a tragic accident."

"That's just it, sir, it weren't no accident," she rasped. "I know that's what the police said, but it's not true."

"Nellie Taylor was found floating facedown in a cold plunge in Doncaster Baths. All the evidence indicated that she slipped on the tiles at the edge of the pool, struck her head, fell into the water and drowned."

The cool, emotionless recitation of the facts ignited the anger and frustration that had been simmering in her since Nellie's death.

"I don't believe it, sir," she said stoutly. "My sister worked in those baths for over ten years, ever since she turned thirteen. Started back in the days when Dr. Doncaster was still giving folks the water cure there. She knew her way around and she was always careful about the wet tiles."

"Accidents do happen, Mrs. Petrie."

"Nellie didn't suffer an accident, I tell you." She clenched the handle of the lantern in her fist. "Someone killed her."

3

"What makes you so certain of that?"

He sounded politely curious.

"Like I said, sir, I don't have any evidence." She swallowed hard and braced her shoulders. "I want you to find the answers for me. Isn't that what you do?"

There was a long silence.

"Yes, Mrs. Petrie, that's what I do," he said. "Tell me more about your sister."

She took another steadying breath and reminded herself to be careful about what she said next. "Nellie worked on the women's side of the baths."

"Her body was found in the cold plunge on the men's side."

"Yes, sir, I know. That's one of the things that makes me suspicious, you see."

"Did she ever have occasion to work in the men's section?"

"Well, yes, once in a while." This was the uncomfortable part, she thought—the part she had hoped to avoid. "Some of the gentlemen will pay extra for a female attendant who will wash their hair or give them a rubdown in a private room."

"I'm aware that such services are available," he said neutrally.

Her stomach chilled with dread. If he believed that Nellie had been a prostitute, he would likely conclude the case was not worth his time.

"It wasn't what you're thinking, sir. Nellie was a respectable, hard-working woman. She was no whore."

"Forgive me. I did not mean to imply that she was."

So polite, she thought, bewildered now. He actually sounded sincere. There weren't many men of his class who would bother to apologize to a shopkeeper such as herself.

"I'm not entirely certain what took place in those private rooms on the gentlemen's side of the baths," she admitted. "All I know is that Nellie worked there occasionally. She said some of the customers asked for her and tipped handsomely for her services."

The man in the doorway of the crypt was silent for so long she began to wonder if he was still there. An unnatural stillness gripped the graveyard.

The gossip that had come to her ears claimed that he could materialize and vanish at will. When she had first heard the stories, she dismissed them as the wildest sort of nonsense. Nevertheless, standing here in a fog-draped cemetery in the middle of the night, it was all too easy to wonder if she had been conversing with a spirit from the Other Side.

Perhaps by day he slept in a coffin inside that very crypt where he had been standing a moment ago.

A thrill of horror electrified her nerves at that thought.

"Do you think that one of Nellie's special gentlemen customers murdered her?" he asked.

"It is the only thing that makes sense to me, sir."

There was another dreadful silence. The fog seemed to be growing heavier, blotting up what little moonlight remained. She could no longer see the outline of the crypt.

"Very well, I will make inquiries for you," he said. "If you're truly certain that you want answers to your questions, that is."

"What do you mean, sir? Why wouldn't I want them?"

"It is not uncommon in affairs of this nature for clients to learn things that they would have preferred not to know about the deceased."

She hesitated. "I understand what you're saying, sir. But Nellie was my sister. Like the rest of us, she only did what she had to do to get by. In her heart, she was a good person. I will not be able to face myself in the mirror if I do not at least try to find out who did that terrible wrong to her."

"I understand, Mrs. Petrie. I will contact you when I have some answers."

"Thank you, sir. I am grateful to you." She cleared her throat. "I hear tell that you charge for your services."

"There is always a fee, Mrs. Petrie."

That sent another shudder through her but she held her ground. "Yes, well, I expect that we had best discuss what I will be expected to pay. I make a fair living selling my parasols, but I am not a wealthy woman."

"I do not charge money for my services, Mrs. Petrie. My fees are more in the nature of favors."

Dread lanced through her. "Begging your pardon, sir, I'm not sure I take your meaning."

"There may come a time when I will have need of a parasol or two. Should that occur, I will send word to you. Do you agree to those terms?"

"Yes, sir," she whispered, baffled. "But I cannot imagine that you'd ever find yourself needing a lady's parasol, sir."

"One never knows. The important thing is that our bargain has been struck. Tell no one that you met with me tonight."

"No, sir, I won't. I promise."

"Good night, Mrs. Petrie."

"Good night, sir." She was not sure what to do next. "Thank you."

She turned and went swiftly back toward the gates. When she reached the entrance of the cemetery, she turned up the lantern and hurried toward the familiar comfort of her snug rooms above the parasol shop.

She had done what she could. The whispers she had heard assured her that, whatever else might be true about the stranger back there in the cemetery, one thing was certain: He could be trusted to keep his word.

2

The second explosion reverberated through the ancient stone walls
that enclosed the secret staircase. The lantern Concordia Glade
clutched in one hand swung gently in response. The low, glary light
splashed wildly into the chilling darkness that surrounded her and the
four young women behind her on the stairs.

Everyone, including Concordia, flinched and caught their breaths.

"What if this stairwell collapses before we reach the bottom?" Hannah Radburn's voice edged precariously toward hysteria. "We'll be
buried alive in here."

"The walls will not collapse," Concordia said with a good deal more
conviction than she felt. She steadied the lantern and pushed her eyeglasses more firmly into place on her nose. "You will recall that we studied
the history of the construction of Aldwick Castle quite thoroughly before
we decided where we would place the incendiary devices. This section
has stood for several hundred years. It is the oldest and strongest part of
the structure, built to withstand catapults. It will not fall apart tonight."

At least, I pray that it won't, she added silently.

The truth of the matter was that the force of the two muffled explosions had greatly exceeded her expectations, to say the least. The first one had taken out the windows in the new wing close to the chamber in which the two men from London had been enjoying their cigars and port after dinner. From her vantage point in the schoolroom in the old section she had seen flames spring up with startling speed and violence.

The second device, timed to burst into flames a few minutes after the first, sounded as if it had done even greater damage.

"That last one was quite loud, wasn't it, Miss Glade?" Phoebe Leyland said uneasily. "I wonder if there was some mistake in the formula we found in that old book."

"The instructions for the mixing of the chemicals were quite clear," Concordia said. "We followed them precisely. It is just that the devices were never meant to be ignited inside a closed room. Naturally they are creating a startling effect. That is precisely what we hoped to achieve."

She kept her tone firm and reassuring. It could be fatal for all of them if she revealed even a hint of the fear that was pounding through her. The lives of the four girls behind her on the staircase were in her hands. If they were to survive and make good their escape, they must remain calm and follow her orders. Hysteria and panic would give rise to certain disaster.

She could hear muffled shouts of alarm from the courtyard. The castle's small staff was responding to the fire. With luck the flames would keep everyone busy long enough for her and the girls to get to the stables.

They had to get out tonight or all was lost. The conversation she had overheard when she eavesdropped on the two men from London this evening had convinced her of that. But secrecy was paramount. She did not doubt for a moment that the coarse, sinister-looking guards who masqueraded as gardeners and workmen on the castle grounds wouldn't hesitate to slit a throat or shoot an innocent at the command of either of the two well-dressed villains from the city.

"It is very dark in here," Hannah said in a small, thin whisper.

Concordia held the lamp a little higher. The stairwell was not only dark, it was narrow and cramped. The descent had not been easy for any of them, but Hannah had a special dread of close, dark spaces.

"We are almost at the bottom of the steps, Hannah," she said reassuringly.

"I smell smoke," sixteen-year-old Theodora Cooper announced.

Her twin sister, Edwina, gasped. "Maybe this wing is on fire, too."

The faint but unmistakable scent drifted ominously up the staircase. Another jolt of fear rattled Concordia's nerves, but she made herself speak with what she thought of as her classroom voice.

"This section of the castle is quite safe," she said. "The only reason we can smell the smoke is because the wind is blowing in this direction tonight. Some of the vapors are seeping in under the door."

"Perhaps we should go back, Miss Glade," Edwina whimpered.

"Don't be silly, Edwina," Phoebe said flatly. "You know very well that there's no going back now. Not unless you want to be taken away by those dreadful men."

Edwina fell silent. So did the others.

Concordia glanced back over her shoulder and smiled at Phoebe.

Like her, the girl wore a pair of spectacles. Behind the lenses of the eye-glasses, her remarkably intelligent blue eyes were filled with a resolve that seemed far too mature for her fifteen years.

During the month that she had been at Aldwick Castle, Concordia had seen similar flashes of a disturbingly adult comprehension of the re-alities of the world in her students. One moment a girl would be caught up in the innocent pleasures and enthusiasms appropriate to a young lady hovering on the brink of womanhood. In the next instant a flicker of fear or melancholia would settle on her, stealing the glow of youth and anticipation from her eyes.

The deep, abiding anxieties that afflicted her students were well founded, Concordia thought. All had been orphaned at some point in the past few months, cast adrift into the merciless seas of life without the support of family or financial resources. Their experience with devastat-ing loss and the fear of an uncertain future gnawed ceaselessly at their valiant young spirits.

Concordia understood. She had lost her parents, and the unconven-tional community that had been her entire world, the year she turned sixteen. That had been a decade ago. The grief and the fear returned fre-quently to haunt her dreams.

"What if the stable is also on fire?" Edwina asked.

"It is on the opposite side of the courtyard," Concordia reminded her. "It will be a long time, if ever, before the fire gets that far."

"Miss Glade is right." Theodora's voice rang with renewed enthusi-asm. "You will recall that we took great care in the placement of the de-vices so that the stables would not be immediately affected."

"The die has been cast," Hannah declared. "We are in the hands of fate."

When she was not obsessed with a seemingly endless list of anxieties, Hannah showed a remarkable gift for drama. She was the youngest of the group, having turned fifteen quite recently, but she often surprised Concordia with her intuitive ability to slip into a role or mimic a person's mannerisms.

"No, we are not in the hands of fate," Concordia said briskly. She looked back over her shoulder. "Do not forget that we have a plan. The only thing that is necessary is to stick to it, and that is precisely what we are going to do."

Theodora, Edwina, Hannah and Phoebe took visible strength from her show of confidence. She had been drilling the importance of The Plan into them for days. It was their talisman in this hour of crisis, just as she had intended. She had learned long ago that as long as one had a plan, one could keep going against great obstacles.

"Yes, Miss Glade." Hannah appeared decidedly more optimistic. Her expressive dark eyes were still very wide but her voice had steadied. "We have all studied The Plan."

"Rest assured, it will work." She reached the bottom of the stairwell and turned to face them once more. "Step One has already been accomplished successfully. We are now ready for Step Two. I will open the door and make certain that the way is clear. Does everyone remember what to do next?"

"We will proceed together to the stables, keeping to the shadows of the old storage sheds along the south wall," Phoebe recited dutifully.

The others nodded in agreement. The hoods of their cloaks were thrown back, revealing the heart-wrenching mix of anxiety and determination in their solemn young faces.

"Does everyone have her bundle?" Concordia asked.

"Yes, Miss Glade," Phoebe said. She clutched her small canvas bag in both hands. It bulged suspiciously in one or two odd places, betraying the scientific instruments stuffed inside.

The apparatus had been part of the collection of books and supplies that Concordia had brought with her to the castle last month.

Earlier that afternoon she had tried one last time to impress upon each girl that only absolute necessities should be packed for this venture. But she was well aware that when one was dealing with young persons, notions of what constituted a *necessity* varied widely.

Hannah Radburn's sack appeared heavier than it should have. Concordia suspected that she had disobeyed instructions and packed one of her precious novels inside.

Theodora's bag was bloated with some of the art supplies she had been told to leave behind.

Edwina's bundle was stuffed with one of the fashionable new gowns that had arrived from London earlier that week.

It was the gift of the expensive dresses that had alerted Concordia to the fact that the situation had become critical.

"Remember," she said gently, "if anything goes wrong, I will give the emergency signal. If that occurs, you must all promise me that you will drop your sacks and run as fast as you can to the stables. Is that quite clear?"

All four immediately tightened their grips protectively around the canvas bundles.

There was a dutiful chorus of "Yes, Miss Glade" but Concordia got a sinking feeling. If disaster befell them, it was going to be difficult to persuade the girls to abandon their possessions. When one was alone in the world, there was a tendency to cling very tightly to whatever had personal meaning.

She could hardly fault her students. She had certainly not set an exemplary example of emergency packing. She would confront the devil himself before she dropped her own canvas sack. It contained a mourning locket with a photograph of her dead parents and the book of philosophy that her father had written and published shortly before his death.

She turned down the lantern. Hannah made a soft, frantic little sound when the stairwell was plunged into deep darkness.

"Calm yourself, dear," Concordia murmured. "We will be outside in a matter of seconds."

She slid the old bolt aside and tugged on the iron handle. It took more effort than she had anticipated to open the ancient oak door. A crack of fire-tinged light appeared. Cold air laced with smoke swept into the stairwell. The shouts of the alarmed men fighting to contain the fire grew much louder.

She could see no one between the door and the first of the old sheds.

"The way is clear," she announced. "Let us be off."

She picked up the darkened lantern and led the way outside. The girls crowded behind her like so many goslings.

The scene that confronted them was lit by a hellish yellow glow. Chaos reigned in the large courtyard. Concordia could see a number of darkly silhouetted figures rushing madly about, calling orders that no one appeared to be obeying. Two men were occupied hauling buckets of water from the well, but it was clear that the small staff of the castle was unprepared to deal with an emergency of this magnitude.

Concordia was stunned to see how much devastation had already been wrought. Only a few minutes ago the flames had been long, searing tongues licking from the gaping mouths of a few shattered windows. In the short span of time it had taken her and the girls to descend the ancient staircase, the fire had grown into an inferno that was rapidly consuming the entire new wing.

"Oh my," Theodora whispered. "They will never be able to quench those flames. I wouldn't be surprised if the entire castle burns to the ground before dawn."

"I never thought the formula would create a fire of that size," Phoebe said, awed.

"We have got just the distraction we require," Concordia said. "Hurry, everyone. We do not have a moment to spare."

She went forward quickly, conscious of the weight of her cloak and gown. It was not just the long skirts and heavy material that made running difficult tonight. Over the course of the past few weeks she had sewn a number of small items that looked as if they could be pawned into hidden, makeshift pockets. The idea was that the stolen goods would eventually be used to sustain them when she took the girls into hiding. But at the moment each item felt like a block of lead.

The girls stayed close behind her, moving easily in skirts that had been stitched together to form wide-legged trousers.

They fled in a tight cluster past the row of sagging, boarded-up outbuildings that had once housed grain and supplies for the castle.

A short time later they rounded the corner of the old smithy. The stables loomed ahead in the shadows.

Concordia was concentrating on the next phase of The Plan when a large man moved out of the shadow of the remains of the ancient windmill and planted himself squarely in her path.

There was enough light from the glare of fire and moon to make out his thick features. She recognized Rimpton, one of the two men who had arrived from London earlier in the day. His coat was tattered and singed.

He held a gun in one hand.

She froze. The girls did the same, perhaps instinctively imitating her in the face of danger.

"Well, now, if it isn't the teacher and all her pretty little students," Rimpton said. "And just where d'ya think you're going?"

Concordia tightened her fingers into a death grip around the handle of the lantern. "We're escaping the flames, you dolt. Kindly get out of our way."

He peered at her more closely. "You're heading for the stables, ain't ye?"

"It would appear to be the building that is farthest away from the fire," Concordia said, putting every ounce of disdain she felt for the brute into the words.

She had disliked Rimpton on sight. There had been no mistaking the lecherous manner in which he had looked at the girls.

"You're up to some trick," Rimpton said.

"Hannah?" Concordia said, not taking her eyes off Rimpton.

"Y-yes, Miss Glade?"

"Kindly demonstrate Araminta's response to Lockheart's surprising revelation in *Sherwood Crossing*."

Rimpton's heavy face screwed into a confused knot. "What the bloody hell—?"

But Hannah had already taken the invisible stage. She launched herself wholeheartedly into the role of Araminta, the heroine of the sensation novel she had finished reading the week before.

Uttering a choked cry of anguish and despair, she crumpled to the ground in a perfectly executed swoon that would have done credit to the most talented actress.

Startled, Rimpton swung his big head around to peer at the fallen girl. "What's that silly little bitch think she's about? I've had enough of this nonsense."

"Not quite," Concordia muttered.

She swung the unlit lantern with all her might. The heavy base crashed violently against the back of Rimpton's skull. Glass crackled and splintered.

Stunned, Rimpton sagged to his knees. Incredibly, he still gripped the revolver.

He was only dazed, Concordia realized, not unconscious. She watched in horror as he tried to regain his feet.

Frantic, she raised the lantern and brought it crashing down a second time, putting everything she had into the blow.

Rimpton uttered a strange grunt and fell flat on his face. He did not move. The gun clattered on the stones. There was enough light to see the dark wetness seeping heavily from the wound and pooling around his head.

There was an instant of shocked silence. Then Hannah scrambled awkwardly erect and picked up her bundle. She and the other girls stared at Rimpton, stricken with the effects of the sudden violence.

"Come along," Concordia said, fighting to sound cool and in control. Her fingers trembled in a very annoying fashion when she bent down to scoop up the gun that Rimpton had dropped. "We are close to the stables. Hannah, that was a very effective piece of acting."

"Thank you, Miss Glade." Hannah spoke automatically. She seemed unable to take her eyes off the fallen Rimpton. "Is he . . . is he dead?"

"He looks dead," Phoebe whispered.

"Serves him right," Edwina said with a surprising show of satisfaction. "He and his friend Mr. Bonner were the two who took Miss Bartlett away. We told you that they did something dreadful to her. Everyone said she'd gone back to London on the train, but she would never have left her new gloves behind the way she did."

"This way, ladies," Concordia said. She no longer doubted the girls' theory concerning the disappearance of her predecessor at the castle. "Stay close."

Her crisp instructions had the effect of freeing the girls from the morbid spell cast by the too-quiet Rimpton. Hurriedly, they regrouped behind her.

She guided them through the shadows, tensely aware that the most difficult part of The Plan lay ahead. The task of getting the horses tacked up in the dark was not going to be easy, although she had made everyone practice the maneuvers many times.

Crocker, the man in charge of the stables, had shrugged and shown little interest when she told him that the girls must be allowed to ride regularly as part of their exercise program. There had been no proper sidesaddles available, but Crocker, after some prodding, managed to produce three worn farmers' saddles and bridles to go with them.

The only horses on the castle grounds were the sturdy, patient beasts used to provide transportation to the village and to haul supplies.

Fortunately, Edwina and Theodora had been raised on a wealthy estate. They had learned to ride from the cradle and were quite expert. They had been able to serve as instructors to Phoebe, Hannah and Concordia. In the way of youth, Phoebe and Hannah had picked up the basic skills very quickly.

Concordia, however, had experienced considerably more difficulty. She doubted that she would ever feel entirely comfortable on the back of a horse.

To her enormous relief, they did not encounter anyone else when they moved into the deeper shadows of the stables. As she had hoped, all of the men were occupied with fighting the fire.

The three horses were alert and agitated. Concordia heard hooves stamp restlessly in the darkness. Soft, uneasy whickers rumbled from the stalls. There was enough fiery light to illuminate the three equine heads turned anxiously toward the entrance. Every set of ears was pricked violently forward. Although the building was not yet in any immediate danger from the flames, the animals had caught the scent of smoke and heard the shouts of the men.

Concordia opened the door of the tack room, moved inside and struck one of the lights she had brought with her.

"Quickly, girls," she said. "We do not have a minute to spare. Put down your bundles and see to the horses."

The students dumped their canvas bags on the floor and rushed to collect blankets, saddles and bridles.

Concordia was relieved to note that the endless drills were now paying off handsomely. The process of tacking up the horses went swiftly and smoothly.

Edwina and Theodora had decided in advance who would ride which horse. The twins took the liveliest of the three mounts, a mare, on the grounds that they'd had the most experience and would be better able to handle her if she got nervous. Phoebe and Hannah were assigned to a good-natured gelding.

Concordia got the second gelding in the stable, a heavy-boned beast named Blotchy. Edwina and Theodora had made the decision based on their assessment of the horse's exceptionally placid personality. Under normal circumstances, it took a great deal of encouragement to get Blotchy to move at anything beyond a jolting trot. His great redeeming characteristic, according to the twins, was that he had virtually no inclination to startle and was unlikely to bolt or throw Concordia to the ground.

She put Rimpton's gun down on a wooden bench and held out the bridle, trying not to reveal her trepidation. Blotchy obligingly thrust his head into the leathers and took the bit. He seemed as eager to leave the premises as she and the girls were.

"Thank you, Blotchy," she whispered, adjusting the bridle. "Please be patient with me. I know I'm a very poor rider. But I need your help quite desperately tonight. We must get these girls away from this evil place."

She led him out of the stall and picked up the gun. With a soft rustle of straw and the squeak of leather, Edwina and Phoebe emerged from the other two stalls, each with a horse in tow.

They got the three horses saddled. The canvas bundles were slung over the hindquarters of each animal and secured with straps.

"Mount," Concordia ordered.

In the systematic manner that they had rehearsed many times, each horse was led to the block. Edwina and Theodora got aboard the mare. Phoebe and Hannah swung onto the other horse with reassuring ease.

Concordia waited until last, never taking her attention off the entrance of the stable.

When her turn came, she pushed the folds of her cloak out of the way, stowed the gun in one of the pockets of the garment and stepped up onto the block.

"I appreciate your patience and understanding in this matter, Blotchy."

She put the toe of her shoe into the stirrup and hoisted herself aboard Blotchy's broad back. The gelding started forward with unaccustomed eagerness. She seized the reins in both hands.

"Steady," she said. "Please."

A lantern flared at the stable entrance.

A beefy-looking man stood silhouetted behind the light. The glow of the lantern danced on the gun in his hand.

"So here's where all the pretty little trollops went," he said. "And their teacher, too. Had a hunch when I didn't find you in your rooms that you'd likely run off."

Concordia's blood turned to ice. She recognized the voice. It belonged to Rimpton's companion, Bonner.

"Step aside, sir," she said, forcing every ounce of authority she possessed into her voice. "I must take the students to a safer location."

"Shut up, you stupid woman." He swung the barrel of the gun toward her. "I'm not a fool. If you'd fled straight from your beds in mortal terror of the flames, you'd all be wearing your nightclothes. Instead you're all dressed for a walk in the park. I know full well what's going on here. You're trying to steal the girls, aren't you?"

"We're attempting to get to safety," Concordia said coldly. "The students are my responsibility."

"I'll wager you found out that the chits are valuable, didn't you? Thought you'd try your hand at turning a profit with 'em, yerself, eh?"

"I have no idea what you are talking about, sir."

Surreptitiously she transferred the reins to her left hand and touched the pocket that concealed Rimpton's gun. Unable to think of any other strategy, she kept Blotchy moving steadily forward.

"You must be a complete fool to think you could get away with stealing Larkin's property and that's a fact." Bonner snorted in disgust. "You're a dead woman, that's what you are."

She slid her free hand into the pocket of her cloak. Her fingers closed around the gun. "Sir, you are speaking nonsense. These students are my responsibility and I must get them away from the fire. The flames are spreading quite rapidly, in case you have not noticed."

"I've noticed. And the more I think about it, the more I'm convinced that damned blaze was no accident." He finally became aware that Blotchy was bearing down on him. "Halt right there."

"You are putting these girls in jeopardy. If they are as valuable as you say, this Larkin person you mentioned will not be pleased to know that they are at risk."

"If you don't stop that damned nag, I'll kill you right now," he warned.

Blotchy abruptly lurched to the left. Concordia did not know if she had confused him with her less than expert handling of the reins or if he simply had had enough of the alarming late-night activity and decided to go his own way.

Whatever the reason, she was forced to remove her hand from the gun in her pocket in order to control the horse and maintain her balance. Blotchy responded to her sudden tightening of the reins by turning in a tight circle and tossing his head.

"Control that bloody horse," Bonner ordered, stepping hurriedly back out of the way.

It dawned on her that he was even less familiar with horses than she. Bonner was clearly a city man, born and bred. Only the wealthy could afford to keep private stables in town. Everyone else either walked or summoned a cab or an omnibus when they required transportation. The villain was expensively dressed, but his harsh accent gave him away. He was a product of the streets, not of Society. It was doubtful that he had ever ridden a horse in his life.

"Have a care with that weapon, sir," she said, struggling with the reins. "If you fire it in these close quarters, all of the horses will take fright. They will likely bolt for the entrance and trample everything in their path."

Bonner looked quickly at each of the three horses. He finally understood that he was the only object standing between them and the entrance. He set the lantern down and took an uneasy step back.

"See to it that you all keep those bloody nags under control."

"We're doing our best, sir, but I fear you are making them restless." She tugged on the reins, urging Blotchy into another tight circle. Halfway around she reached into her pocket, grasped the revolver and pulled it out.

She could only hope to take the man by surprise and pray that she could keep her seat if Blotchy bolted when the gun fired.

She came out of the circle clutching the gun.

Before she could steady herself to fire the shot, the dark figure of a man materialized out of the shadows near the entrance. He glided soundlessly up behind Bonner and made two short, brutal chopping motions with his hands.

The villain jerked violently, as though he had been shocked by a jolt of electricity. He crumpled to the ground.

There was a deathly silence. Concordia and the girls stared at the stranger.

He glided toward Concordia.

"You must be the teacher," he said.

She finally remembered that she was still holding a gun.

"Who are you?" she demanded. "What are you about?"

He did not pause. When he went through the lantern light Concordia saw that he was dressed entirely in black. The light flickered briefly on dark hair and cold, stern features. Before she could get a closer look, he moved out of the light and back into the shadows.

"I suggest we discuss the matter after we are all safe," he said. "Unless you have some objections?"

He had just felled the man from London with a single blow. That certainly seemed to indicate that he was not on the side of the mysterious Larkin. An old axiom flashed across Concordia's memory. *The enemy of my enemy is my friend.*

She could use a friend tonight.

"No objections whatsoever, sir." She put the gun back into her pocket.

"I am relieved to hear that." He looked at the students. "Can these young ladies ride reasonably well?"

"They are all very capable in the saddle," she assured him, not without a touch of pride.

He caught hold of Blotchy's bridle and steadied the gelding. "That is the first bit of good news I have received on what has otherwise proven to be a rather disastrous night."

He unfastened the bundle she had so carefully strapped to the back of the saddle.

"That's mine," she said sharply. "I cannot leave it behind."

"Then I suggest that you hold onto it."

She tucked the bag under one arm, juggling the reins with her free hand.

Powerful fingers closed around her ankle.

Startled, she looked down. "What do you think you are doing, sir?"

It was immediately clear that he was not interested in taking liberties. Instead he deftly slid her foot out of the stirrup, inserted the toe of his boot into the iron and vaulted smoothly up behind her.

He took the reins from Concordia's fingers in one hand and then edged Blotchy closer to the other two horses.

"Please give me the reins, ladies," he said. "The smoke has grown extremely heavy outside. It will provide good cover but it will also make it difficult to see each other if we become separated."

Edwina and Phoebe handed the reins to him without demur.

"Right, then, we're off," he said.

The stranger did something with his knees that made the gelding surge forward.

The violence of the horse's forward lunge caught Concordia by surprise. She very nearly dropped her bundle when she grabbed wildly for the front of the saddle.

"My students are all excellent riders, sir," she got out in a half-strangled voice. "But I regret to say that I, myself, am still something of a novice."

"In that case, I suggest you hang on very tightly. You have caused me more than enough trouble tonight. If you fall, I cannot promise you that I will be in a mood to stop to pick you up."

Something told her he might well mean every word of the warning. She clung to the saddle for dear life.

Beneath the cover of the dense smoke and the noise created by the catastrophic flames and the men's confusion, they galloped out of the stable and pounded toward the southern gate.

Concordia knew that she would always recall two things about that night with vivid clarity for the rest of her life: the astonishing roar of the fire as it consumed the castle and the strength and power of the stranger's body pressed tightly against her as they rode to safety.

3

The stranger brought the small group to a halt on the low mound of a hill on the far side of the river.

Unaccustomed to such sustained exertion, Blotchy and the other two horses were quite willing to stop. They stood, heads drooping, sides heaving, and blew heavily through flaring nostrils.

Breathless from the reckless flight, Concordia looked back toward the fiery scene. The light of the moon bathed the landscape in an other-worldly glow. The flames were a red-gold torch in the night. The acrid scent of the smoke was strong, even from this distance.

"Look." Phoebe pointed. "The fire has reached the old wing. It is fortunate that we did not try to hide in one of the rooms in that section."

"The entire castle will soon be in ashes," Theodora said, her voice soft with amazement.

Concordia felt the stranger's hard body shift slightly behind her when he turned to study the scene in the distance.

"I assume the fire is your work, ladies?" he asked.

He sounded thoughtful, as if he were assessing and analyzing some new, extremely interesting discovery that had heretofore escaped his attention.

"Phoebe and Miss Glade mixed the formula for the incendiary devices," Hannah said. "Edwina, Theodora and I sewed the fuses. They had to be very long and thin so they would not be noticed running along the edge of the wall behind the furniture."

"And they had to be fashioned of material that would not burn either too quickly or too slowly," Theodora added.

"We ran several experiments," Edwina put in.

"Miss Glade hid the devices and strung the fuses in the rooms where we knew that the men from London would likely take their cigars and port after dinner," Hannah explained.

"Miss Glade lit the fuses," Phoebe concluded. "It all went just as we had planned." She paused and turned back to view the flames in the distance. "Except that we did not realize that the devices would ignite such a huge blaze."

"Impressive, indeed," the stranger said dryly. "Well, I have only myself to blame for this miscalculation. There were rumors in the village that there was some sort of girls' boarding school at the castle but I thought it was merely a false story that had been spread around the neighborhood to conceal whatever was really going on there."

He handed the reins back to Edwina and Phoebe.

Concordia was intensely conscious of him crowded behind her in what could only be described as an extremely intimate manner. The immediate danger was past. It was time to regain control of the situation.

"We are indebted to you for your assistance, sir, but I must insist that you tell us who you are."

"My name is Ambrose Wells."

"I want more than a name, Mr. Wells," she said quietly.

He kept his gaze on the fire. "I am the man whose carefully crafted plans have just been cast into complete disarray by you and your students."

"Explain yourself, sir."

"Will you oblige me with your name and the names of the young ladies first? I believe I deserve a proper introduction after what we have just been through together."

She felt herself grow very warm at the implication that she had been rude. Ambrose Wells had been exceedingly helpful this evening, she reminded herself. The least she could do now was treat him with a modicum of civility.

"Yes, of course," she said, softening her voice. "I am Concordia Glade. I was hired to teach these young ladies. Edwina and Theodora Cooper, Hannah Radburn and Phoebe Leyland."

"Ladies." Ambrose inclined his head in a gallant acknowledgment of the introduction.

The girls murmured polite responses. Good manners that had been learned young rarely failed, even in a crisis, Concordia mused.

"Now, may I ask why you happened to be so conveniently at hand to aid us in our escape?" she asked.

He tightened the reins, turned Blotchy's head away from the view of the burning castle and urged the horse forward.

"The answer to your question is rather complicated, Miss Glade. I think it had better wait until we have settled into more comfortable circumstances. Your students are clearly an intrepid lot, but I suspect that they have had enough excitement for one evening. They will soon be exhausted. I suggest we find lodging for what remains of the night."

"Do you think it safe to put up at an inn?" Concordia asked.

"Yes."

She frowned. "No offense, but I do not agree with your opinion on the matter, sir. My plan was to ride as far as possible before dawn, keeping away from the main road. I intended for us to eventually stop in some concealed place—a stand of trees, perhaps—to rest and eat the food we brought with us."

"Did you? That sounds extraordinarily uncomfortable to me. Personally, I think a bed and a meal at an inn would be far more pleasant."

It was becoming clearer by the moment that Ambrose Wells was not accustomed to taking anyone else's advice or direction.

"You do not appear to comprehend the full extent of the danger, Mr. Wells. I fear that once they have recovered their senses, those two men from London will search for us."

"Rest assured, neither of those two villains will conduct any searches either tonight or in the future."

The cold, too-even tone of his voice sent an icy chill of dread through her.

"Are you quite, uh, certain, sir?" she asked uneasily.

"Yes, Miss Glade, I am certain. One is dead. When the other man awakens he will be dazed and disoriented for some time." He adjusted the reins slightly, causing Blotchy to pick up his pace. "I assume it was you who felled the man I found on the ground near the old storage sheds?"

She swallowed heavily. "You saw him?"

"Yes."

"And he was . . . ?"

"Yes."

She gripped her bundle very tightly. "I've never done anything like that before."

"You did what was necessary, Miss Glade."

The second blow she had struck with the lantern had, indeed, killed Rimpton, after all. A shudder went through her. She felt a little ill.

Another thought struck her. She swallowed hard. "I shall be wanted for murder now."

"Calm yourself, Miss Glade. When the local authorities eventually sort out the disaster at the castle, assuming they ever manage to do so, the death will be attributed to an accident that occurred while he was attempting to fight the fire and escape the flames."

"How can you be so sure of that?"

There was enough moonlight to illuminate the wry twist of his hard mouth. "Rest assured, Miss Glade, it will not occur to anyone to consider the possibility that a female who makes her living as a teacher of young ladies might have been capable of dispatching a hardened criminal with a gun."

"What of the man you injured? Won't he tell everyone what happened?"

"When he awakens he will very likely recall nothing of the events immediately before he was knocked unconscious."

She gripped her bundle very tightly. "It occurs to me, sir, that you know precisely what happened at the castle tonight."

"So do you, Miss Glade. It appears that neither of us has any choice at the moment but to trust each other."

4

Shortly after one o'clock in the morning, Ambrose at last found him-self alone with Concordia in the inn's otherwise deserted public room. The flames of the fire that the innkeeper had rekindled for his late-night guests cast a mellow glow across furnishings that had been worn and scarred by generations of travelers.

Upon their arrival, the weary students had been fed cold meat and potato pies by the innkeeper's sleepy wife and then shepherded upstairs to their beds. The proprietors of the establishment had then locked up for the second time that evening and retreated to their own bedroom.

Ambrose poured a glass of the innkeeper's sherry and handed it to Concordia.

She frowned. "I really don't—"

"Drink it," he ordered quietly. "It will help you sleep."

"Do you think so?" She accepted the sherry and took a tentative sip. "Thank you."

He nodded. She was still extremely wary of him, he thought. He could not blame her. He had some questions of his own concerning her role in the affair at the castle tonight.

He went to stand at the hearth, one arm resting on the mantel and considered his companion for a long moment.

Firelight played on her sleekly coiled brown hair and glinted on the round gold frames of her eyeglasses. She was somewhere in her mid-twenties, he decided. Her features lacked the classically correct planes and angles that were traditionally associated with feminine beauty, but he nevertheless found her quite riveting. There was a deeply compelling aspect to her smoky green eyes. In them he saw the hard-learned caution of a far older and more experienced woman.

The tight bodice of her gown revealed the outlines of small, elegant breasts and the curve of a waist that was not quite as tiny as fashion decreed. The recent forced intimacy that had resulted from sharing the back of a horse with her had informed him that the lady possessed a charmingly rounded derriere.

He had never been a strict follower of female fashions, he thought. Concordia's proportions might not conform to those illustrated in the magazines and journals of style but they suited him very well.

There was pride and grace in the way she held herself. Intelligence and a certain vital inner force that he recognized as a sturdy, indomitable spirit marked her in a way that no cosmetics ever could. Even now, exhausted as he knew she must be, there was an irrepressible energy and determination about her that elicited admiration.

No, not admiration, he reflected, *desire.* That was what she elicited in him. It was disturbing, but there was no point ignoring facts.

Part of his reaction was purely physical, he knew. It could be attributed to the familiar aftereffects of danger and those two hours spent riding behind her on the horse. Also, Concordia Glade was still very much a mystery. He was driven by nature and training to look beneath the surface for answers.

But none of those entirely logical reasons fully explained the inexplicable fascination that he was experiencing for this woman tonight.

He watched Concordia take another swallow of sherry. The glass trembled ever so slightly in her fingers. Tension, danger and the effects of fear were catching up with her. He suspected that the worst was yet to come. That would happen when the reality of the fact that she was responsible for crushing a man's skull struck home.

Such soul-shivering realizations tended to occur at night, he had learned. Dark thoughts thrived in the dark hours. If his personal experience with violence was anything to go by, Concordia would likely find herself awakening in cold sweats from time to time, not just in the days ahead, but weeks, months or years from now.

The knowledge that the act had been committed to save her students as well as herself would do little to quell the nightmares. His training had taught him to think of violence as a dangerous form of alchemy. It gave the one who wielded it great power, but it exacted a heavy price.

"If you would prefer, we can conduct this conversation in the morning after you have had some rest," he said, surprising himself with the offer. He had not intended to make it. He wanted answers immediately, not tomorrow. So much had gone wrong today. All of his carefully constructed plans had gone up, quite literally, in smoke. A new scheme had to be formulated as swiftly as possible.

But he could not bring himself to push her any further tonight.

"No." She lowered the sherry and faced him resolutely. "I think it would be best if we answered each other's questions now. To begin, I wish to know how and why you came to be at the castle tonight. What was your purpose there?"

"I have been watching the comings and goings at the castle from the cover of an abandoned farmer's cottage nearby for twenty-four hours. I was waiting for a certain man to arrive. My informant told me that he was due soon. Tomorrow or the next day at the latest. Given events this evening, I think it is safe to say that it is more than likely that he will not show up, however."

"Who is this man?"

"Alexander Larkin." He watched her closely to see if the name meant anything to her.

Her eyes widened behind the lenses of her spectacles. "I heard the name Larkin spoken occasionally at the castle, but always in hushed whispers. It was clear that I was not meant to overhear any references to him. But tonight his name came up again, in a manner of speaking."

"What do you mean?"

"The second villain from London, the one who confronted us in the stables, said something about me being a complete fool to think that I could get away with stealing Larkin's property." Her fingers tightened visibly on the glass. "He also said . . . well, never mind. It is no longer important."

"What did he also say?" Ambrose prodded gently.

"He said, 'You're a dead woman, that's what you are.'" She straightened her already very straight shoulders. "What do you know of this Alexander Larkin?"

"He is one of the most notorious figures in London's underworld, a master criminal or a sort of crime lord, if you like. He worked his way up from the toughest streets in the city. He now lives the life of a wealthy gentleman, but he lacks any genuine social connections and, of course, is not received in Society."

"All of the trappings of the upper classes but not a part of that world." She turned the sherry glass between her palms as though trying to warm her fingers. "Just like any other wealthy man who made his fortune in trade, I suppose."

"He is certainly in trade. Larkin has financial interests in a variety of illegal enterprises including brothels and opium dens. He has been suspected in a number of murders over the years. But he has always been extremely careful to keep a discreet distance between himself and his criminal activities. The result is that the police have never been able to obtain enough evidence to arrest him."

Her mouth tightened. "That would appear to confirm my students' theory about what happened to my predecessor at the castle."

"There was another teacher before you?"

"Yes. A Miss Bartlett. She was there for only a few weeks. One afternoon Rimpton and his companion arrived at the castle. That night the girls were locked in their bedroom. When they were let out the next morning, Miss Bartlett was gone. So were the two men from London.

The castle staff told the girls that Miss Bartlett had been dismissed from her post and that the men had escorted her, together with her trunk, to the train station very early that morning. But the girls were convinced that the men had done something terrible to Miss Bartlett."

"What made them suspicious?"

"Miss Bartlett left a few things behind, including a favorite pair of gloves."

He raised his brows. "An astute observation."

"The girls are far more observant than anyone at the castle gave them credit for." Concordia angled her chin. "Those who find themselves alone and without resources very quickly learn to pay attention to the little things going on around them—things that others might ignore."

"I am well aware of that, Miss Glade."

She gave him a long, measuring look. "Are you?"

"Yes."

He said nothing more, but she appeared to accept his assurance.

"As it happens, I eventually concluded that the girls may have been right about what had happened to their first teacher," she said after a while. "I did not immediately subscribe to that notion, you understand. I am very well aware that young ladies can be extremely imaginative, especially when they have been left to their own devices for long periods of time. For the most part my students were ignored while they were at the castle. Until I arrived, that is."

"I imagine that you kept them well occupied," he said, amused.

"I do not believe in strict regimentation, Mr. Wells, but I have found that a certain amount of order and routine provides a sense of stability that is quite comforting for many young people, especially those who have been orphaned."

He was impressed with her insights. "Please continue."

She cleared her throat. "When the girls showed me the gloves they had found in the room that Miss Bartlett had used while she was at the castle, I admit that I became quite curious. A teacher's pay is not so generous that she can afford to be reckless with her possessions. And the gloves were, indeed, quite new and rather expensive-looking."

He raised his brows, acknowledging the point. "When did the girls tell you of their suspicions?"

"Not for some time. They were very cautious around me at first." She moved one hand in a small, dismissive gesture. "Only to be expected. They have been through so much upheaval and turmoil in their young lives. They are naturally quite careful about whom they take into their confidence."

"You seem to have an excellent understanding of young people, Miss Glade."

"To be honest, by the time they told me of Miss Bartlett's mysterious departure, I had already begun to realize that there was something very odd, to say the least, about the entire situation." She sighed. "Actually, I sensed from the start that matters were not as they seemed at Aldwick Castle."

"What alerted you?"

"You know what they say about things that appear too good to be true."

He considered that for a moment. "I beg your pardon, Miss Glade, but why would a post teaching four young ladies at a remote, tumble-down castle far from the nearest town seem too good to be true? It sounds quite the opposite to me."

"One's perception of a post often depends upon the condition of one's circumstances at the time the post is offered," she said dryly.

"Point taken."

"As it happens, I had just been dismissed from a very pleasant situation at a school for girls not far from London. I was quite desperate for a new position. When the letter from Mrs. Jervis arrived with the offer of the post at the castle, I was extremely grateful and accepted immediately."

He frowned. "Who is Mrs. Jervis?"

"The woman who operates the agency that found me the position at the girls' school. She supplies teachers and governesses to schools and private households."

He nodded. "What information were you given concerning the position at the castle?"

"I was told that a new charity school for orphaned young ladies had been established at Aldwick Castle. I was to be the new headmistress. It was made clear that there were only four students in residence but that more would be arriving in the future. It all seemed . . ." She gave a tiny, forlorn little shrug. "Quite wonderful. My dream come true, if you will."

"What is your dream, Miss Glade?"

"To be in charge of a school of my own." In spite of her exhaustion,

41

she suddenly became more animated. "One where I can put into practice my personal philosophy and ideas concerning the education of girls."

"I see." Curiosity tugged at him, but this was not the time to pursue questions about her dream. "Were you told the name of the benefactor of the girls' academy at Aldwick Castle?"

He did not realize how sharply he had spoken until he saw her stiffen warily.

"The letter from the agency mentioned a certain Mrs. Jones," she said. "I was informed that she was a wealthy, reclusive widow."

"What else were you told?"

"Very little. Only that I would have complete discretion concerning the instruction that I was to provide. Mrs. Jones's single requirement was that the reputation of the students be guarded with great care. After I got to Aldwick Castle, I was delighted with my four students. Phoebe, Hannah, Edwina and Theodora proved to be intelligent, eager pupils. What more can a teacher ask? But, as I said, I knew that something was amiss."

"I think it is safe to say that there never was a Mrs. Jones. What else besides the discovery of Miss Bartlett's gloves raised your suspicions?"

"The housekeeper was a sullen creature who kept to herself as much as possible. I later learned that she was addicted to opium. I was forced to have several stern talks with the cook, who showed no interest in preparing healthy meals for the students. The man in charge of the stables was a lazy drunkard. The gardeners never tended the gardens and"—she paused, eyes narrowing slightly—"they carried guns."

"Guards, not gardeners."

"That was certainly how it appeared to me." She took one more sip of the sherry and slowly lowered the glass. "But the things that concerned me the most were the gowns."

He looked at her. "What gowns?"

"Ten days ago a dressmaker came all the way from London. She brought with her bolts of expensive fabrics and three seamstresses. Several lovely new gowns were made for all of the girls. I was told that Mrs. Jones wanted the students to be prepared to take their places in Society. But that made no sense."

"Why do you say that?"

She did not bother to conceal her impatience with the question. "The young ladies were all born into respectable families. Indeed, Edwina and Theodora once lived a very privileged life. But all of them are now orphans. None can claim any property or inheritances or social connections. They have a few distant relations but none who cared enough to step forward to take them into their homes."

He contemplated that briefly. "I see what you mean. None of them can expect to move into Society."

"Precisely. At best they can only look forward to careers as teachers or governesses. Why provide them with gowns that are suited to the ballroom and the theater?"

"Obviously you suspected the worst."

"Yes, Mr. Wells, I did." One hand clenched in her lap. "I came to the conclusion that my students were being prepared to be sold as expensive, fashionable courtesans."

"It's a possibility, I suppose," he said, thinking it over. "As I told you, Larkin does have extensive interests in a number of brothels."

"You must have seen some of the scandals in the press concerning the trade in young girls who are taken out of orphanages and sent to work as prostitutes. It is quite appalling. And the police have done very little to halt the business."

"Yes, but your girls were not packed off to a brothel. They were sent to Aldwick Castle. A teacher was employed. You said yourself the girls' reputations were to be carefully preserved and guarded."

"I do not believe that my girls were intended to become ordinary prostitutes. Consider the facts, Mr. Wells. All four of my young ladies were brought up in respectable circumstances. They are well mannered, well bred and well educated. They speak with the refined accents of their social class."

"In other words, they did not come from the streets."

"No. I am not naïve, sir. I have been out in the world for some time. I am well aware that there is a market for exclusive courtesans who can emulate ladies who move in respectable circles."

He managed to conceal his surprise. Her casual acknowledgment of certain realities was oddly disconcerting. Women of her class rarely discussed such matters, let alone in a matter-of-fact fashion.

"True," he admitted.

"How much more valuable would those women be if they actually came from good social circles and possessed the airs and graces to prove it? To say nothing of innocence, youth and pristine reputations?"

"I will not argue with you on that account. Nevertheless—"

"Tonight I overheard Rimpton and his companion discussing some sort of auction that was to be held in the near future. I am certain that they meant that my students were to be sold to the highest bidders."

"An auction?"

Her hand tightened in her lap. "Yes."

He hesitated, thinking it through, and then nodded slowly. "You may be right. It would certainly explain a great many curious aspects of this situation."

"What is your interest in this affair, sir? Why were you watching the castle and waiting for Larkin's arrival?" Her expression brightened. "Are you a policeman? Scotland Yard, perhaps?"

"No. I am engaged in a private inquiry on behalf of a client who hired me to discover the truth about her sister's death."

"You're a private inquiry agent?" She was clearly startled. But in the next instant curiosity flared in her fine eyes. "How interesting. I have never met anyone engaged in that profession."

"I hope you continue to find me interesting, Miss Glade, because we are going to be seeing a great deal of each other for the foreseeable future."

"I beg your pardon?"

He left the mantel and went to stand in front of her. "After what occurred at the castle tonight, Larkin will assume that you are aware of some of his plans. He will also want what he views as his property returned. That means that he will do his best to find you and the girls."

She went very still. "I realize that he will not like the fact that I spir-
ited the girls away from the castle. That is why I intend to take them into
hiding for a time."

He reached down, closed his hands around her upper arms and
lifted her gently but firmly out of the chair. "You do not comprehend the
nature of the beast that you are dealing with. I doubt very much that you
have the resources to hide yourself from Alexander Larkin, let alone
conceal the young ladies."

"I was thinking that perhaps if we went to Scotland—"

"You could take your girls to the South Seas and still not be safe, not
if Larkin makes up his mind to track you down. And I believe that he
will try to do just that."

"For a few weeks or even a month or two, perhaps," she agreed
calmly. "But I cannot imagine that he will waste a great deal of time and
energy chasing four girls and their teacher. Surely a crime lord, as you
call him, has more important matters to occupy his attention."

"Nothing is more important to Larkin than his own survival. I think
it is safe to say that he will not rest until he has satisfied himself that you
are no longer a threat to him."

"How can I possibly be any sort of threat to a man like him?" She was
clearly exasperated. "I am a *teacher,* for heaven's sake. I have no social
connections, no power of any sort. I am in no position to do anything
that could cause problems for Alexander Larkin. He must know that as
well as I do."

"You are a loose end, Miss Glade. When Larkin weaves a pattern he
does not leave any dangling threads. As soon as he discovers that you es-

caped with the girls, he will conclude that you know far too much about him and his scheme. Trust me, if he finds you, he will kill you."

She blinked two or three times and then drew a slow, deep breath.

"I see," she said.

Her composure was quite stunning, he thought. Few people, male or female, could have taken the news he had just delivered with such equanimity. Concordia Glade was, indeed, a woman apart.

He released her. "Go to bed, Miss Glade. You need sleep. We will discuss this situation again in the morning."

She startled him with a wry smile. "You can hardly expect me to sleep after what you just told me."

"Perhaps not, but you must try to rest. I intend for all of us to be away from here as early as possible in the morning."

The wariness returned to her eyes. "You sound as if you have some plans of your own for my students, Mr. Wells."

"And for you, also, Miss Glade."

"What are they?"

"Tomorrow we will continue on to the nearest train station. From there, you and the girls will travel to London in a first-class carriage. Any number of people will see you board the train."

"But if what you say about Larkin is correct, he will soon discover that we went to London. He will search for us there."

"He will search for four young women and their teacher."

She studied him with renewed interest. "What do you intend, sir?"

"A feat of magic. Once in London you will all disappear."

"What do you mean?" she asked sharply.

"I will explain in the morning."

She hesitated. He knew that she was torn between bidding him good night and demanding an explanation.

"Good night, sir," she said quietly. "I must thank you for your assistance. I am not at all certain that we could have escaped safely without you."

"I do not doubt for a moment that you would have managed very well on your own, Miss Glade. We have not known each other more than a few hours, but I feel confident in saying that you are, without a doubt, the most resourceful woman I have ever met."

She nodded, evidently unsure how to take the observation, and started up the steps. He heard a soft *thunk* when the hem of her skirt brushed against the first riser.

"Miss Glade, I cannot help but notice that you seem to clank a bit when you walk," he said. "I noticed it earlier when your skirts brushed against the door frame. I must admit, I am curious. Is this some new fashion?"

She paused on the staircase and looked back over her shoulder. "Hardly, sir. I knew that once we were away from the castle we would require money to survive. Over the course of the past few weeks, I helped myself to some of the smaller pieces of silver and several other items that appeared to have some value. I sewed them into my skirts."

He inclined his head, impressed. "A clever trick, Miss Glade. One that is much favored by pickpockets and streetwalkers, I believe."

She bristled in outrage. "I assure you, I am no common thief, sir."

What had possessed him to make such a stupid remark? He should have realized that she would not take it as the compliment he had intended.

"I never meant to imply that you were a thief, Miss Glade," he said.

But he knew it was too late. The damage had been done.

"I only did what I thought I had to do for the safety and security of my students. It was not as if I had a great deal of choice."

"I am aware of that. My apologies, Miss Glade."

"Good night, Mr. Wells."

She stalked up the stairs, skirts clanking and thudding on every step, and vanished into the shadows.

He went back to the fire and stood looking into it for a long time.

It was plain that the teacher did not hold thieves in the highest regard.

Pity.

He was such a skilled one.

5

She went swiftly down the hall to the door of the inn room. So he considered her little better than a common street thief or a prostitute who robbed her customers. Why should she care what he thought of her? She and Ambrose Wells were two people thrown together by a strange twist of fate. When this situation had been sorted out they would go their separate ways and that would be the end of it.

Just as well, she told herself. If he considered her a thief simply because, under extraordinary circumstances, she had stolen some small items that did not belong to her, what would his opinion be if he were to learn of her unconventional past?

Try to maintain some perspective. Petty thievery was the least of her sins tonight. She had killed a man.

Her mouth went dry. A vision of Rimpton lying facedown, blood leaking from the grievous wound, rose in front of her like a scene from a nightmare.

She pushed the image out of her mind. A suitable case of shattered nerves would have to wait for a more convenient occasion. She had other, more important things to concern her now. She must concentrate on taking care of Phoebe, Hannah, Edwina and Theodora.

She entered the small chamber quietly, trying not to disturb Hannah and Phoebe, who shared the room with her.

"There you are, Miss Glade." Phoebe sat up in the shadows, clutching the bedclothes to her throat. "Hannah and I were quite worried."

"Yes." On the other side of the bed, Hannah stirred and pushed herself up on one elbow. "Are you all right, Miss Glade?"

"I am perfectly well, thank you." She lit the candle on the washstand and started removing the pins from her hair. "Why on earth would you think otherwise?"

"Hannah said that Mr. Wells might try to take advantage of you," Phoebe explained in her usual forthright manner.

"Take *advantage* of me." Concordia swung around, wincing slightly when she heard her skirts clink against the side of the washstand. "Good heavens, Hannah, whatever were you thinking? I assure you, Mr. Wells was a perfect gentleman." Aside from that odious remark comparing her cleverness to the tricks of pickpockets and prostitutes, she added silently. But perhaps she was a bit oversensitive tonight.

"Are you certain that he did not try to take any liberties?" Hannah asked anxiously.

"None whatsoever," she assured her. And immediately wondered why she found that fact oddly depressing.

"Oh." Hannah sank back against the pillows, evidently disappointed. "I was afraid that perhaps he might expect you to kiss him."

"Why would he do that?" She unfastened the front hooks of her tight-waisted gown. "We are barely acquainted."

"Hannah suggested that Mr. Wells might play on your gratitude to make you feel that you owed him a kiss," Phoebe explained.

"I see." Concordia stepped out of her gown, relieved to be free of the confining bodice and the weight of the items sewn into the skirts. "No need to concern yourself on that point, Hannah. I am quite certain that Mr. Wells is not the sort to attempt such an ungentlemanly tactic."

"How can you be sure of that?" Hannah queried.

Concordia considered the question while she hung her gown on one of the hooks set into the wall. Why *was* she so certain that Ambrose Wells would not try to take advantage of a woman?

"For one thing, I doubt that he would find it necessary to impose himself on a lady," she said eventually. "I cannot imagine that there is any shortage of females who would be more than willing to kiss him quite freely of their own accord."

"Why would they do that?" Hannah sounded genuinely baffled. "He is not the least bit handsome. Quite fierce-looking, if you ask me. Like a lion or a wolf or some other dangerous beast."

"And he is old," Phoebe pointed out, matter-of-factly.

Concordia stared at their candlelit reflections in the mirror, momentarily bereft of speech. Were they talking about the same person? Ambrose Wells was far and away the most compelling man she had ever met in her life.

"Mr. Wells no doubt appears to be entering his dotage to you,

Phoebe, because you are only fifteen years old," she said, striving to keep her tone light. "I assure you, he is not that much older than me."

Only a few years at most, she added silently. It was that air of grim, worldly experience combined with cool self-mastery that added the age to his eyes, she thought.

Phoebe drew up her knees beneath the covers and wrapped her arms around them. "Perhaps. But I agree with Hannah. I cannot imagine ladies lining up to kiss him willingly."

Concordia sat down at the foot of the bed and unlaced her scuffed ankle boots. "Wait until you are a few years older yourself. I have a feeling that you will discover that men like Mr. Wells are not only quite attractive, they are also extremely rare."

Phoebe's mouth opened in astonishment. Then she burst into giggles. She clapped one hand across her lips to muffle the sound.

Concordia gave her a quelling glare. "And just what are you laughing at, young lady?"

"You *would* kiss Mr. Wells if he asked you, wouldn't you?" Phoebe was barely able to contain herself. "I'll wager you would be one of those ladies standing in line to let him embrace you."

"Nonsense." She blew out the candle. "I would not stand in a line to kiss any man, no matter how attractive he happened to be."

"You really do think that Mr. Wells is handsome," Hannah said, intrigued now.

"But what if there was no line?" Phoebe asked, methodical in her questioning, as usual. "What if you were the only lady Mr. Wells wished to kiss? Would you allow him to embrace you in that case?"

"Enough." Concordia used the moonlight to guide her toward the bed. "I declare this ridiculous conversation to be at an end. I refuse to discuss the subject of kissing Mr. Wells any further. Good night, ladies."

"Good night, Miss Glade," Hannah whispered.

"Good night, Miss Glade." Phoebe settled down onto the pillow.

Concordia reached out to pull the quilt aside and slid beneath the sheets.

She sensed the girls drift immediately into sleep. She envied them.

As she had taught herself to do long ago, she forced her thoughts away from the past and concentrated on the future. Circumstances had changed on her tonight. This was certainly not the first time in her life that such a thing had happened. She needed a new plan. As long as she had a plan, she could keep going forward.

But how was she supposed to incorporate Ambrose Wells into a new scheme? His knowledge of the mysterious Alexander Larkin could prove invaluable. It was clear that he had his own goals in this affair, however. What, exactly, did a private inquiry agent do? Who had hired him? Should she continue to entrust the safety of the girls to his care? And if so, for how long?

The soft, hoarse cry from the other side of the bed brought her out of her moonlit reverie.

Hannah sat up suddenly, gasping for air. "No. No, please don't close the door. Please."

Phoebe stirred sleepily. "Miss Glade?"

"It's all right. I'm here." Concordia was already out of bed.

She moved swiftly around to Hannah's side, sat down and gathered the nightmare-shocked girl into her arms.

"Calm yourself, Hannah."

"So dark," Hannah whispered in the disoriented voice of one who is caught between the world of dreams and full wakefulness. "I'll be good. Please don't close the door."

"Hannah, listen to me." Concordia patted the girl's trembling shoulders. "You are not inside the dark place. Look, you can see the moon. There is plenty of light. Shall I open the window?"

Hannah shuddered. "Miss Glade?"

"I am right here. So is Phoebe. All is well."

"It was the dream," Hannah mumbled.

"Yes, I know," Concordia said. "I expect it was brought on by all the excitement tonight. But you are safe now."

"I'm sorry, Miss Glade." Hannah blotted her eyes with the edge of the sheet. "I didn't mean to disturb you and Phoebe."

"We understand. There is nothing to be concerned about."

She continued to soothe and calm Hannah until the girl's breathing returned to normal.

Eventually Hannah lay down on the pillows. Concordia rose and went back to the other side of the bed.

"Miss Glade?" Hannah whispered into the shadows.

"Yes, dear?"

"When we get to London, may I send a message to my friend Joan at the Winslow school? I am very concerned about her. She did not respond to any of the letters I wrote while we were at Aldwick Castle."

Concordia hesitated, thinking of what Ambrose had said earlier concerning the murderous threat of Alexander Larkin.

"It may not be wise for any of us to contact anyone for a while, Hannah," she said gently. "Don't worry, as soon as it is safe to do so, you may contact Joan."

Phoebe shifted on the pillows. "Are we still in great danger, Miss Glade?"

"We must be careful for a while," Concordia said, choosing her words. "But we have the assistance of Mr. Wells now and he appears to be extremely competent at dealing with situations such as this."

"What sort of situation is this, exactly, Miss Glade?" Phoebe asked, predictably curious.

I only wish I knew, Concordia thought. "It is somewhat complicated, Phoebe. But we will manage, never fear. Now try to get some sleep."

She lay quietly for a long time, listening to the steady, quiet breathing of her companions. When she was certain that Hannah and Phoebe were both asleep again, she closed her eyes.

. . . And saw Rimpton on his knees, trying to get back to his feet. He still held the gun. There was something very wrong with the back of his head. . . .

She awakened with a start, aware that her pulse was pounding.

There was someone in the corridor outside the room. She was not certain what had alerted her, but she could feel the presence on the other side of the closed door.

Ambrose, she thought. It had to be him.

About time he came upstairs to bed, she thought. She hoped he had not spent the past hour getting drunk on the innkeeper's sherry. But even as the notion occurred to her, she set it aside. She had seen enough of him tonight to be quite certain that he was not so lacking in self-restraint. In any event, he had not had so much as a single glass of the stuff earlier when he had served it to her.

She waited for the opening and closing of his bedroom door, but there was only silence. What was he doing? Why didn't he go into his room?

What if she was mistaken? Perhaps it was someone else hovering out there in the hall. Another guest? Edwina or Theodora?

Perhaps one of the men from the castle had managed to follow them, after all.

Fear knifed through her with the force of an electrical shock. She stared very hard at the razor-thin crack of grayish light beneath the door.

For a second or two she was frozen, unable to move or breathe.

With an effort of will she managed to slide out from under the quilts. Neither of the two sleeping girls stirred.

The room had grown very cold, but she could feel the icy trickle of perspiration under her arms. She found her eyeglasses and put them on. Then she made her way to her cloak and fumbled briefly in one of the pockets. Her fingers finally closed around the handle of Rimpton's revolver. She withdrew it quietly.

When she reached the door, she paused again. Whoever he was, he was still there. She could literally feel his presence.

It had to be Ambrose, she thought. But she would not be able to relax until she made certain of it.

Easing the bolt aside, she opened the door a bare inch.

Moonlight spilled from the window at the end of the corridor. Through the narrow opening she could just barely make out the top of the staircase. There was no sign of anyone about. She realized that from her vantage point she could not see around the edge of the door to examine the hallway to the right.

"I take it the sherry was not effective." Ambrose spoke very quietly from the darkness.

She jumped a little and then drew a shuddering breath of relief. Lowering the gun, she opened the door a little wider and put her head around the corner.

At first she could not see him at all. Then she realized why. He was not standing at eye level in the hall; he was sitting cross-legged on the floor, hands lightly curled on his knees. There was a great stillness about him.

"Mr. Wells," she said softly, "I thought I heard you out here. What on earth are you doing sitting there on the floor? You should be in bed. You need your sleep as much as the rest of us."

"Do not concern yourself, Miss Glade. Go back to bed."

She could hardly demand answers at this hour. The last thing she wanted to do was awaken the girls, to say nothing of the innkeeper and his wife.

"Very well, if you insist." She did not bother to conceal her doubts.

"Believe it or not, I do know what I am doing, Miss Glade."

Reluctantly she closed the door and slid the bolt back into place. She made her way to the bed, removed her eyeglasses, put the gun down on the table and got under the covers.

She watched the crack of light beneath the door for a time, thinking about Ambrose's odd behavior. She did not require an answer to her question. She knew why he was out there in the chilly hall, why he had not touched the sherry earlier. He was keeping watch.

She chilled beneath the heavy quilts.

The fact that he felt it necessary to guard them through the night told her just how dangerous he believed Alexander Larkin really was.

6

Ambrose listened to the almost inaudible snick of the bolt of the door sliding into place.

He waited a moment longer, cataloging the sounds of the slumbering inn. That part of him that had been trained to listen for the smallest dissonant note concealed within the natural harmony of the night detected nothing that gave cause for alarm.

He allowed himself to sink back into the quiet place in his mind. There would be no sleep for him between now and dawn, but in this inner realm he could obtain a semblance of rest. Here, too, he could contemplate problems and consider possibilities.

At the moment none seemed quite as pressing or as disturbing as Concordia Glade's words a moment ago. *I thought I heard you out here.*

That was not possible. He knew that he had made no sound. He was equally certain that he had done nothing to disturb the shadows beneath the doors when he made his way down the hall. He knew how to move in the night. He had a talent for it.

I thought I heard you out here.

He let himself drift into the memory of another night. . . .

The boy hovered, shivering, in the deep shadows at the top of the stairs. He listened to the angry, muffled voices emanating from the study. His father was quarreling with the mysterious visitor. He could not make out all the words but there was no mistaking the rising level of rage in both men. It was a dangerous, dark tide that seemed to flood through the house.

His father's voice was tight with fury.

". . . You murdered her in cold blood, didn't you? I can't prove it, but I know you did it. . . ."

"She wasn't important." The stranger spoke in low, angry tones. "Just a chambermaid who learned more than was good for her. Forget her. We're on the brink of making a fortune. . . ."

". . . I won't be a party to any more of this business. . . ."

"You can't just walk away. . . ."

"That is precisely what I'm going to do."

"You surprise me, Colton," the visitor said. "You've been a swindler and a fraud artist all of your life. I believed you to be far more practical."

"Fleecing a few wealthy gentlemen who can well afford to lose several thousand pounds is one thing. Murder is another. You knew I'd never go along with that."

"Which is, of course, why I did not tell you," the stranger said. "Had a feeling you'd be difficult."

"Did you think I wouldn't suspect what had happened? She was just an innocent young woman."

"Not so innocent." The stranger's laugh was mirthless. It ended in a harsh cough. "Rest assured, mine was not the first gentleman's bed she had warmed."

"Get out of here and don't ever come back. Do you understand?"

"Yes, Colton, I understand very well. I regret that you feel this way. I shall be sorry to lose you as a partner. But I respect your wishes. Rest assured you will never see me again."

A sudden, sharp explosion reverberated through the house.

The roar of the pistol shocked the boy into immobility for a few seconds. He knew what had happened but he could not bring himself to accept the truth.

Down below, the door of the study opened abruptly. He stood, frozen, in the shadows at the top of the stairs and watched the stranger move through the light of the gas lamp that burned on the desk behind him.

In spite of the boy's horror, some part of him automatically cataloged the details of the killer's appearance. Blond hair, whiskers, an expensively cut coat.

The man looked toward the staircase.

The boy was certain that the stranger was going to climb the stairs and kill him. He knew it as surely as he knew that his father was dead.

The stranger put one booted foot on the bottom step.

"I know you're awake up there, young man. Been a tragic accident,

I'm afraid. Your father just took his own life. Come on down here. I'll take care of you."

The boy stopped breathing altogether, trying to make himself one more shadow among many.

The killer started up the steps. Then he hesitated.

"Bloody hell, the housekeeper," he muttered on another hoarse cough.

The boy watched him turn and go back down the steps. The killer disappeared into the darkened hall. He was going to check Mrs. Dalton's rooms to see if she was there.

The boy knew what the killer did not. Mrs. Dalton was not in her rooms because she had been given the night off. His father did not like any of the servants around when he conducted his illicit business affairs.

When the stranger discovered that he had no need to worry about an adult witness, he would come hunting for the one person who could tell the police what had happened tonight.

The boy looked over the railing and knew that he could not possibly make it down three flights of stairs to the front door and out into the safety of the night before the killer returned.

He was trapped. . . .

Ambrose's feat of magic went remarkably smoothly the following day. Concordia was more than merely impressed with the timing and the coordination, she was awed. Surely there were very few men in the world who could have organized such a vanishing act.

"The trick is to keep it as simple as possible," Ambrose explained when he saw them off at the train station. "And to remember that people see what they expect to see."

The next thing she knew he had disappeared himself. But just before the train pulled out of the station, she caught a glimpse of a scruffy-looking farmer climbing into one of the crowded third-class carriages. Something about the way he moved told her that the man was Ambrose.

A few hours later, after a number of stops in small towns and villages along the way that afforded the passengers the opportunity to stretch their legs, four well-bred young ladies and their teacher descended from a first-class carriage into a busy London station. They immediately got into a cab. The vehicle melted into the swollen traffic and the afternoon haze.

An hour later, four working-class youths emerged from a thronged shopping arcade. They were dressed in caps, trousers, mufflers and coats. They sauntered in the wake of a flower seller in a tattered cloak.

The small group drifted through a busy vegetable market and climbed into an empty farmer's cart. A tarp was stretched over the back of the wagon to conceal the passengers.

Through an opening in the canvas, Concordia caught occasional glimpses of the neighborhoods through which they traveled. Within a short time, the bustle and clatter of the market gave way to a maze of tiny lanes and cramped, dark streets. Scenes of prosperous shops and modest houses followed. That view, in turn, eventually gave way to one of a neighborhood of elegant mansions and fine squares.

To Concordia's amazement, the farmer's cart eventually passed through the heavy iron gates at the back of one of the big houses and rumbled to a halt in a stone-paved yard.

The canvas was whipped off the back of the cart. Ambrose, wearing a farmer's hat and rough clothing, looked down from the driver's box.

"Welcome to your new lodgings, ladies." He tossed the reins to a tall, lanky middle-aged man dressed in a gardener's attire. "This is Mr. Oates. Oates, allow me to introduce Miss Glade and her four students, Phoebe, Hannah, Theodora and Edwina. They will be staying with us for a while."

"Ladies." Oates touched his cap.

"A pleasure to meet you, Mr. Oates," Concordia said.

The girls acknowledged him cheerfully.

Oates looked oddly pleased and somewhat embarrassed by the polite greetings. He mumbled something unintelligible and turned red.

Two large, sleek dogs with sharply pointed ears and well-defined heads bounded forward and stopped directly in front of the small crowd. Their cold, intelligent gaze stirred the hair on the back of Concordia's neck. The animals reminded her of the portrait of a jackal-headed Egyptian god she had once seen in a museum.

"Meet Dante and Beatrice," Ambrose said.

Concordia eyed the dogs uneasily. "Will they bite?"

Ambrose's smile was not unlike that of the dogs. "Of course. What's the point of having guard dogs that will not rip the throats of uninvited guests? But do not be alarmed. Now that you and the girls have been properly introduced, you are quite safe."

"You're certain of that?"

His smile widened. "Absolutely positive, Miss Glade."

"I say, this was great fun." Phoebe jumped down from the cart without waiting for assistance from one of the men and rubbed the place behind Dante's pricked ears. "I very much enjoyed wearing these trousers. Much more comfortable than the skirts we sewed together." She looked hopefully at Concordia. "May I keep them, Miss Glade?"

"I don't see why not," Concordia said. She relaxed when she saw that the dog appeared to be enjoying Phoebe's attention. "They are quite practical in some ways."

Beatrice trotted toward her and thrust her long nose into her hand. Concordia gingerly patted her.

"I want to keep my boy's clothes, too." Hannah stood up in the back of the cart, hooked her fingers into the waistband of her trousers and struck a jaunty pose. In the blink of an eye she metamorphosed into a youth who would not have looked out of place selling newspapers on a busy street corner. "They are ever so much more comfortable than skirts and petticoats. I feel like a different person in them."

Edwina looked down at her own rough costume and wrinkled her nose. "They may be comfortable but they certainly are not very fashionable."

"It was rather fun masquerading as a boy, though," Theodora said, allowing Oates to help her down from the cart. "Did you see the way people got out of our path in the shopping arcade?"

"I think that is because they were afraid we might try to pick their pockets," Hannah said wryly.

Ambrose looked amused. "You are correct, Hannah, and that is a tribute to your acting skills. I was very impressed." He vaulted easily to the ground and surprised Concordia with a brief, wicked smile. "And that includes you, Miss Glade. I have never seen a more convincing flower seller."

"He's right, Miss Glade," Phoebe said. "You look ever so much older in those poor clothes."

Concordia sighed and unknotted the tattered scarf she had used to cover her hair. "Thank you, Phoebe."

"How in blazes did ye come by this old cart and that broken-down nag?" Oates muttered to Ambrose.

"A helpful farmer loaned them to me."

Oates looked skeptical. "Loaned them, eh?"

"No need to look at me like that, Oates." Ambrose clapped him on the back. "I made it worth his while. He'll be wanting his fine equipage back, however. Will you take care of the matter for me? I told the man I'd leave his horse and cart in Brinks Lane near the theater."

"Aye, sir." Oates climbed up onto the box and flapped the reins.

He did not appear even mildly astonished by the unusual nature of Ambrose's arrival, Concordia thought. She got the feeling that Oates was accustomed to such eccentricities.

"Come, we will go inside and I will introduce you to Mrs. Oates," Ambrose said. "She manages the household and will show you to your rooms."

Before Concordia realized his intent, he took her arm and drew her toward the kitchen door. She was very conscious of the feel of his strong fingers. For some ridiculous reason she wished very badly that she was not dressed in such ragged, unfashionable clothes.

To distract herself from that depressing line of thought, she examined the exterior of the big house as they moved toward the door.

The mansion was a handsome building in the Palladian style with tall, well-proportioned windows and fine columns. It was surrounded by high stone walls and well-tended gardens. The effect was quite elegant, but she could not help but notice that the big house possessed, in a subtle, understated manner, the air of a secure fortress. Dante and Beatrice added the final touch.

The excited, chattering girls rushed enthusiastically into the back hall accompanied by the dogs. Concordia watched them, her insides tightening. Had she done the right thing by bringing them here? Had there been any better choice?

She hesitated briefly before stepping over the threshold of the mansion.

"This is a very grand home, Mr. Wells," she said, keeping her voice low so the girls would not overhear. "I assume it belongs to you?"

"As a matter of fact, it does not."

She stopped quite suddenly. "What on earth do you mean?"

"It is the property of a man named John Stoner."

She frowned. "Is he here?"

"No," Ambrose said. "As it happens, he is not in residence at the moment."

It seemed to her that he spoke a little too casually about the absence of the mysterious Mr. Stoner.

"Are you quite certain that he will not mind having us as house-guests?" she asked.

"Unless he returns unexpectedly, he will not even be aware that he is playing host to you," Ambrose assured her.

She did not like the sound of that. "I don't understand. Where is Mr. Stoner?"

"I believe that he is on the Continent at the moment. Difficult to say, really. Stoner is unpredictable in his habits."

"I see. May I ask what your connection is to this Mr. Stoner?"

He thought that over for a few seconds. "You could say that we are old acquaintances."

"No offense, sir, but that sounds rather vague."

"Do not be alarmed, Miss Glade," Ambrose said very softly. "You have my word that you and your charges will be safe here."

A frisson of acute awareness fluttered across her nerves. Her intuition told her that the girls would come to no harm from Ambrose Wells. She was not nearly so certain about the safety of her own heart.

8

Concordia awoke to the soft *plink, plink, plink* of rain dripping steadily outside the window. It was a peaceful, comforting sound. She lay quietly for a moment, savoring the sensation. This was the first time in several weeks that she had not experienced a rush of anxiety and tension immediately after awakening—the first morning when she had not had to think about the escape plan.

True, things had not gone according to her original scheme, but the girls were safely away from Aldwick Castle. That was all that mattered this morning. Soon she would have to fashion a new plan for the future, but that could wait until after breakfast.

She pushed back the covers, found her eyeglasses and pulled on the wrapper that Mrs. Oates had managed to conjure last night. She gathered the few personal toiletries she had brought with her from the castle and opened the door.

The hall outside her bedroom was empty. Mrs. Oates had mentioned that the only other room in use on this floor belonged to Ambrose. The girls had been given rooms on the floor above.

Satisfied that she had the corridor to herself, she hurried toward the bath with a sense of cheerful anticipation.

She had discovered the wonders of the grand room the night before and was looking forward to repeating the experience. John Stoner might be mysterious in his ways, but he was evidently a firm believer in modern bathing amenities.

The bath was a marvelously decadent little palace graced with vast stretches of sparkling white tiles. All of the fixtures were of the latest sanitary design. Water taps set into the walls supplied hot as well as cold water brought up through pipes affixed to the side of the house. The basin gleamed. There was even a shower fixture over the tub.

The water closet, located in an equally impressive room next to the bath, was a magnificent blend of art and modern engineering. A spectacular field of yellow sunflowers had been painted on both the outside and the inside of the commode. One did not encounter that sort of refinement and elegance very often.

She could get used to this sort of luxury, she thought.

The door of the bath opened just as she reached out to grasp the knob. Startled, she halted and glanced back over her shoulder at the entrance to her bedroom, gauging the distance.

But there was no time to escape.

Ambrose emerged from the white-tiled bath. He was dressed in an exotically embroidered black satin dressing gown. His hair was damp and tousled.

"Mr. Wells."

She clutched the front of her wrapper with one hand and her little bag of toiletries in the other. She was aghast at the knowledge that she must look as though she had just gotten out of bed. It was the simple truth, of course, but somehow that only made matters worse. She was violently aware of the fact that Ambrose was likely quite nude under the robe. And she had on only a nightgown under the wrapper.

He gave her a slow smile that scattered her senses to the four winds.

"I see you are an early riser, Miss Glade."

"Yes, well, I assumed the household was still asleep." She cleared her throat. "I did not realize that you were up and about."

"I also tend to rise early. It appears we have something in common."

Flustered, she took a step back. "I will come back some other time."

"No need to retreat. The bath is all yours."

"Oh. Thank you." She looked past him into the gleaming interior, aware of the warm, steamy air flowing out of it. "I must say it is a very lovely bath."

The corner of his mouth twitched. "Do you think so?"

"Oh, yes, indeed." She was unable to restrain her enthusiasm. "Modern and sanitary in every particular. It even has a hot water shower device."

He shoved his hands into the pockets of his robe and nodded seriously. "I did notice that when I used it a few minutes ago."

She was beyond a blush now. Her face was surely bright red. If only there was a convenient trapdoor beneath her feet. She would give anything to be able to drop out of sight.

She sighed. "You must think me a perfect fool. It is just that I have never been employed in such a modern household."

"You are not working here, Miss Glade." The faint crinkles at the corners of his eyes tightened, giving the impression that he was irritated. "You are a guest."

"Yes, well, it is very kind of you to say so, but we both know that the situation is highly irregular, to say the least, what with the master of the house gone—"

"And I am aware that you are no fool," he concluded, as though she had not spoken. "By the way, if you elect to employ the shower fixture, I advise caution. The damned thing spits hot and cold water out like so many small bullets. In my opinion the entire concept needs a great deal more thought and considerable improvement if the device is ever to re-place a proper bath in a tub."

She cleared her throat. "I'll keep that in mind."

He turned and walked away toward his own bedroom. "When you have finished indulging yourself in the pleasures of our very modern, ex-tremely sanitary bath, I would like you to meet me downstairs in the breakfast room. I have some questions for you."

"What is it you wish to know?" she asked warily.

"Among other things, I would very much like to learn a bit more about you, Miss Glade. You are something of a mystery to me."

Her heart sank. "What do the details of my personal situation have to do with finding Alexander Larkin?"

"Nothing, perhaps." He stopped at the door of his room and looked back at her. "But among my many lamentable failings is that when I have questions, I cannot seem to rest until I get answers."

She gave him a repressive look of the sort that could quiet a room full of chattering young ladies. "I expect you spend a good many sleepless nights, sir."

"Yes, but I do not consider that to be a significant problem." He gave her a slow, devastatingly intimate smile. "I seldom have any difficulty finding other things besides sleep to occupy me at night."

She did not doubt that for a moment. Aware that she was blushing furiously, she stalked into the glorious bath and closed the door very firmly.

9

Downstairs in the peaceful solitude of the breakfast room he drank tea and read the papers, as was his habit. But he was aware that a part of him was waiting for Concordia with a sense of mingled expectation and irritation.

It was such a small thing, but it annoyed him that she seemed so uneasy with the notion of herself as a guest in the household. It was as if she was determined to maintain as much formal distance between them as possible.

He thought about how she had looked in the hall a short time earlier, dressed in a cozy wrapper, her hair in a chaotic knot on top of her head, face still flushed from sleep. His imagination had run wild with a heated fantasy that involved scooping her up in his arms and carrying her into his bedroom.

It was not hard to imagine how she would have reacted to a suggestion of a passionate interlude in his room, he told himself, wincing. She was already extremely wary of him as it was and he could not blame her.

He did not relish the prospect of pressuring her to give up her secrets when she came downstairs in a few minutes. She would resent his intrusion into her private life and that would make things even more difficult between them. But he had no choice.

The questions that he was grappling with had become more complicated of late. He needed answers. Concordia had spent a considerable amount of time at the castle, associating with Larkin's employees. Whether or not she realized it, she was an invaluable source of information, Ambrose thought, turning a page of the newspaper.

He had been giving himself the same lecture from the moment he vaulted up onto the horse behind her and led the girls out of the stable. And he knew very well that he was lying to himself.

From that first instant when he realized that Concordia was the reason his plan had failed, he had known that he wanted more than information from her.

At the very least, it would be pleasant if she demonstrated as much enthusiasm for his company as she had for the damned bath.

"Newspapers," Concordia exclaimed from the doorway. "Excellent. I have not seen any since I left for the post at the castle."

The warm, bright sound of her voice sent a flash of acute awareness through him, tightening his insides and causing his blood to beat more heavily in his veins.

He looked up and saw her standing in the opening. Her dark hair was now pinned into a neat twist at the back of her head. The lenses of her spectacles sparkled. She had on the same severe, unadorned dress she had worn out of the castle. There was no bustle. When a lady prepared for a dangerous flight into the night, she had to make fashion choices, he thought.

He made a note to do something about the wardrobe situation. When one entertained a houseful of ladies who had arrived with only the clothes on their backs, one had to think about things such as gowns and gloves.

"I doubt that you have missed anything of great importance." He put down the paper and got to his feet to pull out a chair. "Just the usual scandals and gossip."

"I'm sure you're right." She sat down and unfolded her napkin. "But when one has been out of touch with current events as long as I have, one comes to miss any sort of news, even that supplied by the sensation press." She pulled the nearest paper toward her. "Speaking of which, what is the latest sensation?"

"A murder, of course." He indicated the story he had just finished reading. "Evidently while you and I were busy dashing about the countryside, a gentleman here in town was dispatched by his mistress after he told her that he intended to cast her aside in favor of another woman. They say she fed him poison. Each of the papers printed various versions, all of which are most likely inaccurate, of course."

"I see." She adjusted her eyeglasses and scanned the piece briefly. "The murder stories do seem to sell best when they are associated with rumors of an illicit love affair, do they not?"

The serious manner in which she made the observation amused him.

"I have noticed that, myself," he said dryly. "It is, in fact, quite startling how often love and death go together."

She lowered the paper and regarded him with a curious frown. "Do you suspect that is the case in the affair that you are investigating, sir?"

He shook his head. "There is nothing to indicate that love or passion is involved in this. From all accounts, Larkin is motivated solely by two things: power and money."

The door that connected the breakfast room to the kitchen opened. Mrs. Oates appeared, her round, cheerful face reddened from the heat of the stove. She carried a large silver platter of scrambled eggs, crisply cooked fish and toast.

"Good morning, Miss Glade." Mrs. Oates smiled warmly. "I trust you had a good night's rest?"

"Yes, thank you," Concordia said. "The young ladies are still in their beds, though. I think it would be best if they were not disturbed. They were quite exhausted."

"Of course, poor dears. Never fear, I'll make certain that they are not bothered." Mrs. Oates set the platter on the table and poured tea into Concordia's cup. "So nice to have a house full of guests. We rarely entertain here." She glanced at Ambrose. "Isn't that right, sir?"

"Yes," Ambrose said.

Concordia cleared her throat very delicately. "Mr. Stoner does not care for houseguests?"

"Oh, my, no, that's not the problem," Mrs. Oates said. "The problem is that there's no lady in the house. You know how it is with gentlemen living on their own. They can't be bothered to plan a dinner party or a ball, let alone invite guests to stay."

"I see," Concordia said. "I hope we won't be too much trouble."

"Not at all, not at all." Mrs. Oates went back through the door and vanished into the kitchen.

Concordia took a spoonful of eggs from the platter. "Mr. Wells, I have been contemplating the extremely unusual nature of our association."

Damnation, he thought. That did not bode well.

"Odd situations necessitate unusual associations," he assured her.

"I am aware of that." She picked up her fork. "But it occurs to me that it would be best if you and I were to put our connection on a businesslike footing, as it were."

"No offense, Miss Glade, but what the deuce are you talking about?"

She looked at him with a level gaze. "You mentioned that you are a private inquiry agent."

"Yes," he said, cautious now.

"Very well. I wish to employ you to make inquiries on behalf of my four students."

He sat back slowly. "There is no need to hire me, Miss Glade. I am already investigating the situation in which you and the girls are involved on behalf of another client."

A speculative light appeared in Concordia's eyes. "You have yet to tell me any of the details of that situation."

"My client has engaged me to look into the circumstances surrounding the recent death of her sister. She believes that it is a matter of murder, not simply an unfortunate accident as the authorities assume."

"I see." She frowned. "How did you come to be at the castle?"

"In the course of my inquiries I spoke with an informant who hinted that there might be a connection between the woman's death and whatever was going on at Aldwick Castle. I went to make some observations. You know the rest."

Her mouth tightened at the corners. "Yours is an exceedingly mysterious business, sir. All the more reason why I would feel more comfortable if we secured our arrangement with a formal contract."

For some reason he found that suggestion thoroughly irritating. "I see no necessity for a contract."

Her fine brows came together above the rims of her spectacles. "In spite of Mrs. Oates's kind remarks, my students and I are not really guests in this household. For heaven's sake, the master of the house does not even know that we are here."

"Don't worry about Stoner."

She ignored that. "You have offered us protection and I have accepted because I think it is in the best interests of my girls to do so. However, I would prefer that we establish a clear understanding of our arrangements. Hiring you would seem to be the most straightforward way to accomplish that."

He propped his elbows on the arms of the chair and put his fingertips together. He wanted to take her to bed and she wanted to do business with him. Matters between them were not proceeding along optimistic lines.

"I see," he said neutrally. Always a safe response, he assured himself.

"Excellent." She smiled, evidently taking his comment for agreement. "Now then, what is your customary fee? I believe that a number of the items I removed from the castle are somewhat valuable. There is a rather nice silver and crystal salt cellar that is surely worth several pounds."

"You mean to pay me in stolen goods, Miss Glade?"

She flushed but her eyes remained steady. "I'm afraid I do not have any money. And, under the circumstances, I am highly unlikely to receive my quarterly wages for my work at the castle."

"Yes, I think that is a safe assumption."

Her chin came up. "If you feel that you cannot accept what you term 'stolen goods' in exchange for your services, sir, then I shall have to consider other alternatives."

"You have no other alternatives, Miss Glade. And I think you know that as well as I do."

She took a deep breath. "Nevertheless—"

"Nevertheless, you want to hire me so that you will feel that you are in control of this situation."

"That is putting it somewhat crudely, but yes, I suppose that is an accurate statement."

"Very well, Miss Glade, if you insist upon paying me, I hereby officially accept your business. Now then, about my fee. You should know that I do not charge money for my services."

"I don't understand, sir."

"I deal in favors."

She stiffened. "Favors?"

"Most of my clients cannot afford to pay me in hard coin of the realm, Miss Glade. So I long ago established a system of barter. It works in this manner. I perform the services required to obtain the answers my clients want. In turn, they agree to repay me at some future date, should I ever happen to need a favor that they are in a position to grant."

"What sort of favors do you generally request?" she asked coldly.

"It varies. Sometimes I need information. Sometimes goods and services. For example, a few years ago I was hired by a housekeeper in a wealthy household. She wanted me to find answers to some questions she had concerning her employer's private activities. After I conducted an investigation and confirmed her fear that her employer was, indeed, a member of a rather nasty club, she determined that she could not continue on in her position. I asked her if she would consider a new post in this household. She and her husband, who happened to be a skilled gardener and very good with tools, accepted positions here."

"That is how you obtained the services of Mr. and Mrs. Oates?"

He nodded. "Nan, the maid, came with them. She is Mrs. Oates's cousin. It has worked out well."

She cleared her throat discreetly. "You say that you, personally, hired Mr. and Mrs. Oates and Nan? Mr. Stoner was not involved in that decision?"

"Stoner had no objections, and as it happened, we were in need of new staff."

"It strikes me as a trifle odd that the master of the house left something as important as the hiring of the staff in someone else's hands."

"Stoner is more interested in his scholarly research, his writing and his travels, than he is in the management of this household."

"How often is Mr. Stoner in residence?"

"He comes and goes at his own whim."

"How convenient for you," she said dryly. "It would appear that you are able to enjoy all of the comforts and advantages of a grand house without the necessity of having to actually pay for it, as it were."

"The situation has worked out rather nicely." He sat forward and picked up his fork. "Then there is my current case. The woman who recently employed me to investigate the death of her sister is a shopkeeper. She has promised to repay me in ladies' parasols should I ever happen to require some."

"Good heavens." Concordia blinked. "What possible purpose might you ever have for parasols?"

"One never knows."

"In some quarters such a manner of conducting one's business would be deemed eccentric, to say the least."

"I do not concern myself with those particular quarters."

"Obviously." She sighed. "Very well, I believe that I comprehend how you conduct your business. What sort of favor might you request from a professional teacher?"

"I have no notion." Thoroughly annoyed now, he put down his fork and assumed what he hoped was an air of intimidation. "Never worked for a teacher before. I shall have to think upon it for a while. I will let you know when I have decided what would constitute suitable payment. In the meantime, you may consider me hired."

Concordia did not appear to notice his intimidating expression.

"It is settled, then," she said with cool satisfaction. "Henceforth, you may consider me your employer."

"It doesn't work like that, Concordia."

"The logic is quite plain. I have hired you to conduct an investigation. That makes me your employer. Now that the nature of our association has been established, I wish to make it clear that, as your client, I expect to be kept informed and involved in this case."

"I do not allow my clients to become involved in my investigations," he said evenly.

"I am not one of your usual clients, sir. Indeed, I am already deeply involved in the inquiry. In point of fact, had I not conducted my own investigation at Aldwick Castle, I would never have initiated the escape plan."

"I will allow you that much, however—"

"In addition, you must also admit that I have been able to provide you with some very valuable information concerning Larkin's scheme."

This was not going well.

"Huh," he said. As a clever riposte it was somewhat lacking, but he could not come up with anything better.

"I will take that as an acknowledgment of the fact," she said. "Furthermore, as matters progress it may very well transpire that I and my girls will be able to supply you with other details or observations that will prove even more useful to you. Can you deny that?"

"No."

She smiled, looking quite satisfied.

He raised his brows. "In hindsight, I suppose it should have been obvious to me that one ought never to engage in a debate with a professional educator."

She was pleased. "Now that the terms of our relationship have been settled, I suggest that we move on to more important matters."

"Such as?" he muttered.

"Solving the case, of course. What is your next step?"

He wanted nothing more than to get to his feet, go to her end of the table, haul her up out of her chair and kiss that look of feminine triumph off her face.

Instead he forced himself to move on to the only subject that seemed to interest her at the moment.

"You mentioned that you got the post at the castle through an agency operated by a Mrs. Jervis," he said.

"That's right."

"Do you happen to know if the ill-fated Miss Bartlett came from the same agency?"

She looked at him in surprise. "I don't know. I never considered the matter. Why do you ask?"

"If you and Bartlett both were employed through the services of Jervis's agency, it would be an interesting link of sorts."

"Good heavens. Never say that you think Mrs. Jervis might be involved in this affair?"

"I have no idea at the moment but I intend to look into the matter. Do you have the address of the firm?"

"Yes, of course. But you can hardly walk through the door and start making inquiries about Miss Bartlett or the post at the castle. If Mrs. Jervis is somehow connected to Larkin's scheme, she will become suspicious and perhaps alert him."

"Believe it or not, that possibility has occurred to me."

"Naturally." She wrinkled her nose and reached for the teapot. "You must forgive me for trying to tell you how to manage your professional affairs, sir. It is the teacher in me, I suppose. I cannot resist the opportunity to instruct."

He startled himself with a laugh. "You did not offend me."

"How will you proceed, if I may ask?"

"I will start by examining Jervis's files."

"She is highly unlikely to allow you to go through her files."

"I do not intend to ask her permission."

Concordia's cup paused in midair. "You are going to break into her office when she is not there?"

"I think that would be the most efficient approach. But I believe I will wait until tomorrow night. This evening I intend to speak with an acquaintance who has some knowledge of Larkin. In addition, it looks as though it is going to rain for most of the day."

She stared at him. "What on earth does the weather have to do with it?"

He shrugged. "I prefer not to conduct that sort of business on wet nights if it can be avoided. Too much danger of accidentally leaving a footprint behind."

"I see." She looked a little dazed. "Well, regardless of the weather, your scheme sounds risky, sir. What if you are caught?"

He raised a finger. "Ah, now that is the truly cunning aspect of my plan. I do not intend to get arrested."

A disapproving frown tightened her brows. "You appear to have some expertise in this sort of thing."

"Such skills are useful in my line."

"I confess, I find you something of a mystery, sir."

"We are even in that case, Miss Glade. Because you are a great enigma to me. Speaking of interesting questions, you mentioned that you took the post at the castle because you had recently been dismissed from one at a girls' school."

Her jaw tensed but her voice remained very cool and even. "That is correct. I was told there would be no reference."

"Why were you let go?"

She put down a slice of toast and gave him a considering look. "I cannot see how knowing the reasons for my dismissal would be of any help in this matter, sir."

He inclined his head in understanding. "There was a man involved, then."

She crushed the napkin in her lap, anger leaping into her eyes. "Of course you would leap to such a conclusion. It is a common enough tale, is it not? It takes so little to shred a woman's reputation, even less to ruin a teacher. Rumors of a love affair, being caught in a compromising position, or even a small indiscretion, and one discovers that one's career has been destroyed."

"Forgive me, I did not mean to dredge up unhappy memories."

"Rubbish. That is exactly what you meant to do, sir. You no doubt assumed that if you made me lose my temper, I would tell you what you wish to know. Well, you have succeeded. For your information, my situation did *not* involve an illicit love affair with a man."

"A woman, perhaps?"

She stared at him, nonplussed. Then she broke into light, lilting laughter.

It was the first time he had heard her laugh. He was enthralled.

Hastily she clapped her napkin over her mouth. "Forgive me," she mumbled into the linen.

He pushed his empty dish aside and folded his arms on the table. "You find my question humorous?"

"Not the question." She recovered her poise and lowered the napkin. "It was the remarkably casual way you asked it that caught me unawares. There are very few gentlemen who could have voiced the suggestion of the possibility of a love affair between two women with such an air of . . ." She paused. "Shall we say, equanimity?"

"I have been out in the world a very long time, Miss Glade. I am well aware that for some, love and passion do not always follow the tradi-tional path. I cannot help but observe that you were not the least bit shocked by my question, merely amused."

She made an offhand gesture and selected another slice of toast. "I was raised in what most would call a highly unconventional manner."

"So was I."

She gave him a long, considering look. He got the feeling that he was being weighed and judged on some invisible scale. He sensed that he had passed the test when she lowered the uneaten portion of toast and sat back in her chair.

"While I appreciate and admire your open-mindedness," she said, "I can state quite honestly that I did not lose my post because of an indis-

creet liaison. My problems stemmed from that unconventional upbringing I mentioned."

"I see."

"You may as well know that you have just been hired by a woman
who has spent her entire professional career concealing her past from
her own employers."

"This is becoming more interesting by the moment, Miss Glade."

"I regret to say that I had very little choice," she continued, her voice
unnaturally even in tone. "There are very few professions open to
women as it is. Those who possess pasts such as mine have an even nar-
rower range of opportunities."

"Believe it or not, I do comprehend the predicament."

"I used a fictitious name to secure my post at the girls' school. I called
myself Irene Colby. The ruse worked well enough in the past. But not
this time. Somehow the truth emerged and the instant it did, I was, of
course, dismissed immediately."

It was an unhappy story, but he could not resist a smile. "You have
used false names to obtain employment on several occasions? How very
inventive of you, Miss Glade. I admire your resourcefulness. What of the
rest of your family? Are they as unusual as you?"

"I can no longer claim any close relations, sir. My parents both died
a decade ago when I was sixteen. There are some cousins on my father's
side, I believe, but I have never met them. They do not consider me a legitimate member of the family."

"Why not?"

"Very likely because I am *not* legitimate," she said lightly.

Too lightly, he thought. "That unconventional upbringing again?"

"Mmm. Yes." She tilted her head slightly to one side to study him. "You are not going to let this matter drop, are you?"

"I did tell you that I like answers," he said.

She hesitated, as though pondering something of vital importance, and then appeared to come to a decision.

"My parents were notorious freethinkers, Mr. Wells. They did not believe in marriage, very likely because both of them were already unhappily wed to other people when they met. They viewed the institution of marriage as a cage, one that was particularly cruel and unfairly confining to women."

"I see."

"I don't think you do." She gave him a steely smile, challenging him to brush off her past. "My father was William Gilmore Glade. My mother was Sybil Marlowe."

The names chimed distantly in his head. It took a few seconds, but finally the old scandal surfaced.

"Not the Marlowe and Glade who established the Crystal Springs Community?" he asked, intrigued in spite of himself.

"I see you have heard of it."

"A decade ago everyone had heard of Marlowe, Glade and the Crystal Springs Community."

Her mouth tightened at the corners. "When it disbanded there were several articles in the sensation press and a number of penny dreadfuls purporting to provide the so-called shocking details of the scandalous activities that were rumored to have gone on inside the Community."

"I recall some of the pieces."

"Most of the reports were utter rubbish."

"Naturally." He brushed that aside with a slight movement of his fingers. "The press is not known for accuracy. It thrives on scandal and rumor, not facts." He paused, frowning slightly. "Why did the Community disband?"

"It fell apart almost immediately after the news of my parents' death in a dreadful snowstorm in America," she said quietly. "They were the Community's founders and leaders. Without them, the others were unable to sustain their purpose and direction."

"What were your parents doing in America?"

"They sailed there with the intention of establishing a sister community." She picked up her teacup. "They believed that America would prove more hospitable ground for their freethinking philosophy."

"My condolences on the loss of your parents at such a young age," he added. "It must have been very difficult for you."

"Yes."

The single word was clipped and neutral. Her expression was cool and veiled. But he could feel the tension simmering inside her. She was waiting for him to mock or condemn.

"I am not well acquainted with the philosophy of the Crystal Springs Community," he said, choosing his words with great care. "But I believe your parents advocated what some would call an extremely liberal view of the relationship between the sexes."

"Thanks to the press, that is all anyone remembers about the Community," she said, suddenly fierce. "But my parents held many other advanced views as well. They believed that women should be educated to the same standards as men, for example. And that females ought to be admitted to colleges, universities and professions on an equal basis with males."

"I see."

"It was my mother's dream to attend medical school." Concordia's self-control returned quickly, masking the brief flash of pain and anger. "When she was refused admission, her parents forced her into a loveless marriage."

"And your father?"

"He was a brilliant man, a philosopher and a scientist who was passionate about modern ideas of all types. He also found himself in an unhappy marriage. He met my mother at a lecture on the rights of women." Her smile was oddly wistful. "They always claimed that it was a case of love at first sight."

"Your tone implies that you do not believe in that phenomenon."

"On the contrary. My parents were proof that it does exist. But in their case it demanded a very heavy price. They destroyed two marriages and created a great scandal in order to achieve their own happiness."

"And they saddled you with the burden of illegitimacy."

She uttered a soft, mirthless laugh. "That is the least of it. The most difficult problems I face arise from the assumptions that others make when they discover that I was raised in the Community."

"These assumptions concern your personal behavior?"

"Precisely, Mr. Wells." She set the cup down on the saucer with enough force to make the fine china clang loudly. "When people discover that I am the offspring of William Gilmore Glade and Sybil Marlowe, they conclude that I practice a similar modern philosophy concerning the relationship between the sexes."

"I can see why you go to some lengths to conceal your past from potential employers."

"There are very few people who are willing to hire a teacher who was raised with such modern notions. As I said, when my past was exposed at my previous post at the girls' school, I was dismissed instantly."

He gave that some thought. "You were perfect for Alexander Larkin's purposes, weren't you?"

"I beg your pardon?"

"You were desperate for a position and you possessed no family connections. If you had disappeared after Larkin was finished with you, no one would have asked any questions."

She shuddered. "A chilling thought."

"I wonder if Miss Bartlett fit the same requirements."

"What do you—? Oh, I see. It does appear that way, does it not? She vanished from the castle, and as far as I know, no one came to inquire after her." Concordia hesitated. "Then again, no one would have mentioned any such inquiries to me. I was just the teacher, after all. For the most part I was ignored."

He nodded slowly, a familiar sense of awareness uncurling inside him. This was the sensation he always experienced when he knew himself to be closing in on the answers he sought.

"Something tells me that you are the key to this affair, Concordia," he said softly. "I think that, when it came to you, Larkin made his fatal blunder, the one that may well bring him down."

"What do you mean?"

"He underestimated the teacher."

10

The innkeeper's wife did not like the man who was questioning her husband so closely. It was not merely because the stranger had made his disdain of their modest establishment evident when he walked through the door a short time ago. She had been in this career a very long time. Wealthy, arrogant gentlemen who treated her neat, respectable, well-kept inn as though it were a hovel were a fact of life. At worst, they got drunk, tried to accost the serving girl and sometimes soiled the sheets. This one was different, though. She doubted that this elegant man would be the sort to commit any of those small, annoying crimes. Very neat and proper, he was. He had come all the way from London on the train the day before, spent the night in the village near Aldwick Castle, toured the ruins this morning and then hired a carriage to go about making inquiries.

Yet in spite of all that dashing around the neighborhood there was not so much as a speck of dust on his fine coat. His shirt collar was clean and crisply ironed.

Over-nice by half, she decided. The type who traveled with his own sheets and towels because he did not trust the cleanliness of inns such as the one she and her husband operated.

She sat in the office, pretending to busy herself with the accounts while Ned spoke with the man. But the door was open. She could see the front desk out of the corner of her eye and hear everything that was discussed.

"Four young ladies and their teacher put up here for the night?" The man from London tossed some coins onto the counter. "They left early yesterday morning?"

Ned did not touch the coins. "Something was said about wanting to be at the station in time to take the morning train to London."

"Did they remark on the fire at the castle?" the stranger asked sharply.

"No, sir. The old castle is a fair ride from here. We didn't get the news of the blaze until after the ladies had left for the station yesterday." Ned shook his head somberly. "Heard the place was burned right down to the ground and that one man died in the flames."

"Yes, that is true." The stranger's words were edged with impatience, as though the loss of the man was more of a nuisance than a tragedy. "The cause of his death is somewhat uncertain, however."

"I beg your pardon, sir?"

"Never mind, it's none of your affair. Is there anything else you can tell me about the young ladies and their teacher?"

"No, sir. Like I said, they arrived very late and left quite early."

The gentleman's jaw flexed. "Wonder what they did with the damned horses?" he said, speaking more to himself than to Ned.

"I can tell ye that, sir," Ned said. "Left 'em at the livery stable next door to the train station."

The man flung a few more coins onto the counter. "How did the teacher pay for the rooms that she and the girls used? Did she have money?"

"Don't know about the state of her finances, sir." Ned raised one shoulder in an elaborate shrug. "She wasn't the one who paid the bill."

The expression on the face of the gentleman did not change by so much as the flicker of an eyelash, but the innkeeper's wife suddenly found it hard to breathe.

"Who paid for the rooms?" the man from London asked in a deadly soft voice.

"Why, the man the teacher hired to protect them while they were on the road," Ned said, stunningly calm.

The stranger's hand tightened abruptly around the gold-headed handle of his walking stick. He studied Ned with eyes as cold as those of a fish. "She hired a bodyguard?"

"Very sensible, I thought. She and her students were obliged to travel at night, after all."

"What was the name of the guard?"

"Smith, I think." Ned opened the register and ran a finger down the page. "Yes, here it is. Mr. Smith. Gave him room number five. The teacher and her girls used three and four."

"Let me see that." The man whipped the register around with a short, brusque movement and studied the name on the page. "The handwriting looks the same as that of the teacher's."

"She signed the register for all of them—the girls, herself and Smith."

"Describe Smith."

Ned shrugged again. "Nothing remarkable about him. Medium height, I'd say. Rather ordinary-looking, to tell you the truth." He glanced back over his shoulder. "Lizzie, can you recall anything about the man who accompanied the teacher and her girls the other night?"

She forced herself to turn slowly, as though the question had distracted her from more important work.

"I believe that he had brown hair," she said politely.

"Is that all you can recall?" the stranger demanded angrily.

"I'm afraid so, sir. Like Ned here said, there was nothing in particular to remark about him."

"Where in blazes would she find a hired guard around here?" the gentleman asked.

They both looked at him, politely blank-faced, and said nothing.

"I'm wasting my time," he muttered.

Without another word he turned on his heel, walked out of the inn and got into the waiting carriage.

Ned scooped up the coins on the counter and walked into the office. He put a comforting hand on Lizzie's shoulder. Together they watched the vehicle roll out of the yard and turn in the direction of the village and the train station.

"Mr. Smith was right when he said that someone would likely come around making inquiries about the teacher," Ned said.

She shivered. "Thank goodness Smith did not ask us to lie in exchange for the money he gave you. I don't think it would have been easy to fool that man."

Smith's request yesterday morning had been simple and quite straightforward. He had put ten pounds on the counter and spoken very politely to Ned. *"There will be questions asked. Feel free to say that the teacher hired me to see her and the girls safely onto the London train. But I would take it as a great favor if you could keep your description of me as vague as possible."*

"In a manner of speaking we did lie," Ned said. "We told the man from London that there was nothing remarkable about Mr. Smith."

"Well, there wasn't," she said. "At least not in regard to his features or his height."

"There was something about him, though . . ." Ned let the sentence fade away, unfinished.

There was no need for words, she thought. They had both been in the innkeeping profession long enough to have become sound judges of human nature. There had, indeed, been something about Mr. Smith, something remarkably dangerous. But the teacher had seemed to trust him and that had been good enough for her. Because there had been something about the teacher, too.

Lizzie had seen the sort of fierceness and determination in the woman that one saw in females throughout the animal kingdom when their young were threatened.

She reached up to cover Ned's fingers with her own. "Never mind, the business is finished, at least as far as we're concerned, and we've nothing to complain of. We've turned a nice profit."

"True enough."

"What is it that still troubles you?"

Ned exhaled deeply. "I'm damned curious about why Mr. Smith didn't ask us to lie outright. Given the amount of money he put on the counter yesterday morning, I expected him to instruct us to say nothing at all about him or his companions."

"Instead, he merely asked us to keep any description of him to a minimum. It does seem peculiar, doesn't it? Ten pounds is a lot of money for such a simple request."

"Got a hunch," Ned said slowly, "that Smith wanted to be certain that the gentleman from London was told that the teacher and her students had a bodyguard."

"Why?"

"Perhaps because he wanted to warn him off." Ned rubbed the back of his neck. "But there is another possibility."

"What?"

"Smith may have wished to distract the elegant man."

"I don't understand."

"If you saw a hungry tiger closing in on a flock of helpless lambs, one way to turn him aside from the kill would be to drag the scent of more interesting prey beneath his nose."

She tightened her hand abruptly around his. "Must you use the word *kill*?"

"Figure of speech, my dear," he said quickly, soothingly.

"I wish I could believe that." She sighed. "I hope we do not see either one of those men again."

The blue and sea green gowns are perfect for Edwina and Theodora," Concordia announced. She looked at the girls and Mrs. Oates. "Don't you agree?"

There was an affirmative murmur of approval.

"Lovely," Mrs. Oates said, studying Edwina and Theodora with warm admiration. "The dresses go ever so nicely with their pretty blond hair."

Edwina and Theodora held the gowns up in front of themselves and examined their images in the mirror. Their faces were aglow with delight. Behind them Hannah and Phoebe were waiting to take their turns in front of the looking glass.

It was five o'clock in the afternoon. Most of the assortment of gowns that had been ordered yesterday morning had yet to arrive from the dressmaker's, but enough had shown up a short time ago to provide everyone with a much needed change of clothes.

In addition, Mrs. Oates had made the trip to one of the large department stores on Oxford Street and returned with a variety of ready-made essentials such as shoes, hats, gloves and lingerie.

Dante and Beatrice, who had already become the girls' constant companions, had been temporarily banished into the hall to avoid any unfortunate canine-related accidents to the pretty clothes. Virtually everyone in the room was bubbling with excitement. Phoebe was the sole exception. She stood defiantly to the side, dressed in the inexpensive boy's trousers and shirt that had comprised her disguise after the return from London.

"You were right when you specified the yellow and brown material for Hannah," Mrs. Oates said, looking quite satisfied with the gown Hannah was trying on in front of the mirror. "The color goes very well with her eyes."

"It has very pretty flounces at the hem," Hannah said. "I wish Joan could see it."

Concordia did not like the whisper of sadness that she heard in Hannah's voice. "Don't worry, she will see your new dress very soon."

Hannah brightened. "It would be wonderful if she could have one just like it."

"Not likely," Edwina said. "At least, not as long as she's at Winslow. All of the students have to wear those dreadful gray dresses. You know that."

"Yes, but when she turns seventeen she will leave and then she can have a gown like mine," Hannah insisted.

"Joan will become a governess or a teacher like most of the other girls who attend Winslow," Theodora said in thoroughly squelching tones. "Women in those careers do not get to wear such pretty clothes."

Hannah's lower lip quivered. She blinked several times, very hard.

"Please do not cry, dear." Concordia thrust a handkerchief into her fingers. "When this affair is concluded, we will see about Joan."

Hannah wiped the moisture from her eyes. "Thank you, Miss Glade."

"Cheer up now and try on these pretty shoes," Mrs. Oates said, holding up a pair of pale yellow high-button boots. "They will go nicely with that gown."

Concordia looked at Phoebe. "What do you think of the pink dress?"

Phoebe scowled at the gown. "I do not want to go back to wearing dresses. I prefer my trousers instead."

"And you look quite dashing in them, indeed," Concordia said calmly. "You may wear them as often as you like. But just in case you want an occasional change, what do you think about the pink gown?"

Mollified by the knowledge that she was not going to be forced back into a dress, Phoebe studied the gown with a critical eye. "It will do for tea, I suppose."

"Right, then, that is settled," Concordia said.

Mrs. Oates nodded sagely. "I expect the gowns will need a bit of taking in here and there, but Nan is a fine hand with needle and thread. I'll send her up to have a look."

Concordia waved a hand at the unopened packages. "Onward to the gloves, ladies."

Edwina, Theodora, Hannah and Phoebe tore into the wrappings.

Concordia went to stand next to Mrs. Oates. Together they watched the girls try on the gloves.

"I am very grateful to you, Mrs. Oates," Concordia murmured. "You did a fine job with the shopping."

"It was no problem." Mrs. Oates chuckled. "Indeed, I quite enjoyed myself."

"I must say, I was astounded that the dressmaker was able to supply so many dresses on such short notice. She must have put off all of her other projects in favor of satisfying this order."

Mrs. Oates raised her brows and looked knowing. "I'm sure she did precisely that."

"The dressmaker is a friend of Mr. Wells?" Concordia inquired smoothly.

"A former client more like. She was no doubt happy enough to pay her bill at last."

Concordia stared at the expensive gowns, shocked. "Good heavens, do you mean to say that the fee Mr. Wells charged for his services amounted to the cost of these gowns?"

"No, no, no, Miss Glade." Mrs. Oates waved that aside with a chuckle. "Mr. Wells paid full price for the dresses. The favor he asked was that they be made up and delivered as quickly as possible. That was how the dressmaker settled her account with him."

"I see. Mr. Wells handles his business in a most unusual manner, doesn't he?"

"Yes, Miss Glade, he does, at that."

"There is something that confuses me, Mrs. Oates."

"Yes, Miss Glade?"

"If Mr. Wells does not charge money for his services and instead merely collects favors when he needs them, I assume that he is a wealthy man."

"He is quite comfortably fixed and that's a fact."

"Yet he occupies another man's house," Concordia added.

"Oh, Mr. Stoner doesn't mind him living here."

"Yet they are not blood relations?"

"No, Miss Glade. Not related in any way. Just good friends."

"*Very* good friends, evidently."

"Aye, Miss Glade. That they are, that they are."

"Mr. Stoner obviously places a great deal of trust in Mr. Wells," she said as tactfully as possible.

Mrs. Oates rocked slightly, acknowledging the comment. "That he does."

Very good friends. Concordia thought about the casual manner in which Ambrose had referred to the possibility that a woman might take another woman as a lover. Was he at ease with the subject because his own personal physical interests were directed at members of his own sex? It might explain the odd connection between Ambrose and the mysterious Mr. Stoner.

It was also, from her purely personal and private point of view, quite depressing.

Then again, it was not as if she had ever had any real expectations of indulging in a passionate liaison with Ambrose Wells, she reminded herself.

"Would you look at the time?" Mrs. Oates gave a small start. "How did it get to be so late? I must be off to see about the preparations for dinner. If you will excuse me, Miss Glade, I'll leave you and the young ladies to the new clothes."

She bustled out the door and disappeared.

Concordia tapped one finger against the top of the dressing table, absently listening to the girls discuss the matching of shoes, gloves and dresses.

So much for her attempt to elicit information about the odd workings of this household. Obviously she would have to take a more crafty approach in the future if she wished to learn anything useful.

The knock on the library door pulled Ambrose out of a deep contemplation of the garden on the other side of the French doors. He surfaced slowly from the meditative trance.

"Come in," he said.

He heard the door open behind him but he did not turn around. He remained where he was, seated cross-legged on the carpet, hands resting on his knees.

Mrs. Oates cleared her throat. "My apologies for intruding on you, sir, but I thought you should know that Miss Glade has started asking questions about Mr. Stoner."

"It was inevitable, Mrs. Oates. With luck, the mystery will occupy her attention while I take care of other matters."

"If I were you, I would not depend on Miss Glade becoming so distracted that she ceases to pay heed to what is going on around here, sir."

"Thank you, Mrs. Oates. I will keep your warning in mind."

"Very good, sir."

"Are the young ladies pleased with their new clothes?"

"All except Miss Phoebe, sir. I believe she has developed a great fondness for trousers."

He smiled. "Ours is an unconventional household. She is free to wear them here."

"Yes, sir. Will you be dining in tonight with Miss Glade and the young ladies?"

"I am looking forward to it." He paused. "But I intend to go out later after our guests are in their beds. There is no need for anyone to wait up for me. I will likely be quite late."

"Very good, Mr. Wells."

The door closed with a hushed sound. Ambrose went back to his meditation on the garden. The past whispered through his thoughts.

HE HAD JUST TURNED EIGHTEEN the night he entered John Stoner's elegant town house through a rear window on an upstairs floor.

His career as a burglar had begun his first night on the street. But his survival instincts had been keen, even at the age of thirteen. He made his way to the nearest cemetery, burgled the lock on the back door of the small chapel and spent the remaining hours until dawn holed up behind the altar.

He did not sleep that night for fear of the dreams he was certain awaited him. He knew, even then, that the events of the night would haunt him for the rest of his life.

He forced himself to do what his grandfather and father had taught him to do before tackling a new enterprise. He made a plan. When it was finished he allowed himself the cold comfort of a few tears.

The next morning, taking to heart the old axiom that the Lord helps those who help themselves, he helped himself to some of the church silver. He selected a rather nice pair of candlesticks and two cups, said a prayer and set out to make his way in the world using the family talents. He knew full well how to go about pawning the items. His father and grandfather had visited the pawnshops often enough in the past when business was not good.

On the whole, a life of crime had proved to be an excellent career choice, he thought as he paused to study John Stoner's bedroom. It was not as if he had not been raised and trained for the work. He came from a long line of professional swindlers, fraud artists and cheats.

The room was empty, as he had anticipated. He had done his research carefully, watching John Stoner for nearly a week before making his plans. In that time he had learned that his intended victim was a scholarly man who had, in his younger days, spent a great deal of time in the Far East.

This was the night the servants had off. A survey of the house a short time ago had disclosed the information that the lights still burned downstairs in the library.

Through the crack in the curtains he had glimpsed Stoner, dressed in an expensively embroidered maroon dressing gown, sitting in front of a comfortable fire. He had a glass of port by his side and was deeply involved in a weighty tome.

Ambrose opened a drawer. The first thing he saw was a pocket watch. He recognized the unmistakable gleam of gold, even in the dim moonlight.

He reached for the watch.

The door to an adjoining room opened without warning.

"I do believe your eyes are even better than my own were at your age," John Stoner said from the shadows.

It was the first time he had been caught while going about his business, but Ambrose had known that sooner or later disaster might strike. He had practiced for just such an eventuality, just as his father and grandfather had taught him. And, as they had always admonished, he had not one plan but two.

Speed and agility formed the basis of Escape Plan Number One.

He did not stop to think, let alone grab the pocket watch. He leaped for the open window and the rope he had left secured to the sill. It would take only seconds to get to the ground.

But he never reached the window. His legs went out from underneath him. A split second later he found himself flat on his back on the floor. The jolt of the fall stunned him and stole his breath.

"Do not move."

Ignoring the command, he sucked in a lungful of air and hauled himself to his knees. His only thought was to reach the window.

A booted foot caught him at the ankle. He plunged headlong back to the floor.

Before he could rise a second time, Stoner leaned over him and seized first one of his wrists and then the other. Ambrose tried to struggle. He was much younger and stronger than his opponent. In addition, he was desperate. He should have had every advantage. Yet in seconds his hands were bound behind his back by a strong cord.

He kicked out with both feet. Stoner sidestepped easily.

"I admire your determination, young man, but I am not going to let you go. At least not yet." Stoner looked down at him. "There is an old saying, 'Do not hurl yourself against a fortress wall. Dig a tunnel beneath it.'"

Ambrose fought the panic that threatened to overwhelm him. He knew that it could destroy him as quickly as any bullet.

Time to fall back on Escape Plan Number Two. He started talking. Fast.

"I beg your pardon, sir. I don't believe I've ever heard that old saying. Shakespeare or Proverbs, perhaps?"

He employed the cool, carelessly cultured voice that he adopted when he dealt with men of this gentleman's world. It was a tone that conveyed the impression that he had been born in the same circles, that he was one of them.

It was nothing less than the truth. His father and grandfather had been scoundrels and rogues by choice, but they had been gentlemen by birth. He was well aware that one's social class was infinitely more important than one's morals.

With a little luck he might be able to talk his way out of this affair. Gentlemen did not like to send other gentlemen to prison.

Stoner shoved his hands deep into the pockets of his dressing gown and inclined his head, as though pleased. "Well done, young man. Not every housebreaker would be capable of making polite conversation at a time like this. You're thinking on your feet, or off them, as the case may be, and that is the important thing."

Ambrose did not have the vaguest notion of what he was talking about, but at least Stoner was making conversation, not summoning the constables.

"I apologize most sincerely for this unfortunate meeting, sir." Ambrose sat up cautiously. "I assure you, matters are not as they appear."

"Indeed?"

"I fear that tonight's work is the result of a few bottles of port and an unfortunate wager made with some of my friends." He grimaced. "You know how it is among men who have Oxford in common. Can't resist a dare."

"What was the nature of the wager?" Stoner sounded genuinely curious.

"As I said, a group of us spent a recent night drinking. Someone, Kelbrook, I believe it was, brought up the stories that have been appearing lately in the sensation press. You may have noticed them? A great deal of nonsense about a burglar who is said to prey exclusively upon wealthy gentlemen."

"Ah, yes, now that you mention it, I do recall reading one or two of those pieces. I believe the journalist who is writing them has nicknamed the rogue The Ghost."

Ambrose grunted in disgust. "The sensation press is very fond of attaching fanciful names to villains in an attempt to make them more interesting to their readers."

"True."

"Yes, well, as I was saying, Kelbrook mentioned The Ghost. My friends and I fell to arguing about how difficult it would be to imitate a successful burglar. I claimed it would not be at all hard to do. Someone else disagreed. One thing led to another and I am sorry to say that I accepted the bet."

"I see. What made you choose my window for this experiment?"

Ambrose exhaled deeply. "I'm afraid that you matched the description of the type of victim The Ghost is said to prefer."

Stoner chuckled. "You really are quite quick, young man, I will give you credit for that. What is your name?"

"Ambrose Wells," Ambrose said, using the name he had invented for himself the night he fled his father's house. If he got out of this he would come up with another.

"What do you say we go downstairs and have a cup of tea while we discuss your future, Mr. Wells."

"Tea?"

"I thought you might prefer it to the other option I am offering."

"What is the other option?"

"A meeting with a police detective. I doubt if you would be likely to get any decent tea in that case, however."

"Tea sounds like an excellent notion."

"I thought you would see it that way. Come along, then. Let us repair to the kitchens. We shall have to see to the business ourselves. This is the servants' night off. But then, you knew that, didn't you?"

———

A MBROSE SAT LASHED to a wooden chair and watched in silent astonishment as his host made tea. Unlike the vast majority of men of his rank and station, John Stoner appeared quite familiar, even comfortable, in his own kitchen. In a matter of minutes he had the kettle on the stove and tea leaves spooned into an elegant little pot.

"How long have you been pursuing your career as a ghost, Mr. Wells?" Stoner asked.

"No offense, sir, but that is a rather awkwardly worded question. Regardless of how I choose to answer it, you will have me admitting that I am The Ghost."

"I think that, under the circumstances, we can dispense with your artful little tale about a wager, don't you?" Stoner carried the pot and two small cups to the wooden plank table and set them down. "Let me see, from what I observed upstairs in the bedroom, you are right-handed. Therefore you will likely be a bit less agile with your left hand, so I shall free that one."

"You could see me that clearly in the shadows?" In spite of his predicament he was rapidly developing a great curiosity about John Stoner.

"As I mentioned, my night vision is not what it used to be, but it is still a good deal better than most men my age."

Stoner sat down on the opposite side of the table and poured tea. Ambrose noticed that the delicate cups had been fashioned without handles. Like the pot, they were decorated with exotic scenes that he could not identify. Not Chinese or Japanese, he thought. But there was something about the designs that let him know they had come from somewhere in the East.

He picked up one of the cups very carefully and inhaled the fragrance of the tea. It was delicate, complex and intriguing.

"Would you mind telling me how you discovered that I was upstairs?" he asked. "I thought you were engaged reading a book in the library."

"I have been expecting you for the past several days."

The elegant little teacup nearly slipped from Ambrose's fingers. "You noticed me?"

Stoner nodded absently, as if it were no great feat. But Ambrose knew that was not the case. None of his previous victims had ever detected him while he was following them about, making notes of their habits.

"I cannot say I was greatly surprised when you showed up here tonight," Stoner said. "From what I had read of The Ghost in the papers, I suspected that he made a thorough study of his victims before he entered their houses. I was interested in your methods. Most burglars lack either the intelligence or the patience to take such a careful approach. They are, by and large, opportunists, rather than strategists."

"I told you, sir, I am not The Ghost. I was merely trying to copy him for the sake of a wager. As you can see, I made a poor job of it."

Stoner sipped tea, looking thoughtful. "Actually, you managed the business quite skillfully. Who taught you your trade?"

"I'm a gentleman, sir. I would not think of lowering myself by going into trade."

Stoner chuckled. "This is going to be a very one-sided conversation if you insist upon evading all of my questions."

"I beg your pardon. You asked me a question. I attempted to answer it."

"The Strategy of False Sincerity is a useful tactic upon occasion and you appear to have a talent for it, but I can assure you that there is no point employing it with me tonight."

For the first time Ambrose started to wonder if John Stoner was a madman.

"I don't understand, sir," Ambrose said.

"Perhaps I am going about this in the wrong manner." Stoner held the little cup between his fingers in a way that implied both elegance and control. "Since you are not disposed to tell me your story, I shall tell you mine. When I have finished with it, we will discuss your future."

13

The offices of the Jervis agency were on the top floor of an ugly
stone building located in an unfashionable part of town. Shortly
after midnight Ambrose let himself inside with the aid of a lock pick.

He moved into the room, closed the door and stood quietly for a
moment, savoring the familiar frisson of excitement that flooded
through him.

He suspected that he had been born with an addiction for the rush of
icy energy that he experienced at moments like this one. It ignited all his
senses and left him feeling as though he could fly like some great night
bird. The drawback was that, like any other powerful drug, there were
aftereffects. It would take some time for the feeling of intense arousal to
evaporate from his bloodstream.

The reception room had been closed up for a long time. An invisible
miasma of stale air and the vague taint of another, more unpleasant odor
drifted through the space.

Tonight there was more than enough moonlight slanting through the undraped window to enable him to see that there was nobody in the room. Yet he would have been willing to wager a great deal of money that death had occurred here at some point in the recent past.

The area around the heavy desk was littered with broken glass, papers and pens. There had been a struggle.

He went through the desk drawers, but there was nothing out of the ordinary inside, just the usual assortment of notebooks, stationery, extra bottles of ink and sealing wax.

He found a black muff in the bottom drawer.

He crossed to the filing cabinets and opened the first one. It was crammed with papers. He struck a light and went through the folders in a swift, methodical fashion.

He was not greatly surprised to discover that there was no file for anyone named Bartlett. There had, after all, been nothing to indicate that she had been employed through the agency. The fact that there were no records for either a Concordia Glade or an Irene Colby, the false name Concordia had used in her previous post, was, on the other hand, extremely interesting.

He closed the drawers, put out the light and stood thinking for a time.

After a while he went back to the desk and reopened the bottom drawer. He took out the muff. There was a small pocket inside, but when he slid his fingers into it he discovered only a handkerchief.

He started to return the muff to the drawer. But something about the proportions of the interior space made him pause. They seemed slightly off. The drawer was too shallow.

Crouching, he felt around inside with his right hand, probing gently with his fingertips. The small depression in the wood was at the very back. It would have been nearly invisible to the casual observer, even in broad daylight.

He'd had some experience with false and secret drawers.

He pressed cautiously and felt a tiny spring respond. The bottom of the drawer rose with a tiny squeak of hidden hinges, revealing a concealed compartment.

The hiding place was empty except for a newspaper that had been folded in half twice, reducing it to a small rectangle.

He took it out of the drawer and opened it once so that it was only folded across the middle. He struck another light and read the familiar masthead. *The Flying Intelligencer* was a particularly lurid example of the sensation press, well known for its dramatic accounts of bloody crimes and its overheated serialized novels.

Why had Jervis gone to the trouble of concealing a newspaper? Perhaps she had put it out of sight so that a prospective client would not catch her with it. *The Flying Intelligencer* was occasionally entertaining, but it was hardly the sort of thing that the proprietor of an agency that supplied teachers and governesses would want to be seen reading.

Still, it seemed rather extreme to conceal it in a secret drawer in her desk. If Jervis's goal was to place it out of sight of visitors, it would have been sufficient to simply drop the paper into the top of the drawer along with her muff.

He slipped the folded paper inside his coat and let himself out of the office.

Downstairs he exited the empty building through a rear door. Out-

side in the alley he turned up the high collar of his coat, pulled the low-crowned hat down to veil his face and walked away into a maze of unlit lanes and cramped streets.

He took a different route out of the neighborhood than the one he had used to enter it, emerging near a nondescript brothel. A number of hansom cabs waited in the street. He chose one at random.

Seated in the cab, he turned down the carriage lamps. It was unlikely that anyone would notice one more drunken gentleman making his way home after a night spent pursuing various vices, but there was no point in taking chances.

He lounged deeper into the darkness of the cab and wondered if Concordia would still be awake when he returned. The urgent desire to see her and talk to her about what he had discovered tonight was disturbing in some ways.

The newspaper crackled softly under his coat. He would wait until he got home to examine it more closely. His night vision was excellent, but not even he could read in the dark.

14

The click of the dogs' nails dancing on the floorboards of the landing was the first indication that Ambrose had returned.

Concordia experienced a profound rush of relief. He was safely home. Now, perhaps, she would be able to shake off the feeling of dread that had descended on her after he had left.

Her second reaction to his presence in the house was a jolt of anticipation. She could hardly wait to learn what, if anything, he had discovered in the course of his investigation of the offices of the Jervis agency.

She heard him say something very softly to the dogs. There was another soft patter of paws on wood and then silence. He had sent Dante and Beatrice upstairs to the floor on which the girls were sleeping.

The deep shadows beneath her bedroom door shifted faintly. Ambrose had paused in front of her room. Expecting to hear his soft knock at any instant, she pushed the covers aside, sat up and groped for her spectacles.

When she got the eyeglasses securely on her nose, she reached for her robe.

Still no knock.

The shadows under the edge of the door shifted again. She realized that Ambrose had changed his mind. He was continuing on down the hall to his own bedroom.

Alarmed, she tied the sash of her robe, slid her feet into the new slippers that Mrs. Oates had provided and rushed to the door. If Ambrose thought he could get away without making a full report to her tonight, he could think again.

She yanked open the door and leaned out into the darkened hall just in time to hear the hushed whisper of sound made by the closing of Ambrose's door.

She stepped into the chilly corridor and walked briskly to his bedroom.

Ambrose opened his door just as she raised her hand to knock. As if he had been expecting her, she thought. He stood silhouetted against the light of the lamp that glowed on the small desk behind him. His black linen shirt was unfastened. It hung loosely outside his trousers.

"You keep odd hours, Miss Glade," he said.

It dawned on her that she was staring at the deeply shadowed wedge of bare, masculine chest that was just visible between the edges of his open shirt.

Mortified, she pulled herself together with an act of sheer willpower, shoved her glasses firmly in place on her nose and reminded herself that she was on a mission.

"No odder than your own, sir," she whispered. "What happened? Did you learn anything of interest?"

"I can't be certain, but I strongly suspect that Mrs. Jervis is dead. There are signs of a violent struggle in her office. I found no files for you or for Bartlett."

"Dear heaven." A numb sensation seized her. She grasped the door frame to brace herself and focused on the most astonishing part of his dreadfully succinct report. "Mrs. Jervis is dead?"

"I have no proof of that yet. I will make inquiries tomorrow morning. But such news would not come as a surprise, given the fact that she may well have been involved with Alexander Larkin."

"If you are right, it means that there have been three deaths thus far in this affair. Your client's sister, Miss Bartlett and Mrs. Jervis." She shuddered and tightened her grip on the lapels of her robe. "Larkin must consider my girls very valuable, indeed."

"I agree." He shoved his fingers through his hair in what struck her as an uncharacteristic gesture of restlessness. "Would you mind waiting a few minutes for the details?" he asked. "I would like to wash my face and hands and clean up a bit. The hansom in which I returned was not the cleanest."

"What? Oh, yes, of course." She stepped quickly back out of his way. "I beg your pardon."

"I suggest you go downstairs to the library. I will meet you there in a few minutes and tell you what little I know."

"Very well." She hesitated uncertainly. "Are you all right? You were not hurt?"

"I am fine." He moved past her with an air of impatience. "Now, if you will excuse me?"

"Sorry," she mumbled.

He crossed the hall and wrapped his fingers around the knob of the door. "I won't be long."

"One moment, if you don't mind," she whispered, unable to restrain herself. "Did you find any clues?"

He looked back at her over his shoulder. "Not unless you count the newspaper."

"What newspaper?"

"The one that is on my writing desk." He angled his chin to indicate the interior of his bedroom. "I doubt if it will amount to a clue, but it looked as though it had been deliberately hidden. I found it tucked away beneath the false bottom of a drawer in Jervis's desk. You may take a look at it if you like."

He disappeared into the bath and closed the door.

She waited until she heard the muffled sound of water flowing through the pipes before she went slowly back to the doorway of Ambrose's bedroom and peered inside.

It was a decidedly masculine room done in shades of green and rich amber. The thick carpet was heavily patterned with giant ferns. The massive four-poster bed and a large wardrobe occupied a great deal of the space. The coat that Ambrose had recently discarded was flung carelessly across the bed.

She could see the folded newspaper on the writing table that stood near the window.

All she had to do was take a few steps, pick up the paper and depart. Yet she found herself hesitating. Entering Ambrose's bedroom struck her as an almost overwhelmingly intimate thing to do.

She drew a deep breath, strode briskly into the room, seized the newspaper and scurried back to the door.

It was only when she was safely out in the hall that she realized she had been holding her breath.

Ridiculous. It was merely a bedroom. Not only that, it was, if she had interpreted the few hints she had picked up from Mrs. Oates correctly, the private quarters of a man who did not have any sexual interest in women.

She hurried into her own room, turned up the lamp and opened the newspaper. Disappointment descended when she realized that she was looking at an edition of *The Flying Intelligencer* that was some six weeks old.

She opened the paper to its full width and turned the first page, looking for markings or notations that might have been made by Mrs. Jervis.

When she turned the second page, two sheets of writing paper fell out and fluttered lightly on the carpet.

She looked down at the papers and saw that they were letters. Both were addressed to R. J. Jervis. Both were signed by S. Bartlett.

She scooped up the letters and read each one quickly, her blood chilling with every sentence.

When she finished, she rushed back out into the hall. The water had stopped.

She rapped sharply on the door of the bath.

"Mr. Wells," she said, struggling to keep her voice from rising. The last thing she wanted to do was awaken any of the students upstairs. "Mr. Wells, you must see what I found in the newspaper."

He opened the door with an air of grim resignation. He had removed his shirt entirely, leaving himself quite nude above the waist.

She could see the glistening dampness of his bare skin where he had splashed cold water on his face and upper body. His shoulders appeared astonishingly broad. The contours of his chest and lean waist would have done credit to a statue of an ancient, mythic hero. A triangle of dark hair angled downward and disappeared beneath his trousers.

"What is it now, Miss Glade?" he asked politely.

She stared at him, aware that her jaw had dropped. "Good heavens, sir, is that a *tattoo*?"

He glanced down at the small flower on his upper right chest. "It is, indeed, Miss Glade. Very observant of you to notice."

"Good heavens," she said again. She drew a deep breath. "I have never met anyone with a tattoo."

"It appears that I have at last succeeded in shocking your extremely modern sensibilities."

"No, no, not at all," she said hastily. "It is just that, well, a *tattoo*?" She peered more closely at the small design. "It is a flower of some sort, is it not? I do not recognize the species."

"I will likely regret this," Ambrose said. He captured her chin and tilted it up so that he could look into her smoky eyes. "But I cannot seem to resist. You have caught me in a very weak moment, Miss Glade. The cold water was supposed to act as an antidote but it does not seem to have been effective."

"Antidote for what? Are you feverish, sir?"

"I am on fire, Miss Glade."

The next thing she knew his mouth was on hers in a kiss that made her forget everything else, including the tattoo.

15

He had not meant to kiss her. Not yet. Not tonight. It was too soon and the timing was wrong. That was why he had tried to send her downstairs a few minutes ago, why he had come in here to douse himself with a great quantity of icy water.

But instead she had come to him. The sight of her standing in the doorway of the bath, dressed in her robe, her soft mouth open in shock at the sight of the tattoo, was too compelling, too intimate.

Logic and good sense did not stand a chance.

He kissed her slowly, heavily, achingly aware that it would no doubt prove to be a grave mistake.

But she was the one who had come knocking on the door of the bath tonight, he reminded himself. And this was Miss Concordia Glade, the very unconventional daughter of the notoriously freethinking William Gilmore Glade and Sybil Marlowe. She was not some inexperienced, milk-and-water miss.

For a timeless instant she simply stood there as if she had been frozen into immobility. He caught the back of her head with one hand and deepened the kiss, desperate for a response that would indicate she felt at least some of what he was feeling.

She trembled. Her mouth softened. A tiny little moan of pleasure sighed through her.

"Mr. Wells," she whispered in soft, wondering tones. "It would appear that you are, indeed, attracted to women, after all."

He went quite still. Then, very cautiously, he raised his head.

"What the devil are you talking about?" he asked.

"It was something Mrs. Oates said. I got the impression that perhaps you and Mr. Stoner were more than just good friends."

"I see." Amusement welled up inside him. "Serves me right, no doubt."

"Never mind. It doesn't matter now."

"No, it does not. Allow me to correct the small misunderstanding."

He tightened his hold on her and kissed her again, very thoroughly this time.

She put her arms around his neck and kissed him back with an enthusiasm that made his head whirl. A hot tide of desire and a euphoric sense of exhilaration surged through him.

He tangled his fingers in her hair and devoured her mouth.

A long moment later he was forced to surface briefly for air.

"After all that we have been through together," he said, "I think it's time you started calling me Ambrose, don't you?"

"Ambrose."

He pulled back slightly and saw that her eyeglasses had become clouded from the effects of their combined breaths.

"My apologies." He smiled and removed her spectacles. "That must have been a bit like kissing a stranger in the dark."

"No," she said. She blinked once or twice and searched his face in an unfocused way. "I know exactly who you are."

"Concordia," he heard himself whisper. "What are you doing to me?"

He pulled her tightly to him, desperate to feel the soft warmth of her against his own heavily aroused body. Nothing else could assuage the hunger that was clawing at his insides.

She clung to him, seemingly as ravenous as he was. He reached down and undid the sash of her robe.

When his hand closed over her breast, she stiffened.

He managed to drag his mouth away from hers. "What is it?"

Her eyes were very wide and shadowed. She released him and took a quick step back.

"Good heavens, I almost forgot." She shoved a hand into the pocket of her robe.

"Forgot what?"

"The letters." She waved two sheets of paper at him. "That is what I came here to tell you. I found them tucked inside the newspaper. They are from Miss Bartlett. She wrote them to Mrs. Jervis while she was at Aldwick Castle. The last one is dated shortly before she disappeared."

He made himself refocus his attention on the two sheets of paper being waved in front of his face. "Let me see those."

She handed them to him. "Miss Bartlett discovered that something was amiss with the situation at the castle. In her first letter she mentions that no mail can be sent or received there. She says she got her letters posted by bribing one of the farmers who delivered produce to the castle kitchens."

He handed her the eyeglasses. "Go downstairs to the library. I will join you in a few minutes."

TEN MINUTES LATER, garbed in his dressing gown, he stood at his desk in the library. The two letters from Miss Bartlett addressed to Mrs. Jervis were spread out before him on top of the blotter.

"It is obvious that she and Jervis were well acquainted," he said.

"Yes." Concordia paced back and forth in front of the desk. "They communicate in the manner of two people who have known each other for some time."

"In the first letter Miss Bartlett tells her that she believes she has stumbled onto some sort of illicit scheme involving the girls she was hired to teach."

"She came to the same conclusion that I did." Concordia's fine mouth tensed. "There can be no mistake about it now. That vile Alexander Larkin was, indeed, attempting to set himself up in the business of procuring high-class courtesans."

He contemplated the letter for a moment. "The implication is that Phoebe, Hannah, Edwina and Theodora may have been experiments, as it were. If all went well, the project was to continue using other orphans."

"Despicable man."

Ambrose thought for a moment. "She doesn't mention Larkin by name. Very likely she was unaware of his connection to the business."

"You did say that he is careful to keep himself at arm's length from his illegal enterprises."

"Yes."

She clenched both hands into small fists. "Dreadful, odious, vile creature."

Ambrose planted his palms on the desk and read aloud from the first letter.

"'. . . There is little doubt about what is going on here. If the first auction is successful, there will be more. I see no reason why you and I should not take a portion of the profits. . . .'"

Concordia stopped abruptly. "It sounds as though Miss Bartlett was suggesting that she and Mrs. Jervis engage in blackmail, doesn't it?"

"Yes. Unfortunately the name of the intended victim is not mentioned in either letter."

She frowned. "You just told me that Larkin would have been careful to make certain that his name was not associated with this business. They must have had someone else in mind to blackmail."

"I think so, yes. And it makes some sense." Ambrose walked around to the front of the desk and lounged back against the edge. "There is more going on here than I have told you, Concordia."

"What do you mean?"

"There have been rumors for months that Larkin has formed a partnership with a gentleman who moves in Society. It may be that the new business associate was the person who approached Mrs. Jervis and asked her to find a teacher for the first four girls in this experiment. Miss Bartlett and Mrs. Jervis may have attempted to blackmail him."

She folded her arms beneath her breasts. "If Larkin's new partner moves in Society, he would certainly have been vulnerable to blackmail."

"And no doubt willing to commit murder to protect himself."

There was a long silence while they both considered that.

"How could Miss Bartlett do that?" Concordia asked after a while.

"Risk blackmail?" He shrugged. "She was making her living in a profession that does not pay well. She saw an opportunity to improve her finances so she seized it."

Concordia shook her head. "I wasn't talking about the blackmail attempt. I meant, how could she consider getting more deeply involved in that dreadful scheme? How could she even think of doing that to the girls placed in her care?"

He smiled a little, recalling that first sight of her in the stable, struggling to control a nervous horse and aim a pistol at a villain so that she could engineer the escape of Edwina, Theodora, Hannah and Phoebe.

"I think it is safe to say that Miss Bartlett's character was very unlike your own," he said gently.

"But she was a *teacher*."

"No, Concordia." He straightened and walked to stand in front of her. "You are a teacher. Miss Bartlett was in another line, altogether."

"What are you thinking?" she asked, using every effort to compose herself.

"That if I had any sense, I would send you upstairs to bed. It is late."

She stilled. "Yes, it is. Very late."

"Much too late for me, certainly."

134

He raised his hands and slid them around the nape of her neck, bent his head and kissed her again. She shivered in the most delicious manner.

He eased her lips apart with the edge of his thumb and drank deep. Her fingers convulsed on his shoulders.

He undid the sash of her robe for the second time that night. The garment parted, revealing the white linen nightgown underneath.

She mumbled urgently when he cupped her breasts in his palms. Through the thin material of the gown he could feel the tight little peaks of her nipples.

He moved his hands lower and found the full, round curves of her thighs.

She shuddered and pushed her fingers up into his hair.

He lifted her into his arms and started toward the sofa. She looked up at him with eyes that were pools of dreams.

He set her down on the sofa and reached out to remove her eyeglasses.

A staccato of sharp, demanding raps sounded on the library door.

"Miss Glade?" Theodora's voice was muffled by the heavy wood panel. "Please come quickly. Hannah has had another one of her nightmares. She is crying and will not stop."

Ambrose saw Concordia tense instantly. The sensual invitation evaporated from her eyes in a heartbeat. She bounded up from the sofa, grabbing at the sash of the robe.

"I must go to Hannah at once," she said. She hurried toward the door and raised her voice. "I am coming, Theodora."

He adjusted his own robe while he watched Concordia rush to the mirror to check her appearance.

When she had set herself to rights, she went to the door and opened it.

Theodora, dressed in a robe and slippers, hovered in the hall, looking appropriately anxious. When she caught sight of Ambrose, her eyes narrowed.

"I went to your bedroom but you weren't there," she said to Concordia. "Then I noticed that there was a light on down here."

"Mr. Wells and I were discussing something of importance that occurred today," Concordia said crisply. She moved out into the hall and paused to look back at Ambrose. "I trust you will excuse me, sir. I had hoped that Hannah would not suffer another nightmare quite so soon."

He studied Theodora, who was watching him with an expression that struck him as somewhat too innocent.

"The timing of this particular bad dream is, indeed, quite interesting," he said.

Concordia was clearly baffled. "I beg your pardon?"

"Good night, Miss Glade." He inclined his head in a small bow. "Rest assured, we will finish our conversation at another time."

She blushed. "Good night, sir."

She went out into the hall and closed the door very quickly behind her.

Ambrose waited for a moment or two. Then he turned down the lamp and let himself out of the library.

He went up the stairs, listening closely. When he reached the landing, he heard muffled whispers and a faint giggle emanating from the
darkened landing of the next floor.

There was a light flurry of footsteps overhead, a hastily closed door
and then abrupt silence.

16

The following morning Ambrose surveyed the crowded breakfast room from his seat at the head of the table. Concordia occupied the chair at the opposite end. He thought she looked very good in that position, as though she belonged there, right where he could see her first thing every day.

Her hair was pinned up into another neat, elegant coil. She wore one of the new gowns he had ordered from the dressmaker. This one was of a pretty bronze material patterned with stripes the color of red sealing wax.

The girls were all in excellent spirits this morning, he noted. A tribute to the resilient powers of youth.

Hannah in particular appeared remarkably cheerful after her supposedly troubled night. Phoebe, seated next to her, was bright and happy-looking in her boy's trousers and shirt. He made a note to send a message to his tailor to commission some more male attire of better quality for her.

Edwina and Theodora sat on the other side of the table, angelic in green and blue. They talked enthusiastically about the tour of the conservatory that Oates had promised to provide.

Ambrose ate his eggs and toast and listened to the lively conversation going on around the table. He was amused and bemused by his own reaction to the presence of Concordia and the girls. For years it had been his custom to spend this hour of the day alone with his newspapers. But this morning the papers sat untouched on a side table. It would have been impossible to concentrate on them in any event, given the students' chatter, he told himself.

He could always read the papers later.

"I intend for us to resume some of our studies this morning," Concordia said decisively.

Her announcement was met with near universal amazement and some consternation.

"But, Miss Glade," Theodora said earnestly, "we do not have any books, or rulers or globes or maps."

Concordia gave Ambrose a challenging smile. "I'm sure Mr. Wells will not mind if we turn the library into a temporary schoolroom."

Ambrose considered that proposition briefly and then shrugged. "No, Mr. Wells does not mind."

"Thank you, sir." Concordia gave him an approving look.

Phoebe turned to Ambrose, dubious. "Are there any books about chemistry in the library, sir?"

"You will find chemistry texts in the second bookcase on the right as you walk through the door," Ambrose said.

"What about ancient Egypt?" Edwina asked. "That is my favorite subject."

"Ancient Egypt is on the balcony just at the top of the staircase. There are also a large number of volumes on China, America, India, Africa and a number of other locales."

She brightened. "Really?"

"Really." He forked up another bite of eggs. "Mr. Stoner spent many years traveling the world. He wrote some of the books that you will find in the library."

The girls were fascinated. Concordia looked politely suspicious.

"You will also find some interesting artifacts that Mr. Stoner brought back from some of his journeys. One in particular may intrigue you. It is called a Cabinet of Curiosities. Legend has it that there are a hundred and one drawers concealed inside but no one has ever been able to find and open that many."

"A cabinet filled with secret drawers." Phoebe was enthralled. "How exciting. May we attempt to open some of them, Mr. Wells?"

"Be my guest."

Edwina looked hopeful. "Does the library include any of Mrs. Browning's work? I adore her poetry."

"Elizabeth Barrett Browning and her husband are both there," he assured her. "Shelved right next to each other. Seemed only fitting."

Theodora leaned forward slightly to look down the length of the table at him. "Are there any watercolor paints and brushes?"

He thought about it. "I believe there may be some art supplies in one of the cupboards. They will be quite old, though. I will have Oates purchase some fresh paints today."

Theodora was pleased. "Thank you, sir. That would be lovely. When Miss Glade arrived at the castle, she brought some excellent paints and brushes with her, but we were forced to leave most of them behind when we escaped."

"I understand," he said.

"What about novels, sir?" Hannah asked. "I am very interested in them, especially the sort that feature secret marriages and missing heirs and madwomen in the attic."

"You refer to sensation novels," he said.

"Yes, sir." Hannah smiled encouragingly.

He helped himself to some toast. "I think I can say with absolute certainty that the library does not contain a single sensation novel."

"Oh." Hannah's face fell.

The enthusiasm on the faces of the other three girls dimmed somewhat, also.

"How unfortunate," Hannah mumbled.

He studied their disappointed expressions.

"This household receives a number of newspapers," he said finally. "Several of them feature serialized novels. You are welcome to read those." He hesitated, catching Concordia's eye. "Assuming Miss Glade does not object."

"Not at all." Concordia buttered a bit of toast. "I am a firm believer in the value of novel reading. It encourages the development of the creative imagination and allows one to experience certain strong passions and emotions that must, of course, be restrained in polite society."

He raised his brows. "You amaze me, Miss Glade. I doubt that there are many in your profession who would agree with your views. I'm certain that the vast majority of educators and most parents, for that matter, consider sensation novels to be a very improper influence on young minds."

"I am aware that my approach to the education of young ladies is somewhat unusual."

"'Unique' might be a more fitting word," he said, amused.

"Perhaps." Enthusiasm lit her eyes. "But I believe very strongly in my theories. One day I intend to establish my own school for young ladies based on the principles that I have developed."

He lowered the uneaten slice of toast, fascinated by the small glimpse of her personal hopes and dreams.

"I believe you did mention that," he said quietly.

"My school will be founded on the same notions of education that inspired my parents," she said. "They were convinced, and I agree, that a broad, wide-ranging curriculum not only develops powers of logic and reasoning in young ladies, it will prepare them for the various professions and careers. It is my firm conviction that young ladies who are equipped to make their own way in life will no longer feel pressured to marry for reasons of financial necessity."

"But, as you have noted, many of the professions and careers remain closed to women," he pointed out.

Her brows snapped together above the rims of her spectacles. "One of the arguments used to keep women out of medical schools and other professional institutions is that they are not properly prepared academically. But the girls who graduate from *my* school will be able to hold their own with male students. What is more, they will emerge resolved to take a stand and agitate for their right to be admitted to the professions."

"I see."

"Mark my words, sir. When a sufficient number of women unite to demand their rights, there will be great changes in the world."

He inclined his head respectfully. "I am impressed with your dedication to your goals, Miss Glade. I wish you the best of luck with your grand plans."

She gave him a glowing smile. "Thank you, sir. Your attitude indicates that you are very advanced in your thinking on such matters."

He grinned. "For a man, do you mean?"

She turned pink. "For anyone, male or female. Generally speaking, there is a great resistance to the notions of equal rights for women, as I'm sure you are aware."

"That may be true of society in general. But this household, like the one in which you were raised, Miss Glade, subscribes to a somewhat unconventional approach to many things."

She cleared her throat. "Yes, well, enough of that topic. We all have a busy day ahead of us." She crumpled her napkin and placed it on the table beside her plate. "If you will all excuse me, I am going to have a look around the library and gather some materials together for today's lessons."

He got to his feet and circled the table to hold her chair. "Let me know if you have any questions about the contents of the library."

"Yes, thank you, I will do that." She rose and walked quickly to the door, where she paused to look at Hannah, Edwina, Theodora and Phoebe. "I will expect you all in the library in twenty minutes."

There followed a dutiful series of "Yes, Miss Glade."

Concordia swept out of the room. The small bustle at the back of her gown caused the bronze-and-red-striped skirts of the dress to sway in an elegant, enticing manner that Ambrose was certain he could have studied for hours.

He became aware of the fact that the room had gone very quiet behind him. When he turned, he discovered that the four girls were watching him with intent, serious expressions.

He went back to his chair at the head of the table and sat down.

"Is there something wrong?" he asked politely.

Hannah, Theodora and Phoebe shifted their gazes to Edwina.

Evidently having decided to accept the responsibility that had been silently thrust upon her, Edwina rose, went to the door and closed it very firmly. She returned to her chair and sat down, resolved.

"We are very concerned about Miss Glade's situation, sir," she said.

Ambrose poured more tea into his cup. "Her situation?"

"In this household," Theodora clarified.

"Right, then." He sat back. "I believe I've got it straight now. You are very concerned about Miss Glade's situation in this household."

Phoebe bobbed her head quickly, seemingly pleased that he had grasped the concept so readily. "That is correct, Mr. Wells."

"The thing is," Hannah said very gravely, "although Miss Glade is quite intelligent and well educated and extremely modern in her notions, she has not had a great deal of practical experience."

He considered each of the girls in turn. "I think you may all be underestimating her. Miss Glade has managed to survive on her own in the world for several years. You must trust me when I tell you that no one can manage that feat successfully without acquiring a good amount of practical experience."

"You are missing the point, sir," Edwina said with a flash of impatience. "Certainly Miss Glade has *some* types of practical knowledge. She knows how to read train schedules and how to rework a gown so that it can be worn for more than one season, for example. But she has had very little experience in the ways of gentlemen."

"I see."

"Ladies who make their livings as teachers are obliged to be extremely cautious in their dealings with gentlemen," Theodora said, earnest and helpful. "They cannot afford the least hint of scandal because it will cost them their posts."

"Therefore they get very little experience in that sort of thing," Hannah added.

Ambrose reached for his cup. "You are all quite certain that Miss Glade does not know how to deal with gentlemen?"

"Miss Glade has spent her entire career working as a governess and teaching in girls' schools," Phoebe said flatly. "That is why we can be sure that she has had very little practical experience in that direction."

Ambrose put down his cup. "This is about the events of last night, isn't it?"

Phoebe, Hannah, Edwina and Theodora exchanged somber glances with one another and then turned back to him. He found himself facing four extremely determined pairs of eyes.

"I see we must be blunt, sir," Edwina said ominously. "Last night we were obliged to rescue Miss Glade because she is too lacking in experience to perceive the dangers of the situation in which she found herself."

"What dangers, precisely, would those be?" Ambrose queried.

They all blushed and exchanged another round of anxious glances. But no one backed down. He wondered if they realized that they were all angling their chins and shoulders in the same determined manner that Concordia did when she was intent upon a goal. They had learned more from her in the past few weeks than they even knew, he mused. Concordia had become a model of feminine behavior for them.

"We are talking about the risks a lady takes when she is alone with a gentleman in the middle of the night," Phoebe said in a quick little rush of words.

"When she is alone with him in her robe and nightgown," Hannah elaborated.

"When the gentleman in question is also dressed in only a robe," Edwina said.

"We do realize," Theodora added, not unkindly, "that because Miss Glade is so clever and because she holds such advanced views, a man of the world might assume that she possesses more experience in certain matters than is actually the case."

He inclined his head. "I comprehend your concerns."

Hannah, at least, appeared satisfied. "We would not want Miss Glade to suffer the fate of Lucinda Rosewood."

"Who is Lucinda Rosewood?" he asked.

"She is the heroine of *The Rose and the Thorns*," Hannah said. "It is an excellent new novel by one of my favorite authors. In chapter seven Lucinda Rosewood is seduced by Mr. Thorne, who takes advantage of her naïve and trusting nature. Afterward, she realizes that she has been ruined, so she flees into the night."

"Then what happens?" he asked, reluctantly fascinated.

"I don't know," Hannah admitted. "I brought it with me when we left the castle, but I have not had time to finish it."

"I see." Ambrose pondered that briefly. "Well, I wouldn't worry about it, if I were you. I expect when you get the opportunity to finish the book, you will discover that Mr. Thorne races after Lucinda Rosewood, apologizes for taking advantage of her and asks her to marry him."

"Do you really think so?" Hannah asked eagerly.

"Don't be ridiculous," Phoebe said in a thoroughly squelching manner. "Gentlemen never marry ladies they have ruined unless the lady in question happens to be an heiress. Everyone knows that."

"Quite right," Edwina agreed. "Impoverished ladies who are ruined always come to a bad end in novels just as they do in real life."

Theodora scowled. "It isn't fair. It is the gentlemen who should come to bad ends, just as Miss Glade says."

"She may be correct in the highest moral and philosophical sense, but the fact is, that is not the way of the world," Edwina declared. She fixed Ambrose with a forceful expression. "But it is precisely because she holds such advanced views that Miss Glade may inadvertently give a worldly gentleman a false impression."

"You have made your point," Ambrose said.

Edwina seemed satisfied with that. She looked around at the others. "We had best be off to the library before Miss Glade comes in search of us."

"I cannot wait to see the Cabinet of Curiosities," Phoebe declared.

"And the books of poetry," Theodora exclaimed.

Ambrose rose and reached for the nearest chair, but the girls were already on their feet and dashing toward the door.

"One moment, if you don't mind," he said quietly.

They halted obediently in the doorway and turned with inquiring expressions.

"Yes, sir?" Edwina asked.

"You were all living in an orphanage before you were sent to the castle, I believe."

It was as if a cloud had materialized overhead in the previously sunny breakfast room. All the light went out of the girls' faces.

"That is correct, sir," Theodora said in a very small voice.

"Did you all come from the same institution?" he asked.

"Yes, sir," Phoebe whispered.

"Please, don't send us back to that dreadful place, sir." Hannah's hands clenched at her sides. Her eyes filled with tears. "We will be very, very good."

Theodora's mouth trembled. Phoebe blinked several times. Edwina sniffed.

Ambrose felt like an ogre in a fairy tale. "Of all the damnable nonsense."

That produced a round of startled expressions. He reminded himself that one did not swear in front of ladies, especially young ones.

"My apologies." He yanked out a handkerchief and shoved it into Hannah's fingers. "Dry your eyes, girl. No one is contemplating sending you back to the orphanage."

"Thank you, sir." Hannah bobbed an elegant little curtsy and hastily turned back toward the door.

Theodora, Phoebe and Edwina made to follow in her wake.

"One more question," he said.

All four girls froze like so many rabbits confronting a wolf.

Theodora swallowed heavily. "What is the question, sir?"

"I would like to know the name of the charity school where you resided before you were sent to the castle."

They gave that a moment's careful consideration, clearly still wary of his intentions.

Edwina finally faced him. "It is called the Winslow Charity School for Girls."

"And the address?" he prompted.

"Number six, Rexbridge Street," Phoebe said. She looked as though the words had been dragged out of her by force. "It is a terrible place, sir."

Hannah was beyond tears now. She had turned quite pale. "Miss

Pratt, the headmistress, punishes anyone who does not obey the Golden Rules for Grateful Girls by locking them in the cellar. Sometimes they have to stay down there in the darkness for days. It is . . . very frightening."

The cellar was the source of her nightmares, Ambrose realized.

"Enough," he said. "None of you will be sent to any institution against your will."

The cloud that had darkened the breakfast room miraculously vanished. Sunlight returned.

The girls dashed off down the hallway. Their lilting voices echoed cheerfully in the big house.

Finding himself alone at last, Ambrose sat down. He looked at the stack of newspapers for a moment and then reached for *The Times*.

After a while he realized that the breakfast room, the place that had always been his early morning sanctuary, felt strangely empty.

17

Shortly after three o'clock that afternoon Concordia felt the now familiar frisson of awareness. She looked up from the menus she had been preparing to give to Mrs. Oates and saw Ambrose standing in the doorway of the library. He carried a box under one arm.

"There you are, sir." She set her notes aside and surveyed him from the depths of the wingback chair. "I was just making out a list of fresh fruits and vegetables that I would like to see included in Mrs. Oates's menus. What kept you? You said you were going out to conduct a few inquiries, but you have been gone for several hours."

"I thought you would be occupied with the girls and their lessons until I returned." He walked across the library and sat down behind his desk. "Where are your students?"

"I sent them off on a tour of the conservatory with Mr. Oates. I suspect that he will do a far more expert job of instructing them in botany than I ever could."

"He will certainly enjoy the task." Ambrose set the box on top of the desk. "Oates has a great passion for his gardening."

"That is obvious." She watched him sit down behind his desk. "Well? Are you going to tell me what you have been about while you were out?"

"Among other things, I made some inquiries in the street where Mrs. Jervis lived."

She caught his use of the past tense instantly. "She is dead, then?"

"Her body was pulled out of the river nearly six weeks ago. Suicide was the verdict."

"If it was, indeed, murder, it occurred very close to the time that Miss Bartlett disappeared."

"Larkin or his partner probably used Jervis's files to find a replacement for Bartlett."

Concordia tightened her grip on the arm of her chair. "Me."

"Yes. After I got that information I paid a visit to a certain institution located on Rexbridge Street."

"The charity school where my students lived? Why did you go there?" Alarm stiffened her entire body. "Surely you are not thinking of sending the girls back to that dreadful place. Because if that is the case, I must tell you it is out of the question. If my young ladies have become a nuisance to you and you would prefer that we leave this house, we will, of course, do so. But I cannot allow—"

"Not again, I beg you." He held up a hand to ward off the lecture. "I went through this with your four pupils this morning. No one will be returning to the Winslow Charity School for Girls against her will. You have my word on it."

She relaxed. "I know it cannot be convenient having all of us here."

"This is a big house," he said. "There is plenty of room."

"Thank you. Winslow is such an unhappy place, by all accounts. I gather that the headmistress, Miss Pratt, was not the least bit modern in her approach to instruction, and the employees of the school were very unkind. That is where Hannah started having nightmares."

"I heard all about the cellar."

"Such a cruel punishment. Every time I think about it, I want to strangle Miss Pratt."

"I don't blame you. Now, if you don't mind, may we return to the subject at hand?"

"Yes, of course." She clasped her hands in her lap and assumed an attentive expression.

"Concerning my expedition to Rexbridge Street." He leaned back in his chair, extended his legs and laced his fingers behind his head. "It occurred to me this morning that the charity school was the one thing all four girls had in common."

"You're right. It is a connection, of sorts, isn't it?"

"Yes. With that in mind I walked through the neighborhood today to study the place."

"Did you go inside?"

"No. I could see no convenient way to do so without calling attention to myself. I would prefer not to do that at this point."

"I understand. But surely you cannot mean to go in at night as you did when you searched Mrs. Jervis's offices?"

"It is a possibility," he conceded, looking thoughtful. "But with so many people living in the building, there is a very high risk of wandering down the wrong hall and accidentally awakening one of the girls or blundering into a member of the staff who happens to be up and about for some reason."

"Quite true."

He looked at her with a considering expression. "You said you wished to be involved in this investigation. Did you mean that in the literal sense?"

"Certainly." Excitement made her catch her breath. "You want me to go into the school?"

"Only if you feel comfortable with the notion of playing the spy."

"It sounds quite thrilling."

He frowned. "It is my fondest hope that there will be nothing the least bit thrilling about this venture. You are to go there on a matter of routine business. You will not say or do anything that refers to Edwina, Hannah, Phoebe or Theodora. Nor will you make any mention of Aldwick Castle or other recent events. Is that quite clear?"

"Yes, absolutely. No one at Winslow knows me so there should be no problem."

"True. Nevertheless, there is no point taking chances. I do not want anyone, especially Miss Pratt, to get a close look at your face."

"I am to wear a disguise?"

"Of a sort." He unlaced his fingers, sat forward and reached for the box he had put on the desk. "I picked this up on the way back here this afternoon. It is the reason that I was late."

He removed the lid of the box, reached inside and took out a large, wide-brimmed hat fashioned of black straw. It was trimmed with black silk flowers and a long fall of heavy black netting.

"A widow's veil." Delighted, she sprang from her chair and hurried to the desk. She picked up the hat and turned it slowly in her hands, noting the circular sweep of the netting. "Very clever, sir. No one who sees me will be able to view my face."

"There are black gloves to match. Wear your dark gray cloak. You will look like any other fashionable widow."

18

Alexander Larkin looked at his business partner seated across from him on the carved marble bench and felt his back teeth grind together. The temperature in the private hot room was high enough to make any normal man sweat, but Edward Trimley appeared as cool and elegant as if he were ensconced in a chair in his club.

But, then, Trimley was a *gentleman,* Larkin reminded himself. The bastard had not been born in the stews. He spoke with cultured accents and carried himself with the refined arrogance that only those in the upper classes could successfully achieve.

Trimley had never had to steal food to survive, Larkin thought. He had never learned to sweat the way you sweated when you faced another man who held a knife and you knew in your vitals that the cove would cheerfully cut your throat just to take your boots.

"Are you certain that the fire was not the result of an accident?" he asked. "The kitchens at the castle were old, after all."

"Trust me, it was no kitchen fire," Trimley said.

Trimley's certainty irritated him. At the start of their arrangement, he had been eager enough to learn everything Larkin could teach him. But lately he had begun to act as if he were the senior partner.

They were both draped in large, white linen sheets. Larkin felt awkward and faintly ridiculous in his. He had to keep a firm hold on the front of the damned thing in order to prevent it from sliding off. But Trimley somehow managed to resemble one of those statues of ancient Romans that the wealthy used to decorate their mansions. Larkin had made certain that a vast number of them were installed in the front hall of the fine, big house that he, himself, had purchased a few years ago.

"What about that gas geyser in the bath in the new wing?" He rose and began to prowl the small, tiled chamber. "Everyone knows they're unpredictable."

"The fire did not start in the bath." Trimley sounded impatient. "I talked to every member of the staff who was there that night. They all agreed that there were two explosions and both occurred in the vicinity of the dining room."

Larkin grunted. "Part of a scheme designed to steal the girls?"

"So it appears."

"Bloody hell." Larkin reached the tiled wall, turned and started back in the other direction. "No one even *saw* the girls and the teacher leave?"

Trimley shook his head. "It was the middle of the night and there was a great deal of smoke and confusion. A couple of men told me that they heard the sound of horses' hooves at one point, but they both assumed that someone had freed the animals so that they could escape the flames."

"Why in hell didn't anyone see to the girls as soon as the fire started?" Larkin demanded. "My men knew that I considered them valuable."

"Evidently Rimpton did tell the others that he was going to take care of the young ladies." Trimley moved one hand in a dismissive gesture. "But he disappeared and never returned that night. The next day his body was found near some old storage sheds."

"And no one even considered the possibility that the teacher and the girls had escaped until the following day?"

"At first it was assumed that they had all perished in the blaze." Trimley shifted slightly on the bench, making himself more comfortable. "It was a reasonable enough conclusion under the circumstances. Given the enormous amount of smoking rubble and fallen timbers, it wasn't easy to conduct a thorough search of the ashes."

"Bloody hell." Larkin felt the old, familiar hot bubbling sensation deep inside him. "All that careful planning wasted. The auction was only days off. I can't believe it's come to this."

The old rage suddenly boiled up, threatening to choke him. He slammed a fist against the gleaming white-tiled wall.

"Bloody damn hell."

That did not satisfy, so he picked up the jug of water that sat on a small table and hurled it into the corner.

The ceramic container exploded. The bits and pieces of broken pottery danced and rang on the tiles.

Instantly he felt calmer, back in control. But he was already regretting the outburst.

He took a deep breath and released it slowly, letting his blood cool. The occasional raw flashes of fury had afflicted him all his life. He could control them now when he chose to do so, but sometimes he let them sweep over him. Generally speaking, they made others nervous. He considered that a good thing. It never paid to have one's employees and business associates get too comfortable.

But the elegant Mr. Trimley did not respond to such showy exhibitions of power the way others did. Larkin sensed that the outbursts elicited nothing but amused disdain in the arrogant bastard.

He tightened his grip on the sheet and swung around quite suddenly, trying to catch Trimley off guard, wanting to see if he could surprise a little fear in the man. But, as usual, there was nothing to be deciphered in his partner's veiled expression.

"Everything depended on those four girls," he muttered. "And now they're gone, thanks to that damned teacher. Why in blazes did she do it?"

"We must assume that she developed some suspicions concerning the fate of her predecessor and concluded that her own life was in jeopardy," Trimley responded calmly.

"That would explain why she fled the castle. But it doesn't tell me why she took the girls with her. It makes no sense. She had to know that they would only slow her down. She must have realized that her odds of a successful escape would have been considerably improved without the added baggage of four young ladies."

"Now that," Trimley said softly, "is a very interesting question. I spent most of the journey back to London contemplating it."

Larkin stopped and turned sharply. "You have some notion of what this is all about?"

"I agree with you that it seems less than rational for a woman who was in fear for her life to burden herself with four girls." Trimley paused deliberately. "But I think that it is safe to say the teacher was not working alone."

"What the devil are you talking about?"

"I do not believe that Miss Glade, clever though she may be, was the one who arranged to remove the young ladies from the castle."

"She had help? One of the guards? Well, it isn't the first time that I've been betrayed by a member of my own organization, but such things don't happen often and that's a fact. Everyone knows the penalty."

"Not one of your people," Trimley said. "I was able to get a bit of a description of him from the proprietors of the inn where he put up for the night with the teacher and the girls." An intrigued expression darkened his eyes. "They described him as well spoken and well mannered. In short, a gentleman."

"They're certain this man was a gentleman?" Larkin asked. "Not just acting the part?"

Trimley quirked a brow. "Forgive me for pointing out that the role of gentleman is not an easy one to play unless one has been born into the part. In any event, it has been my experience that innkeepers, like shopkeepers, are invariably correct when it comes to judging the class of their customers. They have that much in common with you, Larkin, in that their livelihoods depend upon a certain degree of skill in that regard."

Larkin willed himself to ignore that. Trimley considered him good enough to associate with when it came to business affairs, but the bastard's contempt for those he considered his social inferiors was never far below the surface.

"Did these innkeepers have any other useful information?"

"No. Only that the ladies and their escort were bound for London. I checked with the station master. He remembered the girls and their teacher quite well. They traveled first class."

"What of this gentleman who accompanied them?" Larkin asked swiftly.

"Interestingly enough, the station master did not recall any male companion. He seems to have disappeared somewhere between the inn and the train."

Larkin could feel the sweat running down the back of his neck. "Well, at least the man's presence does explain a few things."

"Most especially Rimpton's crushed skull and Bonner's concussion and broken arm," Trimley said.

Larkin frowned. "What's this? I thought you said that Rimpton died in the fire."

"I said he died that night. But I was able to examine the body and I am quite certain that he was killed by human hand, not the flames."

Larkin snorted. "No lady teacher could have done that. You're right. She had help. The question is, what does the lady's *gentleman* associate have in mind? Even if he is aware of the details of our plans, he can't hope to duplicate them on his own. It took us months to make the arrangements for the auction."

"There is no need for him to imitate us in order to achieve a profit,"

Trimley said. "You have a head for business, Larkin. What would you do if you found yourself in possession of certain commodities that you knew to be of great value to someone else?"

Larkin started to relax for the first time since he had gotten word of the loss of the girls. "I'd offer the former owner a chance to repurchase his missing valuables."

"Precisely. I expect that, sooner or later, whoever took the girls will put out the word that he is ready to negotiate. And then we'll have him."

"Bloody hell. We can't just sit around and wait for them to contact us. I'm Alexander Larkin. I don't wait on the convenience of others."

"Calm yourself, Larkin." Trimley got up from the bench and walked toward the door. "The last thing we want to do is draw attention to ourselves. Sooner or later our gentleman thief will find a way to send word to you that he is prepared to do business."

"I don't take orders from you, Trimley." He tightened one hand into a fist. "I'm going to turn the city upside down until I find those girls."

"Suit yourself, but you will be wasting your time."

"Why do you say that?"

Trimley paused at the door. "I would be the last to deny that you have excellent connections in certain quarters in London. But we both know that you do not go into respectable circles. And it appears that is where our man moves."

Larkin went cold in spite of the heat.

Trimley smiled slightly. "Your crude approach has its uses, Larkin, but this situation requires a degree of finesse. Let me handle it. That was one of the reasons you agreed to our partnership, if you will recall. I have connections in places where you will never be allowed to set foot."

Trimley went out into the cold plunge room and closed the door.

Larkin stared at the door for a long time. That finished it, he decided. Trimley had been useful during the past year but enough was enough. When this business involving the four girls was concluded, he would see to it that the partnership was permanently dissolved.

Larkin rearranged his drooping sheet and thought about how he would handle the matter. Getting rid of a gentleman who moved in social circles required some planning, after all. When men from Trimley's class expired in suspicious circumstances, the police were inclined to conduct serious investigations. The press got excited. Inquiries were made.

There had already been too many risky disappearances in this affair, he thought. The last thing he wanted to do was draw the attention of Scotland Yard.

Nevertheless, such things could be managed provided they were handled with great care. Trimley was wrong. The wall that separated respectable society from the other sort was not as impenetrable as he appeared to believe. Death could reach across any class barrier.

19

The Winslow Charity School for Girls was housed in a vast mansion. It seemed to Concordia that the building somehow managed to absorb every trace of the spring sunlight and render the brightness and warmth into cold, unrelenting night.

The office of the headmistress was of a piece with the rest of the place. It was steeped in an atmosphere of unrelenting gloom. The surroundings were well suited to Edith Pratt, the woman who sat behind the large desk.

The formidable Miss Pratt was not nearly as ancient as Hannah, Phoebe, Edwina and Theodora had led her to believe. Pratt was, in fact, only a few years older than herself—thirty at most.

She was not unattractive. Edith was tall and well proportioned with a full bosom, fine features, light brown hair and hazel eyes.

But whatever physical beauty Edith had possessed had long since been submerged beneath a grim veneer. It was obvious that Pratt was a woman who had been bitterly disappointed by life. Concordia suspected that her chief ambition was to ensure that the students in her care learned to expect the same sad reality that Edith herself had discovered.

"My condolences on the loss of your husband, Mrs. Thompson," Edith said.

She did not sound the least bit sympathetic, Concordia thought. If genuine compassion had ever flowed in Edith Pratt's veins, it had been leached out of her years ago.

"Thank you, Miss Pratt."

Concordia stole a quick look around the room from behind her black net veil. The walls were darkly paneled and quite bare of decoration, with the exception of two photographs and a framed plaque.

One of the photographs, predictably, showed the Queen. Victoria was dressed in the somber attire that she had adopted decades earlier following the death of her beloved Albert.

The second picture was of an expensively gowned, heavily bejeweled woman of some forty or forty-five years. Beneath the photograph the words *Mrs. Hoxton, Our Beloved Benefactress* were inscribed in elaborate gold script.

The plaque mounted behind the desk was headed "Golden Rules for Grateful Girls." Beneath it was a daunting list of some twenty admonitions. Concordia read the first one.

A grateful girl is obedient.

She did not read any further.

Edith folded her hands on top of the desk and regarded her with an expression of polite inquiry.

"How can I be of service?" she asked.

"I have come upon a matter of great delicacy, Miss Pratt. It involves some revelations that were made in my late husband's will. I hope that I can depend upon your professional discretion?"

"I have been a headmistress for many years, Mrs. Thompson. I am quite accustomed to dealing with delicate matters."

"Yes, of course." Concordia affected a deeply troubled sigh. "Forgive me. I am still attempting to recover from the shock, you see."

"What shock?"

"It appears that unbeknownst to anyone else in the family, my husband fathered an illegitimate child a number of years ago."

Edith made a *tut-tutting* sound. "Unfortunately, an all too common story, I'm afraid."

"I realize that in your position here at Winslow you often encounter the results of that sort of masculine irresponsibility."

"Men will be men, Mrs. Thompson." Edith gave a small snort of disgust. "I fear there is little prospect of changing their basic nature. No, in my opinion, the only hope of reducing the number of illegitimate children in this world lies with women. They must be taught to practice restraint and self-discipline in all aspects of their lives, most particularly when it comes to the darker passions."

"The darker passions?"

"Those foolish women who allow themselves to be led astray by the blandishments of men will always pay the price and so will their unwanted offspring."

The bitterness in the headmistress's voice spoke volumes, Concordia thought. She would have been willing to wager a great deal of money that at some time in Edith's past, she had fallen victim to some man's faithless promises.

Concordia cleared her throat. "Yes, well, as I was saying—"

"Rest assured that here at the Winslow Charity School for Girls we strive with extreme diligence to instill the tenets of self-discipline, restraint and self-control in each and every student," Edith said.

Concordia suppressed a shudder and reminded herself that she was there to study the interior of the mansion and this office and to observe Edith Pratt, not to engage in a philosophical argument regarding the proper method of educating young girls.

"An admirable goal, Miss Pratt," she said neutrally.

"I assure you it is not an easy task. Young girls are prone to excessively high spirits and reckless enthusiasms. Here at Winslow we make every effort to suppress that sort of thing."

"I'm sure you do an excellent job of crushing high spirits and reckless enthusiasms." Concordia realized that she was clenching one hand into a fist on her lap. She forced herself to relax her fingers. "As I was saying, the result of my husband's dalliance was an infant girl. She was named Rebecca. The mother evidently died a couple of years ago. My husband saw to it that the girl was sent to an orphanage. He never mentioned the matter to me. Indeed, I had no notion that he had a second family until after his death. It has all been extremely trying."

"No doubt." Edith's severe features tightened into a genuinely baffled frown. "How does this concern you, Mrs. Thompson?"

"In his will my husband expressed regret for having allowed Rebecca to be put into a charity home. He evidently felt that the girl should have been brought up in her father's house."

"Nonsense. Your husband could hardly have expected you to raise his illegitimate daughter. That would have been asking far too much from a decent, well-bred lady endowed with any delicacy of feeling whatsoever."

But what of the feelings of the innocent child? Concordia wanted to scream. Doesn't the little girl's pain and suffering matter? It was the duty of the adults involved to take care of that poor little girl. It wasn't Rebecca's fault that she was born on the wrong side of the blanket.

Concordia could feel her pulse pounding with the force of her emotion. Get ahold of yourself, she thought, or you will ruin everything. This isn't a real-life tragedy. You are acting a part in a play.

But she knew all too well that the tale rang true because there were, indeed, many real-life Rebeccas in the world.

"Perhaps," she said through her teeth. "But the fact remains that my husband deeply regretted the decision to put the child in an orphanage. In his will he requested that I make every effort to locate Rebecca so that I could provide her with a small inheritance and a photograph of her father."

"I see. You say there is an inheritance involved?"

Edith was suddenly showing a good deal more interest in the matter, Concordia thought.

"Yes. Not a large one, you understand."

"Oh." Edith's brief spark of concern faded.

"The problem," Concordia said, determined to stick to the script, "is that there is no record of which orphanage my husband chose for the girl. I am, therefore, attempting to call on as many of them as possible in hopes of identifying the one in which Rebecca was placed."

"Well, if she was sent to a workhouse or one of the orphanages that takes in children who lack respectable connections, she will likely have gone into service by now."

"Rebecca is only nine," Concordia said, forgetting her role again.

"Old enough to be put to work in the kitchen of a respectable household, certainly," Edith said. "Children who are destined to become servants must be taught early in life that they will be expected to work hard if they wish to obtain good posts and keep themselves off the streets."

"Do you send your girls into service, Miss Pratt?"

"I should say not." Edith appeared deeply offended. "Winslow accepts only orphans from the better classes. Our young ladies are educated to become governesses and teachers. They usually remain here until the age of seventeen." She frowned. "They could certainly start to earn their keep at an earlier age, but it is difficult to convince a school or a family to employ a teacher who is younger than seventeen."

"Indeed," Concordia said stiffly. Her own age had been one of many things she had been forced to lie about when she sought her first post, she recalled. She had claimed to be eighteen. "Do all of your students eventually find suitable employment?"

"Those who learn to comport themselves in a modest, unassuming manner and who strive to live according to the Golden Rules for Grateful Girls generally find a post, yes." Edith spread her hands. "Naturally, there is the occasional failure."

"I see." Concordia realized that she was clenching her hand again. "What happens to them?"

"Oh, they usually find themselves on the streets," Edith said casually. "Now then, about your husband's illegitimate daughter. We have thirty-seven girls here at Winslow. There are two Rebeccas, I believe. I will be happy to check the records to see if either of them has any connection to a family named Thompson."

"That is very kind of you."

Edith cast a considering look at the row of filing cabinets. "I am a very busy woman, Mrs. Thompson. It will require some time to conduct a proper search of the files."

The hint could not have been more obvious.

"Naturally, I insist upon compensating you for your trouble." Ambrose had been right, Concordia thought. Edith expected a bribe. She reached into her muff and withdrew the banknote that Ambrose had provided for just this purpose. She placed it on the desk.

"Very well, I shall see if there is a file for a Rebecca with a father named Thompson." Edith made the banknote disappear into the pocket of her gown. "Do you happen to know the mother's name?"

"No, I do not."

Edith rose and crossed the room to the filing cabinets. She opened the one labeled P–T. Concordia could see that it was crammed with folders and papers. She felt her insides clench. So many sad little histories trapped in that dark drawer, she thought.

A knock sounded on the office door.

"Come in, Miss Burke," Edith said without looking around.

The door opened. Concordia saw the faded little wren of a woman who had opened the door for her a short time ago.

"I'm sorry to disturb you, Miss Pratt, but you did say that you wanted to be notified immediately when the men who deliver the coal arrived."

"Quite right, Miss Burke." Edith slammed the drawer closed and whirled around with an astonishing display of vigor. "You must excuse me for a few minutes, Mrs. Thompson. It is necessary that I have a word with these deliverymen. We are using far too much coal here at Winslow, considering that it is spring. I intend to reduce the standing order."

"Of course," Concordia murmured, thinking that it had been rather chilly to date this year.

Edith strode across the office and went out into the hall. With an apologetic nod at Concordia, Miss Burke shut the door.

Concordia found herself alone in the office.

She looked at the filing cabinets. Then she looked at the closed door. Edith Pratt's forceful footsteps were receding rapidly.

The opportunity was simply too good to ignore.

She jumped to her feet, hurried to the filing cabinets and yanked open the A–C drawer.

There were several Coopers but no Edwina or Theodora.

She closed that drawer and tried the one that should have contained a file for Phoebe Leyland.

That search, too, proved futile.

There was no file for Hannah Radburn, either.

It was as though the girls had never existed.

Disappointment and frustration flashed through Concordia. There had to be some record of the four. They had all come from the Winslow Charity School for Girls.

Recalling Ambrose's success with the search of Mrs. Jervis's desk, she went to Edith Pratt's heavy desk.

The first thing she saw was a large, leather-bound journal.

She flipped it open and found herself looking at an appointment calendar and schedule typical of the sort most headmistresses kept. It came as no surprise to discover that Edith Pratt maintained meticulous records. The details of daily classroom assignments, weekly menus and the monthly change of sheets on the beds were all carefully noted in small, very precise handwriting.

The sheets were only changed monthly? Outrageous, Concordia thought. Fortnightly was the rule in respectable schools and households. Evidently Pratt had found yet another way to save money. True, the washing, drying and ironing of sheets took up a great deal of time and effort, but it was absolutely necessary to perform the task frequently and regularly in order to achieve a healthful standard of cleanliness.

She studied the entries for the past week but nothing out of the ordinary jumped off the page. Unable to think of anything else, she turned back to the month that Phoebe, Hannah, Edwina and Theodora had been removed from the school and sent to Aldwick Castle.

Two days prior to the day that the girls recalled having been summoned to the office and told to pack their bags, the name *H. Cuthbert, Dorchester Street* was written down and underlined twice. The words *bill for 4 pr. new gloves & 4 new bonnets* were jotted down directly beneath the address.

She searched the schedule for a few days prior to the date but saw no other useful notes.

Closing the journal, she reached down and opened the largest of the desk drawers. A file labeled *Correspondence* caught her eye.

It was a very slim folder.

She sifted through it quickly. Most of the letters were from potential employers requesting descriptions and details of the physical looks and educational accomplishments of the school's most recent graduates. There was, Concordia noticed, a strong demand for *modest* young women of *plain* and *unremarkable* appearance. Few wives wanted to hire governesses who might prove attractive to the men in the household.

She was about to drop the file back into the drawer when a signature at the bottom of one of the letters caught her eye. W. Leyland.

Phoebe's last name was Leyland.

Footsteps echoed loudly in the hall.

There was no time to peruse the letter. Concordia yanked it out of the file and jammed it into the inside pocket of her cloak.

She hurried around the corner of the desk and went to stand at the window, making a pretense of looking out at the street.

The office door opened abruptly.

"That takes care of that little matter," Edith announced. She was flushed with satisfaction. "There will be no more fires in any of the rooms until the end of October."

"You were about to check your files for a record of Rebecca," Concordia said, turning away from the window.

"Yes, of course."

Edith went to the cabinet containing the *T*s, rummaged around briefly and then shut the drawer.

"Sorry. There is no file for a nine-year-old illegitimate girl named Rebecca who was fathered by a gentleman named Thompson."

"Thank you, Miss Pratt." Concordia went to the door. "You've been most helpful."

Outside in the hall it took all of her self-control to walk sedately toward the front door. Every instinct she possessed was urging her to flee the suffocating atmosphere of the school.

The wan-looking Miss Burke opened the door for her and uttered a weak farewell. Concordia got the impression that the woman longed to follow her out of the mansion. But Miss Burke was evidently as much a prisoner of the school as any of the students.

Concordia breathed a small sigh of relief when she reached the street. It occurred to her that during the entire time she had been inside the school she had not seen a single student.

That was not surprising. Hannah, Phoebe, Edwina and Theodora had explained that for the most part the girls were restricted to the upper floors of the old mansion. The exceptions included the two meals a day served in the dining hall and the thrice-weekly twenty-minute exercise sessions outside on the walled grounds at the back of the big house.

At the corner Concordia paused to look back at the dark mansion one last time. There was a flicker of movement in one of the upstairs windows. She glimpsed a pale face looking down at her. She thought about Hannah's friend Joan, who was somewhere inside the school.

Concordia shivered. She was fortunate. She could walk out of that dreadful place today. But that young girl up there and thirty-six others were trapped in the shadows.

Her eyes blurred as she rounded the corner and started down the street toward the cab in which Ambrose waited. She pulled out a handkerchief.

None of the passersby took any notice of her when she dabbed the moisture from her eyes. Widows, after all, were expected to burst into tears at odd moments.

D id you take complete leave of your senses?" Ambrose demanded from the opposite carriage seat. "What the devil did you think you were doing?"

It dawned on Concordia that he was furious. His reaction baffled her.

When she had returned to the cab a few minutes ago, she had expected praise and admiration for her display of initiative. Instead, she was receiving a blistering reprimand.

"I merely took a quick look through the files while Miss Pratt was out of the room." Annoyed, Concordia crushed the black veil up onto the brim of her hat and glared at him. "I fail to see why you are so agitated, sir. Had you been in my shoes, I'm certain you would have done the same thing."

"What I would or would not have done is beside the point. I gave you very precise instructions concerning how you were to conduct yourself while you were in that place. I specifically said that you were not to do anything that might arouse suspicion."

"No suspicions were aroused, I assure you."

"Only because you had the good fortune not to be caught in the act of searching the files."

"It was not good fortune that prevented me from being caught," she retorted. "It was my own caution and cleverness. Furthermore, I resent being lectured to in this fashion by a gentleman who appears to have made a career out of taking very similar risks."

"We are not discussing my career."

"That is true, isn't it?" She gave him a falsely sweet smile. "In fact, you have told me very little about yourself. You are a man with many secrets, are you not, Mr. Wells?"

"Do not try to change the subject. It is your actions that we are discussing here."

"For heaven's sake, you are acting as if you have the right to give me orders. I would remind you that I am the client."

"And I am the expert in this affair. It is only reasonable that you take instructions from me."

"Indeed? And just what do you know about the filing arrangements commonly used in girls' schools? Very little, I expect. I, on the other hand, have spent my entire career working in such places."

"You are a teacher, damn it, not a detective."

"This is ridiculous. Why on earth are you overreacting so dramatically to what was, essentially, nothing more than a bit of clever sleuthing on my part?"

"If I am overreacting, it is because you scared the hell out of me, Concordia Glade."

She blinked. "I beg your pardon?"

He groaned and reached for her. His hands closed around her upper arms. Before she realized his intent, he hauled her onto his thighs.

"There is no hope for me, is there?" He sounded resigned. "You are going to drive me mad."

She clutched at her hat, which had been knocked askew by the abrupt change in the seating arrangements. "What on earth are you talking about?"

His mouth trapped hers with a fierceness that stopped the words and stole her breath.

The world outside the swaying, jostling cab ceased to exist. A shimmering, glittery sensation swept through her. She put her fingertips on Ambrose's shoulders. This was the second time he had kissed her, she reflected. It provided an excellent opportunity to practice what she had learned the first time.

She opened her mouth in an experimental fashion. He muttered something low and urgent and immediately deepened the embrace.

A very satisfactory experiment, she concluded.

By the time he raised his head she was hot and flustered and her eyeglasses were fogged.

She yanked off the spectacles. "This is really most annoying."

He watched her very steadily, his expression unreadable. "I suppose you want an apology."

"For clouding my eyeglasses?" She wiped the lenses carefully with a clean handkerchief and held them up to check for smudges. "I hardly think that is necessary. It is not your fault that when warm, moist air, such as one's breath, comes in contact with a glass or mirrored surface, it creates a foglike vapor. It is merely a scientific fact."

She popped the spectacles back onto her nose and discovered that Ambrose was gazing at her with a wry, bemused expression.

She frowned. "Is there something wrong, sir?"

He shook his head as though dazed. "Nothing that I could even begin to explain in a remotely rational manner."

She could feel the muscled strength of his thigh and the unmistakable hardness of his aroused body pressing against the side of her leg.

She was the cause of that particular physical change in his anatomy, she thought, rather dazzled by the newfound sense of feminine power.

The cab jolted over some rough pavement. The movement caused her to settle into an even more intimate position. Reality came crashing back. They were in a hired cab, for heaven's sake, she thought. It was certainly not the place for this sort of thing.

She cleared her throat. "Perhaps I should return to my seat."

His mouth curved faintly but the heat in his eyes stirred her senses in a way that made it difficult to breathe.

"Perhaps you should, Miss Glade."

Well, at least he no longer appeared angry, she thought. That seemed like a good sign. Taking command of herself, she collected her skirts and moved back to the other side of the cab.

"Now then, if you have finished lecturing me, perhaps you would like to know what I found in Miss Pratt's office," she said.

He frowned. "I thought you said there were no files for any of the girls."

"True. It was as if they had never resided in the school," she said patiently. "However, I found two items of interest in her desk. The first was a note in Pratt's appointment journal concerning a bill for four pairs of new gloves and four new bonnets to be sent to an H. Cuthbert on Dorchester Street."

"Who is Cuthbert?"

"I don't know, but his name was written down in the journal only two days before the girls were handed over to Miss Bartlett to be escorted to the castle. I think the fact that the bill was for exactly four pairs of gloves and four bonnets has to be something more than a mere coincidence, don't you? Obviously the girls were being outfitted for the journey to the castle."

His brows climbed. "My apologies, Concordia. You are, indeed, starting to sound like an expert detective."

"Thank you." Pleased, she reached into the pocket of her cloak. "The other item of great interest that I discovered was a letter signed by a W. Leyland."

Recognition flashed in his eyes. "A connection to Phoebe?"

The hunter in him had returned to the fore, she thought, greatly relieved. It was much easier to deal with Ambrose when he was in this mood.

"Perhaps," she said. "I have not yet had an opportunity to read it." She opened it carefully. "As you can see, it is somewhat wrinkled. The moment I discovered it in the drawer, I heard Miss Pratt returning. I was obliged to stuff it rather quickly into my pocket."

"In other words, it was a very near thing. Just as I feared, you were almost caught."

She smoothed the letter on the cushion of the seat. "For the sake of our mutual goal in this matter, I suggest that we do not return to that subject."

His jaw flexed but he did not pursue the matter.

"Read it to me," he said.

She picked up the letter.

To Whom It May Concern:

I write to inquire whether or not my niece resides in your school. Her name is Phoebe Leyland. She was lost in a boating accident four months ago. Her body was never recovered. The authorities are convinced that she drowned.

Unlike most girls, Phoebe was taught to swim and was quite expert. It has occurred to me that she may have survived the accident but perhaps lost her memory as a result of the shock or a blow to her head.

On the off chance that Phoebe was found and placed in an orphanage because of her inability to identify herself or to recall the details of her past, I am writing to as many institutions as possible to ask that records be searched for a girl matching my dear niece's description. Following are the particulars . . .

Concordia quickly read a description that matched Phoebe in every way.

When she was finished, she looked at Ambrose.

"It is signed W. Leyland," she said quietly. "Phoebe often speaks fondly of a maiden aunt named Winifred Leyland. Her father had intended that she go to live with Winifred after he died. But an uncle on her mother's side of the family took her in instead. The uncle and his wife told Phoebe that Winifred had succumbed to a fever."

"And then they sent Phoebe to the orphanage."

"Yes." Concordia tapped the letter. "It doesn't make any sense. If the uncle and his wife wanted to be rid of an unwanted niece, why not send her to live with Winifred Leyland? Why did they pack her off to Winslow and tell her that her aunt was dead?"

Ambrose settled back against the seat, looking thoughtful. "In my opinion, the most interesting aspect of this matter is that the aunt and uncle also appear to have gone out of their way to inform Winifred Leyland that Phoebe had drowned."

Concordia's fingers clenched around the letter. "Why would anyone do such a cruel thing to an orphaned girl and the only other person on the face of the earth who wanted her? It is monstrous."

"I suspect that Larkin or his partner compensated the aunt and uncle very well for their cooperation and silence."

She stared unseeingly down at the letter. "You mean they *sold* Phoebe to those dreadful men?"

"That is certainly how it appears. It is obvious that Edith Pratt was involved in the business, too. Larkin and his associate probably paid her to take the girls into the school with no questions asked and hand them over when they were ready to move them to Aldwick Castle."

"I suspect that they paid Edith Pratt quite handsomely for her assistance," Concordia said, closing her fingers into a small fist. "She appeared rather expensively dressed for a headmistress of a charity school. What are you thinking, sir?"

Ambrose leaned back in his seat. "I believe it is time that I interviewed the four people who know more about this affair than anyone else."

H e sat down behind his desk and looked at Hannah, Phoebe, Edwina and Theodora. They were seated in front of him in a neat row. Curiosity, expectation and excitement lit their faces.

Concordia occupied the wingback chair near the window. Unlike the girls, she appeared serious and more than a little anxious. He knew that she was concerned that his questions would force the girls to recall some of the unhappiest moments of their young lives. He wasn't looking forward to this any more than she was, but he could see no way around it.

He needed answers, and Phoebe, Hannah, Edwina and Theodora very likely knew a good deal more than they realized.

"Miss Glade said that you would like our help with your investigation," Theodora said.

"We will be happy to assist you," Edwina assured him.

"Does this mean that we are now assistant detectives?" Phoebe asked eagerly. Behind the lenses of her spectacles her eyes sparkled with enthusiasm.

"That is precisely what it means," Ambrose said.

"How thrilling," Hannah whispered. "Just like in a novel."

Concordia smiled for the first time since they had gathered in the library. "That is true, Hannah. The four of you are, indeed, involved in a mystery story of your very own. We are attempting to identify the villain of the piece."

"What do you want to know?" Phoebe asked.

He looked at her. "For starters, Phoebe, we have some reason to believe that your aunt, Winifred Leyland, may still be alive and that she is searching for you."

"Aunt Winifred?" Phoebe stared at him, clearly stunned. "Alive? But Uncle Wilbert said she died of a fever."

Ambrose glanced at the date of the letter in front of him. "As of a little more than two months ago, she was alive and living in a village named High Hornby."

"That is her home," Phoebe whispered. "She has lived there for many years. But why would Uncle Wilbert and Aunt Mildred say that she died?" Her face started to crumple.

Concordia was out of her chair and at Phoebe's side in a heartbeat. She put her arm around the girl's shaking shoulders.

"It's all right, dear," she said quietly. "Rest assured, if your aunt really is still alive, we will find her."

Phoebe sniffed a couple of times and looked blankly at Concordia. "I don't understand, Miss Glade."

"None of us do, as yet," Ambrose said. "But we will sort it all out eventually. Now then, your aunt's letter indicates that she was told that you drowned in a boating accident. Do you have any idea how that tale might have come about?"

Phoebe shook her head slowly. "My father used to take me boating on the river. He taught me to swim in case I ever fell into the water. But I haven't been in a boat since shortly before he took ill and died."

Ambrose folded his hands on top of the desk and looked at the girls. "I know this will be painful for all of you. But I want each of you to think back to the time when you were taken to Winslow. I want the names and addresses of the relatives who delivered you to Edith Pratt."

The request seemed to confuse the girls.

"But my uncle did not take me to the school," Phoebe said, brow crinkling a little.

Concordia frowned. "Do you mean to say that he sent you off alone on the train?"

"No," Phoebe said. "Uncle Wilbert took me to an inn. There was a gentleman waiting in a private carriage. I was told to get into the carriage and that the man inside would escort me to my new home. It was a very long journey."

Hannah's eyes welled. "That is how it was with me, too. My aunt gave me over to a stranger who took me away in a private carriage. I have not seen her since."

"That is how we came to leave our home, too," Edwina said. "Isn't that right, Theodora?"

Theodora nodded mutely and seized a handkerchief.

"Dear God." Concordia sank to her knees in front of the girls and grabbed their hands in her own. "You never mentioned that each of you was sent off alone with a man. You must have been terrified. Did he . . . hurt you in any way?"

"No." Edwina shrugged. "He was not rude or unkind. As I recall, he barely spoke a word to us during the entire journey. Isn't that right, Theodora?"

"He spent most of the time reading some newspapers," Theodora agreed.

"The gentleman who took me to Winslow ignored me for the most part," Hannah said. "I was not afraid of him, just of where we were going."

Phoebe nodded in agreement. "He did not hurt me, Miss Glade, truly."

Concordia gave them a watery smile. "You relieve my mind."

Ambrose looked at them. "Did this gentleman who escorted you to the school give you his name?"

All four girls solemnly shook their heads.

"Can you describe him for me?" Ambrose asked.

Edwina glanced at Theodora. "He reminded me of Mr. Phillips."

Theodora nodded quickly. "Yes, that's true."

Ambrose picked up a pen and reached for a sheet of paper. "Who is Mr. Phillips?"

"Father's man of affairs," Edwina explained. "He retired shortly before our parents died."

"The gentleman who took me to the school acted just like a man of affairs also," Hannah said.

She hunched her shoulders, lowered her chin and squinted while she pretended to read something in her hand.

"Yes, that is exactly how he sat in the carriage for the entire journey," Phoebe exclaimed.

Ambrose met Concordia's questioning eyes and shook his head.

"Not Larkin," he said quietly. "The gentleman partner, perhaps."

Concordia turned back to Theodora. "You are a very fine artist, dear. Can you draw this man?"

Everyone looked first at her and then at Theodora. Ambrose realized that he had gone very tense with anticipation.

"I could try," Theodora said slowly. "But it has been several months since I saw him. I will not be able to recall his features precisely."

"We all saw him," Phoebe reminded her. "Perhaps if you start to draw him, Theodora, we could each add bits and pieces and come up with a useful picture."

"A brilliant suggestion, Phoebe." Ambrose rose. "Come and sit here at my desk, Theodora. I'll find some more paper."

"It would help if Hannah assumed his posture in the carriage seat again," Theodora said, sitting down in Ambrose's chair.

Hannah immediately elevated her shoulders. Ambrose was impressed with the transformation that came over her. She went from being a lively young lady to a stooped, middle-aged gentleman with poor eyes in an instant.

"He was partially bald," Theodora said, picking up a pencil. "I recall that quite clearly."

"And what hair he did have was a very pale gray," Edwina added. She wrinkled her nose. "His suit and shoes appeared to be quite cheap."

The girls crowded around Theodora, offering suggestions.

"A mustache and whiskers," Phoebe said. "And don't forget the spectacles."

Theodora was suddenly very busy with her pencil and paper.

An hour later, Ambrose was once again alone with Concordia in the library. They stood together in front of the desk and looked at the portrait that Theodora had produced.

"He does have the appearance of a somewhat less than prosperous man of affairs, doesn't he?" Ambrose said, studying the picture. "The girls were right."

"I told you, they are very observant." She studied the image. "Do you think that is Larkin's mysterious gentleman partner?"

"No. I believe it is far more likely that he is precisely what the girls believed him to be, a man of affairs."

"Why do you say that?"

He lounged on a corner of the desk. "From start to finish this situation has the appearance of being a rather complicated piece of business. A great many financial arrangements were made. Teachers were hired. Relatives were paid to hand over unwanted young relations. Carriages were procured in order to avoid traveling by train. The list of details must have been quite extensive."

"I see what you mean. A man like Larkin or his partner could not have been bothered to make all those arrangements. He would have employed someone else to handle the details."

Ambrose spread his hands. "Who better to perform such tasks than a genuine man of affairs?"

She brightened. "You are thinking about the H. Cuthbert in Pratt's appointment schedule, aren't you? The one to whom she sent a bill for four pairs of gloves and four bonnets."

Ambrose contemplated the picture again. "I believe I will pay a visit to Dorchester Street this afternoon."

"Excellent notion. I will go with you."

"Concordia—"

"Whoever this Cuthbert is, it appears he was involved in stealing my four girls. I am going with you, Ambrose."

22

T hank you for seeing us without an appointment, Mr. Cuthbert."
Ambrose held a chair for Concordia and then took his own seat.
He adjusted the crease in his trousers, placed the point of his walking
stick on the carpet between his knees and stacked his gloved hands on
the hilt.

Concordia murmured something vague and coolly polite. Herbert
Cuthbert did not appear to hear the thinly disguised loathing in her
voice, but Ambrose was very aware of it. Fortunately the black net veil of
her hat concealed her expression.

"Not at all, sir," Cuthbert said. An eagerness bordering on desperation glistened in his pale eyes. "As it happens I had some time free this
afternoon."

Ambrose suspected that the roles he and Concordia had chosen to
play today, that of an upper-class couple of obvious means, was the real
reason Cuthbert had discovered some free time in his appointment
book.

Theodora had captured the essence of H. Cuthbert, he thought. He was, indeed, a less than prosperous man of affairs. Judging by the faded curtains and the shabby furnishings of his office, he could not afford to turn down potential new clients.

"Very kind of you," Ambrose murmured into his beard.

The false hair, which included wig, mustache and whiskers, was laced with a great deal of silver and gray. It was not his favorite costume because it tended to become uncomfortably warm after a time. But it was an effective disguise. The impression of advancing years was further enhanced by his conservatively cut coat and the heavy scarf around his neck.

Hannah, Phoebe, Edwina and Theodora had examined him with great interest before he and Concordia left the house an hour ago. They had been delighted by the change in his appearance.

"You look even older than you really are," Phoebe declared. "Rather like someone's elderly grandfather."

"But still quite fit for a gentleman of such advanced years," Concordia had assured him in a suspiciously serious manner.

Cuthbert fixed him with an expression of attentive inquiry. "How can I be of assistance, Mr. Dalrymple?"

"I will come straight to the point. Mrs. Dalrymple and I are searching for a young lady. She is a distant relative who lost her parents some months ago and was sent to an orphanage. We wish to employ you to locate her."

Cuthbert's expression congealed. Something that might have been panic flared in his eyes. "Beg your pardon, sir. I'm a man of affairs. I handle financial matters. Wills, investments, that sort of thing. I do not search for lost relatives."

"Not even when there is a fortune involved?" Concordia asked coldly.

Cuthbert was having some trouble breathing. His cheeks flushed an unhealthy shade of red. He fiddled nervously with the knot of his tie, evidently trying to loosen it.

"A fortune, you say, Mrs. Dalrymple?" Acute interest was rapidly replacing the startled fear in his expression.

"Indeed."

She was taunting him, Ambrose thought. As he had feared, her animosity toward Cuthbert was threatening his plan. It was time to take control of the situation.

"We will not bore you with all of the unfortunate details," he said smoothly. "Suffice it to say that an elderly relative on my wife's side of the family died recently. She had been bedridden and decidedly senile for some time. It was assumed that her money would go to my wife. It was not discovered until after the aunt expired that she had changed her will, leaving everything to the girl I mentioned."

Cuthbert cleared his throat. "I understand how upsetting this sort of thing can be, but I really don't see how I can help."

"You can find her for us, that is how you can help," Ambrose said, letting impatience edge his words. "The damn will stipulates that if the young lady is not available to receive the money, the entire inheritance goes to an even more distant cousin. We cannot allow that to happen. My wife was supposed to receive the inheritance."

193

Cuthbert contrived to appear sympathetic. "An unhappy state of affairs, I grant you. But locating the girl would not be a simple task. There are, as it happens, a vast number of orphanages and charity homes in London." He paused, frowning. "How old is this young lady?"

"By my calculations, she turned fifteen within the past few months," Concordia said.

Cuthbert sighed. "That makes the situation even more complicated. By the age of fifteen many orphans have been sent out into the world to make their livings. Can't have a lot of lazy, shiftless young people hanging about, frittering away their time and taking advantage of the kindness of their benefactors, you know."

"If that is what occurred in this instance, surely there will be a record of where the young lady is currently employed," Ambrose said.

"That may be true," Cuthbert agreed slowly. "Nevertheless—"

Ambrose rapped the point of his cane once, very sharply on the floor. Cuthbert twitched violently in reaction.

"Let me make myself quite clear," Ambrose said. "I consider finding the girl a matter of considerable importance."

"I understand. Nevertheless—"

"The chit is worth a great deal to us," Ambrose continued meaningfully. "I am willing to reward the person who helps me locate her very handsomely. Do I make myself clear?"

Cuthbert grunted. "How handsomely?"

"Shall we say a thousand pounds?"

Cuthbert's mouth opened and closed twice before he found his voice. "That is a very generous reward, indeed." He cleared his throat.

"I suppose I could make a few inquiries. Ah, what is the name of the young lady?"

"Hannah Radburn."

Cuthbert stiffened. He looked as though he was being strangled by his tie.

"Radburn?" he whispered hoarsely. "Are you certain?"

"Quite certain," Concordia said icily.

Ambrose reached into his coat and took out a piece of paper. "My wife wrote down a list of particulars concerning Hannah. Place and date of birth, the names of her parents and so forth. Please be thorough in your inquiries. Wouldn't want to get the wrong girl, now would we?"

Cuthbert looked hunted. "Sir, I, uh—"

"If it transpires that she has, indeed, left the orphanage, as you suggested," Ambrose continued without pause, "we would be extremely grateful if you could provide us with some clue to her present whereabouts."

"Orphaned girls do not always end up in the most favorable positions when they go into service," Cuthbert said weakly. "I regret to say that a few just seem to disappear."

"I expect you mean that they end up on the streets or in brothels," Concordia snapped. "And just who do you think is to blame for that state of affairs? As long as women lack the same opportunities to seek honest employment that are available to men—"

Ambrose got to his feet, put one hand on her shoulder and squeezed once, quite firmly.

Concordia lapsed into a simmering silence.

Ambrose looked at Cuthbert, who was staring at Concordia with an expression of utter astonishment.

"You must excuse my wife, sir," Ambrose said. "She has not been herself since we discovered that her entire inheritance was left to Hannah Radburn."

"Yes, of course." Cuthbert collected himself. "Very upsetting state of affairs. More than enough to shatter a lady's nerves."

"Indeed," Ambrose said. "To return to the matter at hand, the fact is we must locate Hannah, even if she has been ruined. The girl's worth her weight in gold, literally. As I said, I'll pay a thousand pounds if you produce the chit."

Cuthbert sighed. "I may not be able to produce her, as it were. But I might be able to find out where she is currently residing. Would that be worth anything to you?"

"It would be worth five hundred pounds, no questions asked, if you can provide me with even the name of anyone who knows anything about Hannah," Ambrose said softly.

Cuthbert's eyes were stunned. "Five hundred pounds just for a name?"

"We are quite desperate to find her," Ambrose said. "Any clues at all will be greatly appreciated. If she is, indeed, in a brothel or in some other unfortunate circumstance, I certainly do not expect you to retrieve her. I will take care of that end of things."

Cuthbert flapped his hands. "Sir, this is a most unusual piece of business."

Ambrose gripped the handle of the cane very tightly and narrowed his eyes. "Get me a name and you shall have at least five hundred pounds. Do I make myself clear?"

"Quite clear," Cuthbert rasped.

"Very well then, we will not take up any more of your time." Ambrose removed a card from the pocket of his coat. "If you come across even the smallest shred of information concerning Hannah Radburn, send word to me at my club immediately. The management knows how to contact me. I will come around to see you as soon as I get your message."

He dropped the card on the desk. Concordia got to her feet.

He could feel the angry tension in every inch of her body as they walked to the door. Neither of them looked back at Cuthbert.

23

Outside the afternoon haze and fog were thickening rapidly. A cab appeared out of the mist. Ambrose hailed it and opened the door for Concordia.

She got inside, sat down and arranged her skirts. She was still vibrating with anger. She wanted nothing more than to storm back into Cuthbert's office and tell him that she intended to inform the police of what he had done. But that small satisfaction would have to wait.

"That dreadful Cuthbert most certainly recognized Hannah's name," she said.

"Yes." Ambrose leaned forward and rested his forearms on his thighs, fingers loosely clasped between his knees. He contemplated the busy street. "That much was obvious. He was alarmed, but I have dealt with his sort before. In the end, his greed will overcome his anxieties."

"I agree. But what do you suppose he will do? He can hardly pretend to find Hannah for you. She has, for all intents and purposes, disappeared."

"If I am right, Cuthbert knows a great deal about this matter. He will try to sell me some information."

She cleared her throat very delicately. "You told Mr. Cuthbert that he could send word to you at your club."

"Yes."

"I was not aware that you belonged to a club, sir."

"They are excellent sources of gossip and rumors," he said somewhat absently. "In my business I depend upon both."

"I see." She kept her voice as casual as possible. "If you are a member of a club, I assume the other members know you?"

He continued to contemplate the street, but the corner of his mouth twitched a little. "They know an eccentric gentleman named Dalrymple."

"Fascinating." She smoothed her gloves. "I will admit that I am not particularly knowledgeable about such arcane matters, but I was under the impression that a gentleman was considered for admission to a club only upon the recommendation of a member in good standing who knew the candidate quite well."

"I am very well known to the gentleman who recommended me."

She wrinkled her nose. "Mr. Stoner?"

"Stoner's name opens many doors in this town."

She sighed. "You are enjoying this game, are you not?"

He appeared politely surprised by the question. "What game is that?"

"You know very well what I mean. Asking you personal questions is like trying to examine moonlight. One can see it quite clearly but one cannot quite grasp it."

He was silent for a moment. The corners of his mouth no longer kicked up.

"I am not in the habit of explaining myself to others," he said eventually.

"Neither am I."

He leaned back and rested his arm on the back of the seat. "I am aware of that."

"It appears that, for the sake of our careers, we have each gone to great lengths to construct a curtain of privacy around our personal lives."

He reflected on that for a moment and then inclined his head in a somber fashion. "What is your point?"

"My point, sir," she said gently, "is that when one has lived with secrets for a long time it can be difficult to shed the habit."

Shadows moved in his eyes. For a moment she thought she had gone too far.

To her surprise, he leaned forward and drew the edge of one finger along the underside of her jaw.

"Sometimes it is better not to break old habits," he said.

"I broke mine when I told you about my past in the Crystal Springs Community."

"Rest assured, I will keep your secrets."

"I do not doubt that. But there has not been an even exchange between us, Ambrose. I have trusted you. Can you not trust me?"

He sat back in his seat again, drawing in on himself. She could almost hear the click of invisible locks.

"It is not a question of trust," he said.

"Are your secrets so terrible, then?"

His brows rose in a subtle warning. "I am not one of your students, to be comforted with the offer of sympathy and a kind ear, Concordia. I have lived with my secrets a long time."

She tensed at the rebuff. He was not going to confide in her and that was that.

"Very well." She folded her hands together in her lap. "You are entitled to your privacy, sir. I will not press you."

He returned to gazing meditatively out the window. The silence lengthened between them. When she could not abide it any longer, she tried to think of a way to break it.

"I wonder what Mrs. Hoxton would say if she knew what was going on at the Winslow Charity School for Girls," she mused.

Ambrose frowned. "Who the devil is Mrs. Hoxton?"

"The benefactress of the school. Her picture was on the wall of Edith Pratt's office, directly across from a photograph of the Queen."

"Was it, indeed?" He raised his brows. "In that case, your question is a very interesting one. I wonder what this Mrs. Hoxton does know about the goings-on at the school."

"Nothing at all, I expect."

"What makes you so sure of that?"

Concordia grimaced. "Judging from what little the girls told me about her, Mrs. Hoxton is typical of many women in her position who engage in philanthropy. They do so only because they believe that a bit of charity work elevates their status in Society. The Mrs. Hoxtons of this world take no real interest in the schools and orphanages that they support."

"Did the girls ever see this Mrs. Hoxton?"

"Only once. She made an appearance at Christmas and stayed just long enough to bestow a pair of mittens on each girl. Phoebe, Hannah, Edwina and Theodora said that all of the students were summoned into the dining hall for the occasion. Miss Pratt made a little speech along the lines of how fortunate they all were to have such a gracious, generous benefactress, the girls sang some carols and then Mrs. Hoxton took her leave."

He shook his head in disgust. "That must have made for a memorable Christmas for the students."

"I think it is safe to say that Mrs. Hoxton does not take a great deal of interest in the day-to-day operation of her charity school."

"I believe you," Ambrose said. "Nevertheless . . ."

"Yes?"

"It might be interesting to ask Mrs. Hoxton a few questions about her generous charity work."

Concordia stared at him, astonished. "You're going to interview Mrs. Hoxton?"

"Yes. It will have to wait until tomorrow. It is too late today."

"Are you acquainted with her?"

"Never met the woman," he admitted.

She widened her hands. "She is evidently a very wealthy woman who moves in Society. How on earth will you persuade her to allow you through the front door?"

"I intend to call upon a higher power."

"I beg your pardon?"

He smiled slowly. "Society is composed of several ascending circles. Mrs. Hoxton will view any person who moves at a level that is higher than her own as a god of sorts."

"I see. And do you happen to know one of these higher-ranking gods?"

"In Society, one is always outranked by someone." Ambrose shrugged. "Unless, of course, one happens to be the queen. Something tells me that Mrs. Hoxton is nowhere near that particular circle."

HERBERT CUTHBERT sat alone in his office and pondered his unexpected good fortune. There were two ways to play this new hand of cards he had just been dealt, he decided—two ways to turn a profit.

He would have to be very careful about how he handled the matter, of course. Larkin and Trimley were both extremely dangerous men. They would, however, be very eager to receive the information that he was in a position to give them. With luck, their gratitude would translate into a sizeable sum of money.

As for the second arrangement, that would pose no significant problems that he could see. He would simply sell a fraudulent name to Dalrymple, pocket the five hundred pounds and take himself off to his favorite gambling hell.

His luck had changed at last.

24

W hoever he is, the bastard managed to locate Cuthbert." Trimley
paced the hot room. "Do you realize what this means?"

Larkin lounged on the bench, a cup of cold water in one hand, and
savored the satisfaction that was flowing through him. Trimley, he
thought, was finally starting to show signs of strain. The man was actually sweating. His elegant Roman toga was slipping, too.

About time.

But then, he had always known that Trimley's nerves would weaken
sooner or later. Trimley was soft at the core. He lacked the hard, tem-
pered steel that could only come from being raised on the streets.

"It means," Larkin said, stretching out his legs in a leisurely manner as
though ensconced in a comfortable club, "that we are in a position to set
a trap. I must admit I am curious to find out just who this Dalrymple is."

"It is obvious who he is. He's the one who stole the girls from the
castle."

"Not necessarily," Larkin said. "He may be working for someone else, someone who wants to take my place, perhaps."

He never did his own dirty work anymore, he mused. Perhaps whoever was behind the theft of the young ladies kept a similar distance between himself and his business activities.

Trimley clamped a fist around the knot of his toga-style sheet, barely managing to keep it from sliding off his shoulder. "Either way, we will get him when he goes to see Cuthbert."

"That would be very stupid." Larkin drank some water. "I am not a stupid man, Trimley."

"What the devil are you talking about? We have to stop Dalrymple before he gets any closer. Matters are slipping out of control. Can't you see that?"

"Matters are still in hand, Trimley," Larkin said patiently. "If this Dalrymple is, indeed, involved in this thing, he can lead us to the girls and the teacher. I want him followed after he visits Cuthbert's office. Once we have recovered the young ladies and Concordia Glade, we will deal with him."

Trimley's jaw jerked once or twice but he did not argue. "Yes, that makes sense, I suppose. But what of Cuthbert? He expects to be paid for informing us of Dalrymple's visit."

"He will receive his reward."

Trimley came to a halt. "Damn it to hell, don't you understand? If this Dalrymple managed to track down Cuthbert, the police may well do the same."

"There is no reason to think that the police have any interest in this affair. But be that as it may, I promise you that Cuthbert will not talk."

"I would not depend upon that, if I were you."

Larkin almost smiled. Trimley was definitely starting to fray around the edges.

"Calm yourself, Trimley. Cuthbert will not give us any more trouble."

25

Dorchester Street was drowning in a sea of fog and shadows. A row of gas lamps stood sentinel against the night, but the balls of glary light did not penetrate far into the dense mist.

Ambrose stood in a doorway at the corner and surveyed the scene.

The message from Cuthbert had reached him less than an hour ago. The urgency in the cryptic, scrawled note had been unmistakable.

I have news of interest. Meet me at my office. Eleven o'clock tonight. Come alone. Kindly bring a bank draft for the agreed-upon amount.

The shops on the street level were locked and shuttered. Most of the windows in the rooms above the ground floor were also darkened, but Ambrose saw a thin outline of light around the edges of the curtain that masked the window of Cuthbert's office.

The street was empty except for a lone cab. The driver, shrouded in a heavy coat, his hat pulled down low over his ears, was slouched on his

box. He looked as if he had gone to sleep. His bony nag stood waiting patiently, head lowered, no doubt lost in a dream of fresh hay and a
warm stall.

Ambrose watched for a while longer. Nothing and no one moved in
the shadows. The rim of light continued to burn steadily in Cuthbert's
window.

One thing was certain: He was not going to learn anything more if he
remained in the shadows of the doorway.

He walked toward the entrance to Cuthbert's office, allowing the
heels of his shoes to echo hollowly on the pavement. Mr. Dalrymple was
not the furtive sort. He was a respectable, prosperous gentleman who
maintained a membership in an exclusive club and patronized an expensive tailor. He had come here on a matter of business tonight and he
was in a hurry to conclude it.

The door of Cuthbert's building was unlocked. Ambrose let himself
into the dark hall and waited a moment, absorbing the feel of the space.
When he sensed that it was empty, he climbed the stairs to the floor
above and looked down the corridor.

The only light was the razor's-edge glow that came from beneath
Cuthbert's office door.

He went along the hall, moving silently now. Methodically he
checked the office doors on either side of Cuthbert's. Each was securely
locked.

Satisfied that Cuthbert was the only one present on this floor, aside
from himself, Ambrose went to the office and checked the knob. It
turned easily in his hand.

He did not bother to knock. Instead he thrust the door open very quickly, giving no warning of his presence.

The attempt at a startling effect was for naught. Cuthbert was not at his desk. The office was empty.

He studied the lamp on the desk. Why had it been left burning? Had Cuthbert gone off for some reason, intending to return shortly to keep the appointment with Mr. Dalrymple?

Or had the man of affairs become frightened and fled in such a great hurry that he had not taken the time to lower the lamp?

Ambrose closed the door and turned the key in the lock. He did not want to be unpleasantly surprised while he searched the premises.

He had spent a lot of time on this case dealing with files of various sorts, he reflected. Not like the old days when the object of his searches had been intriguing little items that glittered and flashed and gleamed in the light.

Ah, but the snap and crackle of the exhilarating energy was still as potent as it had always been. Pity he could not find a way to bottle and sell this intense experience. The potential for profit would have been enormous.

He made short work of the small filing cabinet. There was nothing to interest him amid the assortment of aged business papers. Judging by the names and addresses in the various files, most of Cuthbert's clients were single women of modest means. There were a number of widows, retired housekeepers, governesses and others who survived on meager pensions and small investments.

He closed the last drawer in the filing cabinet and went to the desk, expecting little. He was not disappointed. Most of the drawers and cubbyholes were filled with the usual assortment of paper, business cards, pens, pencils and spare bottles of ink.

Inside the center drawer was a small leather-bound journal. He flipped through it quickly. The pages were filled with figures and sums. A journal of accounts, he concluded. One could often learn a great deal about a man by examining his finances.

He tucked the little journal into his coat pocket, closed the drawer and went to the window. Flattening himself against the wall, he peered through a crack in the curtain.

Down below in the street nothing had altered. Fog still veiled the gaslights. The dark shape of the cab with its dozing driver was still parked where it had been earlier. Ambrose detected no movement.

He went back across the office, unlocked the door and let himself out into the darkened hall. Once again he paused for a moment, using his excellent night vision to examine his surroundings.

Satisfied that there was no one else about, he went back downstairs.

Outside on the street he walked deliberately toward the hackney. His footsteps rang loudly in the fog-bound silence.

"Driver, I'd like a word with you, if you please," he called, using his Dalrymple accent.

The driver stiffened and turned his head very quickly to watch Ambrose approach. His features were all but lost in the shadows cast by his high collar, heavy scarf and low-crowned hat.

"Sorry, sir, I'm not for hire tonight. Waitin' for a fare."

"Are you, indeed?" Ambrose kept walking.

"Aye, sir. If it's a cab yer needin' I expect you'll find one in the next street."

"I do not require a cab," Ambrose said. "I merely want to ask you a few questions."

He was less than ten paces from the vehicle now. The lights inside the carriage had been turned down. The curtains were drawn across the windows.

Out of the corner of his eye he could see a damp patch on the pavement directly below the crack at the bottom of the closed passenger door. Either the nag or the driver had relieved himself during the long wait for a fare, he thought. Not enough volume of liquid for a horse, though, and no taint of the familiar, extremely pungent stench.

"Rest assured, I'll make it worth your while." Ambrose reached into his pocket and withdrew some coins.

The driver shifted uneasily. "What is it ye want to know?"

"I'm looking for the man of affairs who keeps an office in that building that I just left. We had an appointment tonight but he failed to appear. Did you happen to see anyone come or go from that address before I arrived?"

He was closer now, only a couple of strides away from the cab. There was something quite troubling about the damp pavement. Why would a cabdriver relieve himself directly beneath the door of his own vehicle when there was an alley not more than a few steps away?

"I didn't see no one," the driver mumbled.

Electricity danced through Ambrose. His already painfully alert senses shifted into that intense, near-preternatural state in which even the slightest movement, sound or shifting of shadows took on great significance.

"What of your fare?" he asked. "You must have seen him recently."

"Got himself a little doxy in this street. She lives in a room over one of the shops. He went up there about an hour ago. Told me to wait. That's all I know."

"Indeed," Ambrose said, studying the dark pool on the pavement.

He was directly alongside the carriage now. He grasped the handle of the door and yanked it open.

An arm that had evidently been wedged against the door flopped down and dangled grotesquely in the opening. Ambrose saw the shadowy outline of the rest of the body crumpled on the floor of the cab.

There was just enough light from the outside carriage lamp to gleam on the blood that had flowed from the mortal wound in Cuthbert's chest.

"It appears your fare finished his business somewhat earlier than he intended," Ambrose said.

26

"Yer a right stupid bastard, that's what ye are." The driver straightened and reached inside his heavy overcoat. "Should have minded yer own business."

Ambrose already had one foot on the step beneath the driver's box. He grabbed the handhold with his left hand, rose halfway up the side of the vehicle and rammed the tip of his walking stick into the driver's belly.

The man grunted and doubled over in pain. The knife that he had just taken out of an inside pocket clattered from his hand and tumbled onto the pavement.

Footsteps pounded from the direction of the alley. Ambrose looked over his shoulder and saw a second man charging toward him. The glare of a nearby gas lamp glinted on the barrel of a revolver.

He jumped back down to the pavement and dove beneath the wheels of the carriage, rolling into the deep shadows on the far side of the vehicle.

The gun roared. The bullet thudded into the wooden panels of the four-wheeler.

Startled out of his dozing slumber, the horse snorted, tossed its head and lurched forward violently. The man on the box, still gasping for air, scrambled about and managed to seize the reins.

"Bloody stupid nag."

Ambrose got to his feet and vaulted quietly up onto the back of the hackney. He crouched there. His training had taught him that people rarely looked up until they had searched everywhere else first.

"Where are ye, ye bloody bastard?" The second man turned nervously from side to side in an attempt to spot his quarry. He peered under the carriage. "If ye come out quietly with yer hands in the air, I'll let ye live."

The hackney jerked violently in response to another lunge from the horse.

"Get that damn nag under control," the man with the gun shouted at his companion, clearly unnerved by the manner in which events had spiraled out of control.

Ambrose rose and dropped down over the side of the carriage, feet-first. He struck the man below with his full weight. The impact sent them both to the ground.

"Get outta the way, Jake," the driver shouted.

Ambrose got to his feet in a quick, twisting move and leaned over to scoop up the gun. Out of the corner of his eye he saw the driver reach into his heavy leather boot.

A second knife. Should have thought of that.

He dodged behind the back of the hackney.

The hurtling blade missed him by inches and thudded into the side of the vehicle.

The second man was on his feet, running toward the front of the hackney.

"Bastard's got my gun," he yelled at the driver. He grabbed the hand-hold on the side of the vehicle and hauled himself up beside his companion. "Get away from that bloody cove."

The driver loosened the reins. The horse, in a complete panic now, surged forward. The carriage swayed precariously but remained upright.

Ambrose stood in the mist-draped street, aware of the cold thrills of dark energy still flashing through him. He listened to the clatter of hooves and carriage wheels until the sound faded into the night.

EMPLOYING HIS CUSTOMARY TACTIC to find a cab late at night, he walked to the nearest tavern and chose a hansom at random.

Twenty minutes later he ordered the driver to stop in a pleasant little square lined with handsome town houses. There were no lights on in any of the residences.

He made his way around to the alley that lined one row of houses, unlatched one of the gates and walked through the well-tended garden.

He used the head of his cane to rap lightly on the back door.

A short time later the door opened. The sandy-haired man in a dressing gown who responded was approximately his own age, albeit somewhat taller.

Ambrose knew from past experience when he and Felix Denver had put the question to a scientific test in a wide-ranging variety of venues, including several taverns, two theaters and an assortment of public houses, that women considered Felix to be the better-looking of the two.

"I trust this is important, Wells. I've got company."

Ambrose smiled slightly. It was the great misfortune of the ladies of London that Inspector Felix Denver of Scotland Yard was not interested in women in anything more than a friendly, social way. Whoever was upstairs in his bed tonight, that individual was of the masculine gender.

"Sorry to disturb your rest, Felix."

Felix raised the candle in his hand to get a better look at Ambrose's face. He grimaced. "I would reconsider the whiskers and mustache, if I were you. They do nothing to enhance your appearance."

"No, but they do conceal it and that is all that concerns me. I came here because I wanted to let you know that the situation has become more complicated."

"It always does when you're involved, Wells."

He told Felix what had happened in the street in front of Cuthbert's office.

"All this blood and mayhem merely for the sake of transforming four respectable young women into high-class courtesans doesn't seem logical," he concluded. "Larkin is a businessman at heart. He prefers not to take unnecessary risks. There is something else going on here. I can sense it."

"I suspect that the four girls you and the teacher rescued may be part of a much vaster trade in young women that is being carried on by

Larkin and his new gentleman partner," Felix said. "If the business is sufficiently lucrative, it would explain why the proprietors are willing to kill to protect it."

"Have you learned anything new from your inquiries?"

"The responses I got from the telegrams I sent merely confirm what you already suspected. All four of the girls at the castle supposedly died in various tragic accidents. None of the relatives appear to be in deep mourning."

"Phoebe Leyland's aunt may be the exception. She evidently made some inquiries of various orphanages after her niece disappeared. I suggest you send someone to speak with her."

"Do you have an address?"

"Yes." Ambrose gave it to him and then stepped back. "I am going home. It has been a long night." He glanced up at the darkened bedroom window. "There is someone waiting for me."

Felix smiled a little. "Makes a change for you, doesn't it?"

"Yes," Ambrose said. "It does."

27

Concordia gripped the lapels of her dressing gown, turned and paced the length of the library again. She had lost count of how many times she had walked this path in the past hour. Her anxiety increased with every step.

Ambrose should have been home by now. Something terrible had happened. She could feel it in her bones. He should not have gone alone. He should have allowed her to accompany him.

The big house was silent and still around her. The girls had gone upstairs to their rooms hours ago. Mr. and Mrs. Oates and Nan had vanished to their quarters after checking all the locks. Dante and Beatrice had wandered in to join her when everyone else had taken to their beds and were now dozing in front of the low-burning fire.

She came to a halt in front of the old Cabinet of Curiosities and looked at the clock. The hands had only advanced five minutes since she had last checked the time. Another shiver flickered through her. The room was comfortably warm, but the heat from the fireplace was not at all effective against the small frissons of dread that had been disturbing her nerves all evening.

Ambrose should have taken her with him when he went to meet with Cuthbert. When he returned she would make it very clear to him that he was not to leave her behind again. She was his client, his employer. She had rights in this matter.

Dante raised his head and regarded her intently. She knew that he had sensed her anxiety.

"Has your master told you his secrets?" she asked the dog.

Beatrice opened her eyes.

Both dogs rose and padded across the carpet to where she stood. She bent down and rubbed them behind their ears.

"I'll wager that neither of you cares a jot about your master's secrets," she said. "When this affair is concluded, I will probably never see him again, so why am I obsessed with discovering whatever it is he is intent upon concealing?"

Dante lowered himself onto his haunches and leaned blissfully against her leg. Beatrice showed a number of teeth in a vast yawn. Neither beast bothered to respond to the question.

The clock ticked into the heavy silence.

She opened the front doors of the cabinet and looked at the beautifully decorated box of secrets. The design of the exotically painted and inlaid woods was distinctive, quite unlike any pattern she had ever seen. The carefully worked, exquisitely detailed triangles and diamond shapes had clearly been intended to deceive the eye.

"You are just like this cabinet, Ambrose Wells," she whispered. "For every compartment that is discovered, there is another one that remains hidden."

Phoebe, Hannah, Edwina and Theodora had amused themselves by trying to locate all of the secret drawers. She unfolded the drawing they had left inside the cabinet to mark their progress. It was clear from the diagram that thus far they had identified only twenty-three compartments. The location of each one was carefully marked on the sketch.

She studied the picture for a long moment. Then she examined the interior of the cabinet. There were a lot of drawers left to find.

She drew the tips of her fingers along the surface of one of the intricately inlaid panels, feeling for the invisible crevices that marked some of the drawers, pressing gently to test for the hidden springs and levers that opened others.

Experimentally she opened some of the compartments that Phoebe and the others had explored. Most were empty. A few contained small relics that had evidently been stored in the chest and then forgotten. There was a little unguent jar with Roman markings in one drawer, a ring set with a red carnelian in another.

It would be amusing to discover a drawer that the girls had not yet succeeded in locating, she thought. The search would pass the time while she waited for Ambrose to return.

She set to work.

Twenty minutes later she had failed to find a single new compartment.

"This is a lot harder than one would think," she informed the dogs.

Dante and Beatrice had returned to the hearth. They twitched their ears but did not open their eyes.

She walked around the cabinet, examining it from every angle, intrigued by the puzzle of the thing. Then she returned to the front and took a closer look at one of the drawers that had already been discovered.

A sudden thought occurred to her. To test it she inserted her hand inside one of the compartments and felt around very carefully with her fingertips.

Nothing.

She went on to explore some of the other drawers. When she came to the one labeled number fifteen on the sketch, her fingertips skimmed across a tiny depression at the very back of the compartment.

She pressed tentatively and heard the faint, muffled squeak of tiny hinges and springs.

Without warning, an entire section of drawers swung open to reveal a second, interior cabinet that had been concealed within the outer one.

"Very clever," she murmured to the dogs. "I will not tell the girls. They'll have more fun if they discover this secret for themselves."

She probed with her fingertips, her curiosity heightened by her small success. When she pushed a series of triangles-within-triangles, a long, narrow compartment slid open.

A faded newspaper, folded in half, was inside. It had no doubt been tucked away in the cabinet years ago and forgotten.

She removed and unfolded it. Several columns on the front page were taken up with a lurid report of a suicide and a financial swindle.

The date of the paper was nearly twenty years old.

She started to read the report.

The body of a gentleman believed to have been engaged in a number of remarkably clever financial swindles was found in his house in Lexford Square on Tuesday.

Evidently consumed by remorse for having brought ruin upon so many innocent investors, Mr. George Colton put a pistol to his head and took his own life sometime during the night. The housekeeper discovered the bloody scene when she arrived to take up her duties the following morning.

The distraught woman was unable to supply many coherent details, but she did express grave concern for Mr. Colton's young son who is missing. . . .

Dante and Beatrice bounded to their feet, dashed toward the door and disappeared down the hall.

Ambrose was home at last.

She listened for his footsteps in the hall while she closed up the cabinet. When the outer sections were shut, she realized she was still holding the old newspaper. She put it down on a nearby table and turned toward the door of the library.

Ambrose appeared in the opening, the dogs at his heels. He had removed the false whiskers and beard. She sensed the dangerous energy that crackled invisibly in the air around him. She had been right, she thought, something terrible had happened.

"Imagined you'd be in bed," he said from the doorway.

"Are you all right?" she asked. She took an anxious step forward, wanting to go to him, to touch him and make certain that he was not injured. "I've been very worried. Were you hurt?"

"Do I look that bad?" He walked into the room, shrugging out of his coat.

"For heaven's sake, Ambrose, tell me what happened."

"Cuthbert is dead." He slung his coat over the back of the sofa. "I never got a chance to speak with him."

"Dear Lord." She sat down very suddenly on the arm of a leather reading chair. "I knew something dreadful had happened."

"There were two men at the scene." He went to the table where the cut-glass brandy decanter stood and picked up the bottle. "Got the impression they were waiting for me, perhaps hoping to follow me after I left Cuthbert's office."

She watched him down a considerable amount of the brandy in a single swallow. A fresh jolt of alarm swept through her. "You *were* hurt." She sprang to her feet and rushed toward him. "Shall I send for a doctor?"

"I am not hurt. The very last thing I need is a doctor." He downed another large dose of the brandy.

"There is dirt and grime on your clothes. Did those two men assault you?"

He considered that briefly and then inclined his head. "Yes, I believe they did assault me. I tried to assault them right back, mind you. I regret to say that I was not quick enough."

"*Ambrose.*"

"Sorry to report that they got away." He frowned. "They took Cuthbert's body with them. I expect they will have dropped it into the river by now."

"This is terrible. What are we going to do?"

"Well, for starters, I suggest we both go to bed."

"Are you mad?" She swept out her hands. "You can't just walk in here, announce that you found another dead body and then tell me to go upstairs to bed."

"I think it would be best if we saved this discussion until tomorrow morning."

"We will discuss this now."

Something dark and dangerous moved in his eyes. "This is my household. I give the orders here."

"Really, sir?" She raised her chin. "I was led to believe that this was Mr. Stoner's household."

He shrugged. "In Stoner's absence, I am in command."

"How very convenient for you."

"Not at the moment." He glanced at the table where she had placed the newspaper. "What is that?"

She followed his gaze. "An old paper. I found it in one of the drawers in the Cabinet of Curiosities."

"Bloody hell." He crossed the space with two quick, gliding strides, picked up the newspaper and looked at the front page. "I had forgotten about this."

He started toward the fire. Brooding anger and old anguish etched his hard face.

"Ambrose, wait." She launched herself forward and grabbed his arm. "Why do you wish to burn it? What is so important about that newspaper?"

"There is nothing important about it. Not anymore." He reached over with one hand and pried her fingers loose from his sleeve. "It is merely old news, Miss Glade."

"Stop." Unable to restrain him physically, she stepped directly into his path. "I have had enough of secrets and cryptic remarks. I want answers, sir. I mean to have them before this night is over."

"You want answers?" He halted, inches away, raised his hand and captured her chin with his fingers. "What an astonishing coincidence. As it happens, I want something, too, Miss Glade."

She could scarcely breathe. She would not let him intimidate her, she vowed.

"And what is it that you want, sir?"

"You," he said.

By rights his wintry smile should have iced her blood. But for some reason she was suddenly unbearably warm.

"You are trying to frighten me," she whispered.

"Yes, Miss Glade, I am, indeed, trying to frighten you."

"Well, you won't succeed. I'm not leaving this room until you answer some of my questions."

"You want answers. I want you. It is an interesting dilemma, is it not?"

"I am quite serious about this."

"So am I. The good news is that, unless you run, not walk, to that door and take yourself straight upstairs to bed, one of us is going to get what he wants tonight."

"I beg your pardon?"

"The bad news," he continued very deliberately, "is that it won't be you. Do I make myself clear, Miss Glade?"

Comprehension struck her with the force of a lightning bolt. She stared at him, disoriented with shock. Then a thrilling anticipation sparkled through her.

She could insist upon getting answers later.

"Are you threatening to ravish me, sir?" she asked. "Because if so, I think it would be best if I removed my glasses first. You know how they tend to fog up when you become passionate."

He closed his eyes, bent his head and rested his forehead against hers. She heard the newspaper drop to the carpet behind her.

"What am I going to do with you, Miss Glade?" he whispered.

She slipped her arms around him. "I thought you intended to ravish me. It sounds like an excellent plan."

He threaded his fingers through her hair. Pins popped free and dropped to the carpet.

"I am lost, aren't I?" he murmured.

"I don't know. Are you?"

"Yes."

He raised both hands and removed her eyeglasses with great care. She felt him reach around behind her to set them on the mantel. There was a soft clink when he put the spectacles down on the marble.

In the next moment his mouth was on hers. The aura of dark energy that she had sensed in him was suddenly transformed into another kind of force. It flooded her senses, igniting a dizzying response.

"Ambrose."

She pressed herself against his solid chest.

He reacted to the small, muffled cry and the tightening of her embrace by scooping her up into his arms. Without breaking off the kiss he carried her across the room toward the door.

Dante and Beatrice, evidently assuming that everyone was about to depart the library, got to their feet and bounded ahead so as not to be left behind. She heard the dogs' claws on the polished wooden floorboards in the hall.

When Ambrose reached the opening, however, he did not go through it. Instead he used one booted foot to shut the door.

"Lock it," he said against her mouth.

"What? Oh, yes. Right."

She reached down and fumbled with trembling fingers.

"Hurry," he whispered.

"Sorry."

She finally managed to get the door locked. The instant Ambrose heard the unmistakable click of iron against iron, he carried her back across the room to the sofa.

He set her on the cushions, straightened and turned down the gas jet so that the library was lit only by firelight.

She watched, fascinated, as he unfastened his shirt with quick, impatient movements. He left the garment hanging loosely and sat down on the edge of the sofa. She heard one boot hit the floor with a soft thud and then the other.

He turned and leaned over her, caging her between his arms. For a moment he just looked at her, as though he needed to commit her to memory because she might vanish at any moment.

"I knew that you would be waiting for me," he said.

She looked up into his haunted eyes and smiled.

"Is that a bad thing?" she asked gently.

"I am not accustomed to having someone waiting for me," he said, as if that explained everything.

In some strange way, it did, she thought. An oddly wistful sensation whispered through her.

"Neither am I," she said.

"I want you."

"It's all right." She touched his jaw with her fingertips. "I want you, too."

He never took his eyes off her while he untied the sash of her dressing gown.

She could see some of the curling hair on his chest and the strange flower tattoo. Intrigued, she slipped her hands inside the edges of his open shirt and flattened her fingers on his bare skin, enthralled by the heat and strength of him.

The dressing gown fell away, leaving her in her nightgown. He reached down her leg. When she felt his hand on the inside of her bare thigh, she drew a sharp breath. The intimacy of his touch left her shaken, utterly consumed with a great need.

He kissed her throat and undid the bodice of the nightgown. Then, quite suddenly, she felt the edge of his teeth on her nipple. The sensation electrified her senses.

She clenched her hands in his hair. A violent shudder swept through her.

"Ambrose."

He opened his trousers and pushed himself against her bare thigh, hard and heavy and demanding.

When he touched the damp, aching place between her legs, she became shatteringly aware of the compelling tension that was building within her there. She lifted herself against his hand and he responded with slow, deliberate strokes of his fingers that drove her to the brink of madness.

Sensation after sensation coursed through her, leaving no room for uncertainty, let alone any sense of modesty. She was caught up in the whirlwind and she could not wait to see where it would take her.

Desperately curious, she circled him with her fingers. He responded with a hoarse groan that could have reflected either intense pleasure or intense pain.

"Did I hurt you?" she asked anxiously.

"I am in agony."

"Oh, Ambrose, I never meant—"

"Do it again," he ordered roughly.

She explored him while he rained kisses on her throat, shoulders and breasts.

Abruptly, but with obvious reluctance, as though he yearned for more but feared he could not tolerate the sensation, he levered himself up and away from her. His fingers closed around one of her ankles. He raised her leg.

Assuming that he was going to complete their union, she braced herself.

But he did not enter her. Instead, to her great shock, he draped her leg over the back of the sofa and moved down the length of her body. When she felt his tongue on her in the place that he had just finished caressing, she was so stunned, she could not utter a single word, let alone protest.

By the time she finally found her voice, it was too late. Her entire body was clenched as tight as a fist.

Without warning a dazzling sense of release burst through her. The sensation was so overwhelming that she barely noticed that Ambrose had changed positions and was now looming over her.

She opened her eyes just in time to catch a glimpse of his intent, fiercely shadowed features, and then he was sinking himself into her body.

It was too much. She could not endure the alchemical brew of pain and pleasure. Her lips parted on a small scream.

Ambrose sealed her mouth with his own, silencing her before the cry escaped.

He groaned and then, as though he could not help himself, as if he had lost some portion of the self-control he valued so highly, he began to move within her.

She clutched his shoulders and clenched her teeth against the uncomfortable, impossibly tight feeling, knowing that he needed this release, aware that it was a gift that she could give him.

He stroked into her again and again. Then, quite suddenly, he went absolutely rigid. It was as if he was engaged in a battle of some kind.

"Hold me," he begged against her throat.

The words seared her soul. The discomfort she had been experiencing did not matter. The only important thing in the entire universe in that moment was holding Ambrose as close as humanly possible.

His climax surged through him.

Time stood still and the night burned.

28

A long time later she felt Ambrose move. He eased himself away from her body and got to his feet. She opened her eyes and watched him close his trousers. The act made her acutely aware of her own nakedness.

The atmosphere in the room had changed. The night was no longer white hot. In spite of the glowing embers on the hearth, there was a chill in the air.

She sat up quickly and pulled the dressing gown around herself.

Ambrose went to the mantel, retrieved her spectacles and came back to the sofa. He positioned the eyeglasses gently on her nose, took her hand and pulled her to her feet.

"Are you all right?" he asked quietly.

"Yes, of course." She adjusted the folds of the wrapper, ignoring the slightly bruised sensation between her legs and the small stains on her nightgown. All perfectly natural under the circumstances, she thought. "Why would you think otherwise?"

He smiled wryly. "Determined to play the unconventional, freethinking, modern woman to the hilt, aren't you?"

"It is not an act. I *am* unconventional, freethinking and modern."

"You were also a virgin."

She frowned. "See here, you are not going to allow yourself to be guilt-stricken about that small fact, are you? If so, I can assure you that regrets are entirely unnecessary. I certainly do not have any."

"Are you quite sure of that?"

"Positive. All in all, it was an extremely instructive experience."

"Instructive." He did not seem to know quite what to do with the word.

"I would even go so far as to call it enlightening." She went to the mirror on the wall and fumbled with her hair. "There is a great deal to recommend virginity when one is a young woman, but it is a far less interesting condition when one has arrived at a certain age."

"I see."

She met his eyes in the mirror and was unable to resist a chuckle. He looked so serious and intense. "Calm yourself, sir. It was the right time. You were the right man. Had you not taken the initiative tonight, I would no doubt have felt compelled to do so and that would have been *so* very unconventional."

He came to stand behind her and put his hands on her shoulders, watching her in the mirror. "How did you know that I was the right man?"

She hesitated, uncertain how to put it into words. She could not tell him that she loved him. It would only add to his guilt.

"I just knew." She put one of her hands on top of his. "I was very attracted to you from the start."

He tightened his grip on her shoulders and bent his head slightly to kiss her ear. "I had a similar reaction to you."

Her spirits rose. "Did you?"

He startled her with one of his rare smiles. Then he released her and went toward the brandy table. "Told myself it was merely the effect of having shared the back of a horse with you for an extended period of time, of course."

She turned around very slowly. "It was a very intimate experience, wasn't it?"

"It was, indeed. One that I will certainly never forget."

Better to leave it at that, she thought. A modern, free thinking, unconventional woman would certainly do so.

He poured brandy into two glasses and set down the decanter. "Shall we drink a toast to your new, enlightened status?"

"Certainly." She took the glass from his fingers, feeling very worldly. She was now a woman of experience.

He raised his own glass. "To you, Concordia Glade."

"And to you, Ambrose Wells." She took a small sip, lowered the glass and looked pointedly at the newspaper on the floor. "Whoever you are."

The ghosts returned to his eyes.

He picked up the newspaper and looked at the front page for a long time. She knew that he was reading the piece about the suicide.

"Who was he?" she asked gently.

He did not look up from the paper. "My father."

"Oh, Ambrose, I was afraid of that." She went to him and put her hand on his sleeve. "I'm so very sorry." She glanced at the date on the old newspaper. "How old were you at the time?"

"Thirteen." He refolded the paper with great care and put it on a nearby table.

"Dear heaven." She tightened her grip on his arm. "To lose a parent in that way is such a dreadful thing."

"My father did not commit suicide." He took another swallow of brandy and lowered the glass. "He was murdered."

She frowned. "You know that for certain?"

"Yes." He turned away, freeing himself from her hand. "I was there that night. I was the only one, with the exception of the killer, who knew the truth."

"Ambrose, you must tell me what happened."

He slanted her a strange, veiled look. "It is not a pretty story."

"Obviously. But now that you have told me this much, I must know the rest."

He turned the glass between his palms, seemingly lost in the play of the light on the faceted crystal. She knew he was choosing his words carefully, deciding how much to tell her.

"My father sent me upstairs early that night," he said. "He gave me strict instructions not to come back down for any reason. He was expecting a late-night visit from a gentleman with whom he had business dealings."

"What of your mother? Where was she?"

"My mother died when I was born. My father never remarried."

Tragedy upon tragedy, she thought. "I see."

"My father had been tense and distracted all day. I knew that the man who was to call on him was the cause of his agitation, but I did not know the nature of the threat. I was still awake when the visitor arrived. He came to the back door. I got out of bed when I heard my father greet him, went to the top of the stairs and stood in the shadows. I saw the two go into the study."

"What happened?"

"There was a quarrel, a violent one. My father and the other man were partners in an illicit financial scheme." He glanced at the newspapers. "The press got that much right."

"They argued about their business affairs?"

Ambrose nodded. "Something had gone wrong. A maid had discovered some details of the swindle. My father's partner had murdered her to ensure her silence."

"Dear God," she whispered.

His mouth twisted humorlessly. "I told you, this was not a cheerful tale."

"Go on, Ambrose."

"My father told his partner that he could not abide murder and that he intended to end their association. The partner had a pistol." Ambrose gazed deeply into the firelit brandy. "When I heard the shot, I knew what had happened. I was . . . transfixed with fear and shock. It was as though I had found myself in a waking nightmare."

She put her hand on his arm again. This time he did not pull away.

She got the impression that he did not even realize that she was so close. He was lost in the terrible memories that he saw in the brandy.

"I was still standing there in the darkness at the top of the staircase when the stranger came out of the study. He looked around and then he started toward the stairs. He knew I was in the house. He did not intend to leave any witnesses."

She tightened her grip on his arm.

"I just stood there, mesmerized. He could not see me from the bottom of the steps, but I knew that by the time he reached the first landing he would almost certainly notice me. Then he appeared to remember the housekeeper."

"What about her?"

"I think he reasoned that she was more of a threat as a witness because she was an adult. He was right. In any event, he decided to deal with her first. He turned and went back down the stairs toward the kitchen."

She put her arms around him and held him as tightly as she had earlier when they had been locked in a passionate embrace.

He hesitated as though he did not know what to do with the offer of comfort. Then, slowly, he wrapped his arms around her and let her hold him.

"Mrs. Dalton, thank God, was not there that night. My father had sent her away for the evening, to make certain that she did not overhear anything incriminating when he confronted his partner. But I knew that once the killer had assured himself that the housekeeper was not a problem, he would resume his hunt for me."

237

"What did you do?"

"When he disappeared to search for Mrs. Dalton, it was as though I had been freed from a trance. I could move and breathe again. I knew I had only a very short span of time to find a hiding place upstairs, but I had one major advantage. I was, of course, quite familiar with the interior of the house. There was a cushioned window seat in my father's bedroom. It opened up to form a cupboard, but when the lid was closed, it appeared solid."

"You hid inside the window seat?"

"Yes. I had to remove the blankets that had been stored inside first. I shoved them under the bed. I managed to get into the window seat and lower the lid just as the killer started up the stairs. I heard him make his way down the hall, searching every room on the floor."

"What a terrifying experience."

"The worst part was that the bastard kept calling to me, urging me to come out of hiding. He said that my father had just killed himself and that he would take care of me."

She shuddered and tightened her hold on him. "And all the while he meant to kill you."

"He went through every room. I heard him open the wardrobes and cupboards. When he came into the bedroom where I was hiding, my heart was pounding so loudly I was certain he would hear it. I tried not to breathe, not to move so much as the tip of my finger. I was certain that he would open the window seat and find me."

"But he didn't."

"No. I heard him swearing in frustration and rage. But he was also nervous about delaying his escape from the house. He did not want to linger at the scene of the crime any longer than was absolutely necessary. He concluded that I was not there and left. I stayed where I was for a time because I knew that he might be watching from outside, perhaps waiting to see if I turned on a light."

"What did you do?" she asked.

"When I could not bear it any longer, I climbed out of the window seat and went downstairs without turning on any lights. The lamp in the study still burned. When I got to the doorway I could see my father lying there on the floor." Ambrose watched the dying fire. "There was . . . a great deal of blood."

"You were so young to look upon something so terrible," she whispered.

"I never even got to say good-bye." He flexed one hand. "Sometimes I wonder what would have happened if I had gone downstairs earlier, while my father and the stranger were still quarreling."

Alarmed, she stepped back to look at him. "Ambrose, no, you must not think that way."

"Perhaps my presence could have altered the outcome."

She hushed him by putting her fingers against his mouth. "Listen to me. I know what you are thinking and it is wrong. You bear no blame or responsibility for what happened that night. There was nothing you could have done."

"I was there and I was helpless."

"You were a boy, only thirteen years old. Indeed, it is astonishing that you managed to outwit the killer and save yourself."

He did not respond but neither did he attempt to free himself from her arms.

"Did the police ever catch the man who murdered your father?" she asked after a while.

There was a short pause.

"No," Ambrose said. "They did not catch him."

Anger on his behalf shot through her. "Do you mean that in the end there was no justice done?"

He looked bemused by her display of outrage.

"It took some time," he said quietly. "You could say that there was justice of a sort, but no true revenge."

"What do you mean?"

"Evidently the killer became very anxious after he failed to find me. He went to America for four years. When he returned, I was waiting for him. I had made elaborate plans."

"What happened?"

Ambrose's mouth tightened at the corners. "By the time he returned, he was dying of consumption."

"And you decided to let nature take its course, didn't you?"

"Nature and the smoke of London." He shrugged. "It seemed to me that killing him would have been akin to an act of mercy."

"Did you go to see him?"

"No. I sent a message to him, letting him know who I was and that I was out there, somewhere, watching and waiting for him to die. He lasted less than six months."

"What happened to you after your father was killed?" she asked. "Did you go to live with relatives?"

"I had no close relatives. My grandfather died a year before my father was killed. There was no one else."

"Did you end up in an orphanage or the workhouse?"

"No."

"What did you do? You were only thirteen years old."

He raised his brows. "I was no innocent, Concordia. I come from a long line of rogues and criminals. My grandfather moved in Society, but he survived by stealing the jewels of the wealthy people who invited him into their drawing rooms and ballrooms. My father was a professional swindler. By the age of thirteen, I had been well trained to survive by my wits. Given my particular talents, education and background, there was little doubt about my career path."

She cleared her throat. "I see."

"On the night my father was killed, I changed my name. Shortly thereafter I began to make my living climbing through upstairs windows and stealing valuables." His face was expressionless. "Now do you comprehend? I am a professional thief, Concordia. I was born into the business and I practice it with some success."

"Not any longer," she said fiercely. "Now you are a professional private inquiry agent."

He shrugged. "Not much difference, truth be told. Similar set of skills required, and I still do a great deal of my work at night."

She grabbed the edges of his shirt. "You know very well that there is a vast and significant difference between the kind of work that you do now and what you did to survive all those years ago."

He looked down at where she was crumpling his shirt. When he raised his head, there was an odd expression in his eyes.

"Do not try to make me out a hero," he said. "I am no knight in shining armor."

She gave him a wobbly smile. "But that is exactly what you are. Admittedly, the armor may be a bit tarnished in places, but that is only to be expected after several years of wear and tear."

His mouth twisted wryly. "Whatever I am today, I owe to John Stoner."

"Who is he, Ambrose?"

"I suppose you could say that he is in the same line as you are."

"Is he a teacher?"

"I think you could call him that, yes. If I had never met him, I would still be stealing jewels, paintings and small antiquities for a living."

"I doubt it." She stood on tiptoe and brushed her mouth lightly against his. Then she turned and walked toward the door. "Good night, Ambrose."

"Concordia—"

She unlocked the door and opened it. "Whoever John Stoner is, he is no magician. He could not have made you into a hero if you had not already possessed the raw material."

29

He poured himself another glass of brandy after Concordia left. Then he sat, cross-legged, on the carpet in front of the dying fire, looked deep into the flames and thought about the conversation in John Stoner's kitchen all those years ago. The memory was as clear to him as if the events had happened yesterday.

"WHEN I WAS about your age, I found myself in a situation that is not unlike the one in which you are tonight." Stoner poured more of the fragrant tea into the tiny cups. "I was alone and on my own. I eked out a living in the gaming hells. Occasionally I resorted to cheating when I could not pay my rent. I was rather good at it."

"Cheating at cards?"

Stoner shrugged. "What can I say? It's a talent. But cheating at cards is extremely risky work. Back in those days it was not anything out of the ordinary for men to conduct duels at dawn over a disputed hand of whist."

"My grandfather used to tell me that. I believe there was a saying, 'Pistols for two, breakfast for one.'"

Stoner smiled reminiscently. "The world was a different place in those days. The queen, God bless her, had not yet come to the throne. Waterloo was still an all-too-recent memory, and ladies' gowns were a good deal more revealing and more charming than the current fashions."

"More revealing?" Ambrose asked, greatly interested now.

"Never mind." Stoner cleared his throat. "In any event, my future looked extremely unpromising until I chanced to encounter a gentleman who was a master of a secret society founded on the principles of an ancient philosophy that included arcane fighting arts and certain meditation exercises."

Curiosity flickered in Ambrose. "Who taught him such strange things?"

"He learned them from a group of monks who lived on a remote island in the Far East. I will not bore you with all of the details. Suffice it to say that the gentleman offered me the opportunity to travel to the island to study the philosophy and the fighting arts taught by the monks."

"Did you go?"

"Yes," Stoner said. "I spent nearly five years studying in the Garden Temples of Vanzagara. Afterward I set out to see something of the world. Egypt, America, the South Seas. I was gone from England a very long time. When I returned I discovered that much had changed."

"In addition to the fashions in ladies' gowns, do you mean?"

"Yes." A melancholy mood seemed to have descended upon Stoner.

There was a faraway expression in his eyes. "I learned that no one cared much about the arts of Vanza anymore."

"What of the gentleman who arranged for you to travel to the island?"

"I have no doubt that he and perhaps some of the others who had studied Vanza in their younger days kept the Society's secrets and very likely taught the way of the Circle to their sons. But their heirs considered themselves men of the modern age. They had no patience for secret societies and the like."

"Is it still possible to travel to Vanzagara to study in the Garden Temples?"

Stoner shook his head. "Twenty years ago the island was destroyed by an earthquake. The monastery where I learned the arts vanished forever."

For some inexplicable reason, Ambrose felt a crushing and utterly incomprehensible sense of disappointment.

"Unfortunate," he said, not knowing why he said it. What did he care about the monks or their lost philosophy? He, too, was a man of the modern era.

"When I returned to England five years ago, I realized that I had no place here," Stoner continued.

"Why was that?"

"Perhaps I was gone too long. Or maybe I was simply left behind when the rest of the world moved forward. Whatever the case, I have only my books, my research and my writing to occupy me these days."

Silence fell. Ambrose was uncomfortable with the wave of sympathy that washed through him. *Get ahold of yourself, man. Stoner just knocked you flat and now he has you tied to a chair. He will likely turn you over to the constables when he has finished spinning his old man's tales. There is no call to feel the least bit sorry for him.*

"Is it difficult to learn the ways of Vanza?" he heard himself ask.

Stoner considered that briefly. "It certainly requires some degree of natural talent to master the fighting arts. But anyone who can climb the side of a house the way you did tonight could manage the techniques quite nicely, I should think."

"Huh." Ambrose drank more of the fragrant tea and thought about how useful the arts of Vanza would be in his profession.

"The thing is," Stoner said gently, "the fighting skills are only one aspect of Vanza. The least important, in truth."

"No offense, sir, but I'm not inclined to believe that. Not after the way you dealt with me a short time ago."

Stoner smiled. "At the heart of true Vanza lies self-control. A master of Vanza is first and foremost a master of his own passions. In addition, he learns to look beneath the surface and consider all factors of a situation before he acts."

Ambrose thought about that. He decided that he liked the notion of being a master of something, even if it was just his own passions. And learning to look beneath the surface sounded like a useful skill.

There was another round of silence.

Ambrose shifted a little in his chair, testing the cords that bound his ankles and wrist. Nothing gave.

"What will you do now?" he asked after a while. "Hand me over to the police?"

"No, I don't think I'll do that," Stoner said.

Hope flared. "If you set me free, sir, I give you my oath that you will never see me again."

Stoner ignored that. He contemplated Ambrose for a while longer.

"As far as I am aware, I am the last Master of Vanza left in England, perhaps in the world," he said finally.

"That must be a very strange sensation."

"It is. Tonight when I watched you climb the side of my house it occurred to me that perhaps I might take on a student."

Ambrose sat very still. *"Me?"*

"I think you would make an excellent pupil."

Ambrose could feel the electricity flashing across his nerves. It was the same sensation he had gotten the night he left his father's house, carrying only what fit into his pack, the unmistakable knowledge that his whole life was about to change.

"There's something you should know, sir." He picked his words very carefully. "I've got what you might call a business associate."

"The young man keeping watch across the street?"

Ambrose was dumbfounded. "You saw him, too?"

"Of course. The two of you are remarkably clever, but you both lack the wisdom that only time and proper instruction can provide."

"The thing is, I couldn't abandon my associate to go into training with you." Ambrose shrugged. "We're friends."

Stoner nodded in an agreeable manner. "I don't see why I cannot take on two students. It is not as though I have anything else of great importance to occupy my time."

30

He stopped in front of Concordia's door the next morning and listened closely. There was no sound of movement inside. She was still asleep.

That was good, he assured himself, walking quickly to the stairs. She needed her rest after the late-night activities in the library.

But what if she wasn't asleep? What if she was huddled in her room, sobbing silently, regretting what had happened between them?

No, Concordia wouldn't hide from him, regardless of how she felt about matters this morning. She was the sort of woman who faced things squarely and moved forward.

He, on the other hand, was not feeling nearly so brave. The sharp fangs of troubled second thoughts had been gnawing at him ever since he had awakened.

He'd been a fool.

Dante and Beatrice bounded up the staircase to meet him halfway. He paused to scratch their ears.

What the devil had he been thinking to tell Concordia so much about his past? he wondered. He had kept his secrets for more than two decades. The only other people who knew or had guessed most of the truth about his past were John Stoner and Felix Denver.

What had made him throw caution to the winds last night?

He continued down the stairs, the dogs at his heels.

He could not blame it on the fires of passion. He'd experienced that condition often enough to know that it did not make him inclined to confide. Quite the opposite, in fact. He had always been especially careful not to let down his guard when he was with a woman.

It was the shock of seeing that old newspaper, he decided. That was what had made him careless.

No, couldn't blame it on that, either. He reached the foot of the staircase and went toward the library. He was generally quite adept when it came to dealing with startling incidents.

He paused just inside the library, struck by the fierceness of the emotion that swept over him. All of the heat and intensity of last night's encounter came back in a great rush. He had never wanted any woman as much as he had wanted Concordia last night.

Footsteps pattered on the staircase. Phoebe, Hannah, Edwina and Theodora were on their way downstairs to breakfast. He was not looking forward to facing Concordia's valiant guardians this morning. He could only hope that they had remained fast asleep in their beds while he was making love to their teacher.

Making love.

The words jarred and jangled and then settled quietly into place. He had *made love* to Concordia.

He crossed the room to the table where he had left Cuthbert's journal and picked up the small leather-bound book.

"Good morning, Mr. Wells," Edwina said very formally from the doorway. "May we come in? We wish to have a word with you."

He looked up from the journal. Edwina was not alone. Theodora, Phoebe and Hannah were clustered behind her. There was a solemn, determined look on each young face.

So much for hoping that they had remained blissfully unaware of what had occurred in the library last night.

"Good day to you, ladies." He closed the journal. "What can I do for you?"

"We want to talk to you about Miss Glade," Phoebe announced, typically direct.

From somewhere deep in the recesses of his ancestral memory he dredged up the motto that had been drilled into him by his father and grandfather. *When cornered, the first rule is to never admit guilt.*

"I see," he said neutrally.

Theodora took the lead, moving farther into the room. "We saw her coming up the stairs very late last night. She was in a condition that can only be described as dishabille, sir."

Rule Number Two: Redirect the blame back onto the accuser.

"Did you?" He raised his brows. "I'm surprised that you all look so fresh and rested this morning, given that you were awake and spying on your teacher at such a late hour."

"We weren't spying," Hannah said quickly. "We just happened to see her on the stairs."

"Because Dante came to my room and scratched on the door," Phoebe explained. "When I got up to let him in, I heard Miss Glade coming up the staircase."

"Phoebe woke the rest of us," Edwina concluded.

He nodded. "That explains how you all just happened to be hovering on the landing when Miss Glade retired to her bed."

They exchanged uneasy glances.

"The thing is," Edwina said very solemnly, "her hair was down."

"Just like Lucinda Rosewood's in *The Rose and the Thorns*," Hannah added. "After she came in from the garden with Mr. Thorne. That was where Mr. Thorne ravished her, you see."

Ambrose nodded. "In the garden."

"And then he abandoned her," Hannah said sadly. "Remember? I told you that part the other morning at the breakfast table."

"I believe you also mentioned that you had only been able to complete half the novel," he said. "Have you had an opportunity to finish it yet?"

"Well, no," Hannah admitted. "But it is quite obvious that it will end badly for Lucinda Rosewood. The thing is, we do not want Miss Glade to be ruined in the same way."

Edwina drew herself up very straight. "Under the circumstances, Mr. Wells, we feel quite strongly that you must ask Miss Glade to marry you."

"I see," he said again.

They watched him with expressions of anxious anticipation.

It was Concordia who broke the tautly stretched silence.

"Good morning, everyone," she said briskly from the doorway. "What is everyone doing here in the library? It's time for breakfast."

Startled, all four girls swung around very quickly to face her.

"Good morning, Miss Glade," Edwina got out in a little rush. "We were on our way to the breakfast room."

"We happened to notice that Mr. Wells was in here and we stopped to say good day to him," Phoebe said.

Theodora gave Concordia an overly bright smile. "Mr. Wells was just telling us some of the history of the artifacts in the cabinet on the balcony."

"That's right," Hannah said. "Very educational."

"Indeed?" Concordia smiled. "How nice of him."

"In point of fact," Ambrose said coolly, "we were not discussing ancient artifacts."

"You weren't?" Concordia was starting to look bewildered.

"Your charming pupils cornered me here this morning to inform me that, under the circumstances, they feel that I am honor bound to propose marriage to you, Miss Glade."

Concordia's mouth dropped open. She turned very pink. Her hand closed forcibly around the door frame as though to steady herself.

"Marriage?" she got out in a hoarse little whisper. Clearly horrified, she glowered at the four girls. "You have been discussing *marriage* with Mr. Wells?"

"We had no choice," Hannah said, straightening her shoulders. "We saw you on the stairs last night, Miss Glade."

"Your hair was down," Phoebe added.

"It appeared that you had been ravished," Theodora said. "So, naturally, we told Mr. Wells that he must marry you."

"That is what a gentleman is supposed to do if he ravishes a lady," Edwina explained. "But sometimes the gentleman doesn't do the right thing and then the lady is ruined forever."

"We don't want that to happen to you," Edwina concluded.

Concordia turned her stricken gaze on Ambrose.

He got a sinking sensation.

"I was just about to explain to the young ladies that ours is not a conventional situation," he said quietly. "I was going to remind them that you are a modern, unconventional woman who does not feel obligated to follow the old-fashioned, straitlaced rules that Society dictates for women."

"Quite right." She pulled herself together with an obvious effort. "Furthermore, appearances are often deceiving." She beetled her brows at Phoebe, Hannah, Edwina and Theodora. "How many times have I told you that one must not leap to conclusions without sufficient and very solid evidence to support them?"

"But, Miss Glade," Phoebe said, "your hair was down."

"The pins had given me a headache earlier in the evening," Concordia said. "I removed them."

Hannah frowned. "But, Miss Glade—"

"Appearances aside," Concordia continued brusquely, "I would also remind the four of you that it is incumbent upon all well-mannered people to respect the privacy of others. It is not the place of young ladies who are still in the schoolroom to intrude into the affairs of their elders. Do I make myself clear?"

The unhappy hush that followed in the wake of the lecture made it clear that the girls were not accustomed to such stern talk from their beloved Miss Glade.

"Yes, Miss Glade," Edwina whispered.

Hannah's mouth quivered. "Yes, Miss Glade."

Phoebe bit her lip.

Theodora inclined her head unhappily. "We're sorry, Miss Glade. We only meant to help."

Concordia softened immediately. "I know that. But rest assured that nothing occurred between Mr. Wells and me last night that need cause any of you the least bit of concern. Isn't that correct, Mr. Wells?"

"I would remind everyone present that in a situation such as this, there is more than one person's reputation involved," Ambrose said.

They all looked at him.

"I beg your pardon?" Concordia said. She sounded as though she spoke between clenched teeth.

"It is true that Society is concerned primarily with the reputation of the lady, but there is also the not insignificant matter of the gentleman's honor," he said quietly.

Concordia's expression turned stony. "Mr. Wells, this conversation appears to have lost direction. I suggest that we all repair to the breakfast room immediately."

He ignored the interruption. "Given that I am the gentleman in question, I cannot help but feel that I have some rights in this matter."

"I fail, utterly, to see how your rights have been in any way affected, sir," Concordia said. Her voice had become very tight.

"Naturally, I would not wish you to think that I do not fully respect your modern sensibilities, Miss Glade," he continued. "So I believe that a compromise is in order. I would like to offer an alternative to the usual method of dealing with this sort of situation."

Phoebe, Hannah, Theodora and Edwina began to look quite interested.

"What are you talking about, sir?" Concordia asked, spacing each word with ominous emphasis.

"It appears to me," he said, "that there is a very modern, indeed, an extremely unconventional approach that might be employed in this matter that should suit all parties concerned."

"Mr. Wells," Concordia said darkly, "you are not making any sense. Perhaps you did not get enough sleep last night."

"I slept very well, thank you," he assured her.

Hannah took a step forward. Her face was alight with curiosity. "What is this modern, unconventional approach you mentioned, sir?"

He smiled directly at Concordia. "I believe it would satisfy everyone involved if we leave it up to Miss Glade to decide whether or not to propose marriage to me."

Concordia stared, evidently rendered mute by the shock of his suggestion.

Phoebe, Hannah, Edwina and Theodora reacted with astonished delight.

"Letting the lady propose to the gentleman is a very modern notion, indeed," Phoebe declared.

"Excellent plan, sir," Edwina said to Ambrose.

"Thank you," he said, trying to appear modest.

Hannah glowed. "Just think, if Lucinda Rosewood had been able to insist that Mr. Thorne marry her, she would not have been ruined."

"Very clever," Theodora enthused. "It solves the problem quite brilliantly, does it not, Miss Glade?"

Concordia finally found her tongue. "There is no problem to be solved."

No one paid any attention to her.

"It is certainly a very original notion," Phoebe said. "I wonder if it will catch on in the future?"

Hannah pursed her lips. "But what if Miss Glade does not ask Mr. Wells for his hand in marriage?"

Theodora's brows bunched together. "Or what if she does ask him but he refuses?"

That brought an abrupt halt to the conversation. The girls looked at Concordia.

She released her grip on the door frame and made a show of checking the time on the face of the little chatelaine watch she wore at her waist.

"Gracious, it is really quite late, isn't it?" She gave everyone a polished grin. "I, for one, am famished. If you will excuse me, I believe I will go have my breakfast."

She turned around and walked off down the hall. The heels of her shoes rang lightly on the polished floorboards.

When she was gone, the girls swung back to confront Ambrose with accusing eyes.

He spread his hands. "That is the one troubling aspect of doing things in a modern, unconventional style, I'm afraid. Granted, it makes for an interesting change. Unfortunately, one cannot always be assured that, when all is said and done, one will find that one is any better off than when things were done the old-fashioned way."

31

Concordia adjusted the black glove on her left hand with a snapping motion of her fingers and peered at Ambrose through the black net veil that concealed her face. She was very conscious of the chaotic mix of strong emotions that was still twisting through her. She did not know whether she was unsettled, angry or depressed.

She decided in favor of anger. It seemed the safest course.

"I cannot believe that you allowed that conversation in the library to become so outrageous this morning," she began. "Don't you know that when one is dealing with young people, one must take great care to remain firmly in control of the subject matter of the discussion at all times?"

Ambrose regarded her from the opposite seat of the cab. He was wearing whiskers, a mustache and spectacles. Together with a frumpy coat that had been padded around the midsection, a stiff, high collar and conservatively cut trousers, he appeared every inch the unfashionable man of affairs.

"I regret to say that my own experience with persons, especially young ladies, of that age is considerably more limited than yours," he said.

It worried her that she could not tell if he was teasing her. She should *know* if he was amusing himself at her expense, she thought.

They were on their way to Mrs. Hoxton's residence. This was the first time she had been alone with Ambrose since the disastrous meeting in the library before breakfast. She had convinced herself that she had regained her composure, but now she was discovering that her nerves were still distressingly unsettled.

"Really, sir, what were you thinking to put that notion into their heads?"

"What notion was that?" he asked.

"Do not try to play the innocent with me. You know very well that I am referring to that extremely poor joke you made in the library."

He somehow managed to appear crushed by the accusation. "I do not recall making any jokes this morning."

His bold-faced denial was too much. She lost what little remained of her temper.

"I am talking about your ridiculous comments regarding the appropriate behavior of a lady and a gentleman following . . . following . . ." Words failed her. She was obliged to resort to waving her gloved hands about in an embarrassing manner. When she realized what she was doing, she quickly clenched them together in her lap. "You know very well what I mean."

"Following a night of inspired passion that left the gentleman in question too enchanted, enraptured and enamored to be able to think clearly the next day?"

"Any man who can insert *enchanted, enraptured* and *enamored* together in one sentence is thinking with perfect clarity."

He sank deeper into the cushions. "I thought you, of all people, would appreciate how deftly I handled that awkward scene with your pupils."

"You consider the suggestion that it is up to me to do the right thing by you an example of deft handling?"

"Well, you must admit that it was, at the very least, quite a modern way of dealing with the matter."

She sighed. "You are impossible, sir."

There was a short pause.

"Would you have preferred that I did the traditional thing?" he asked neutrally. "Should I have asked you to marry me this morning?"

She tensed and fixed her attention on the view outside the window. "Because of a single night of passion in which we engaged as equals? Of course not. You did not take advantage of me, sir. There is no need for you to atone with an offer of marriage."

"What if I were to make the offer?" he said.

She scowled. "I would refuse it, of course."

"Because you are so very modern and unconventional?"

He was deliberately goading her now, she decided.

"No," she said brusquely. "I would refuse it because I would know that it was your own sense of gentlemanly honor that had obliged you to make the offer. I will not marry any man for such a reason."

He gave her an unreadable look. "I believe that you may be overestimating the degree to which I am guided by my gentlemanly honor."

"Nonsense. You are a deeply honorable man, Ambrose. I sensed that much the first night we met. And that is why I would be forced to refuse any offer you made. I could not marry you under that sort of duress."

"Duress," he repeated. "What an unpleasant word."

"Yes, well, there you have it. A marriage contracted for reasons of old-fashioned, misguided notions of honor or to appease the dictates of respectable Society is all too likely to result in a lifelong sentence in a prison without walls for both parties."

"An opinion held by your parents, I presume?"

She could not respond to that comment. It was the truth. How often had she heard her parents take precisely that stand? Indeed, she had grown up with that admonition ringing in her ears.

"You fear that if you were to contract a marriage for those reasons it would be a betrayal of the memory of your parents and all that they taught you, do you not?" Ambrose asked gently.

She collected herself and raised her chin. "I would not subject either of us to a miserable marriage."

"Are you certain, then, that we would be miserable together?"

Her mouth went dry.

Fortunately, the cab rumbled to a halt at that moment. Ambrose reached for the door handle.

"Given your obviously devout feelings on the subject," he said, "it appears that we are left with my ingeniously modern, unconventional approach."

"I beg your pardon?"

"As I told you this morning in front of your students, I shall leave the matter of marriage up to you. If you decide to ask me for my hand, you know where to find me."

HE WAS WELL AWARE that he had gone too far with that last remark and that he would no doubt soon regret it.

It had been obvious all morning that Concordia was balanced on some internal tightrope fashioned of inflamed nerves. In hindsight, it had clearly been a mistake to raise the subject of marriage in the first place, let alone suggest such an unconventional approach to it.

But what was he supposed to do after Phoebe, Hannah, Edwina and Theodora cornered him in the library?

At the time it had seemed a positively brilliant way out of an untenable situation. He knew very well that if he had asked Concordia to marry him that morning, she would have refused. For his part, he was grimly aware that he would not have tolerated the rejection well. By placing the burden of proposing on her shoulders, he had attempted to ease them both out of a potential quagmire.

It only went to show that for all its emphasis on self-control and calm, logical thinking, his Vanza training had its limits. Two generations of Colton family wisdom had not been of much use, either. But then, in spite of their larcenous ways, his father and grandfather had both been hopeless romantics. Evidently it was a family characteristic.

HE WELCOMED THE INTERVIEW with Mrs. Hoxton. It was an excellent excuse to focus his attention on something other than his increasingly complex relationship with Concordia.

The door was opened by an imposing butler who, after a brief consultation with his employer, showed them into a heavily over-furnished drawing room.

It was apparent that Mrs. Hoxton's decorator had been intent on incorporating every fashionable element. The result was a murky kaleidoscope of colors, patterns and textures.

Plum-colored drapes pooled on a carpet of gigantic blossoms of blue, lilac and cream. The heavily bordered wallpaper featured a profusion of massive pink blooms against a maroon background. Every piece of furniture was upholstered in chaotic prints. Large urns filled with artificial bouquets stood in the dark corners. Framed pictures were hung from floor to ceiling.

Concordia sat down on one of the velvet-covered chairs. "Thank you for seeing us on such short notice today, Mrs. Hoxton. Very kind of you."

Ambrose was impressed with the smooth manner in which she had slipped into her role. If he hadn't known better, he would have believed her to be exactly what she purported to be—a wealthy, fashionable widow.

"Not at all, Mrs. Nettleton." Mrs. Hoxton's round face glowed with an ingratiating smile. "Any friend of Lady Chesterton's is, of course, welcome in this household."

The association with the wealthy, socially powerful Countess of Chesterton was extremely tenuous. Ambrose had, in fact, invented it a few minutes ago when he had jotted the lady's name on the card that he handed to the impressive butler.

The gossip he had picked up in his club concerning Mrs. Hoxton's social-climbing aspirations had proved accurate. She had been unable to resist the lure of entertaining a "close personal friend" of Lady Chesterton's.

"This is my man of affairs." Concordia waved a black-gloved hand somewhat vaguely in Ambrose's direction. "No need to pay any attention to him. I brought him along to take notes. He deals with all the boring details associated with my rather extensive financial affairs."

"I quite understand." Mrs. Hoxton gave Ambrose a cursory glance and instantly dismissed him as beneath notice. She turned eagerly back to Concordia. "What did Lady Chesterton tell you about me?"

"Cynthia gave me your name and assured me that you could advise me on the matter of establishing a charity school." Concordia accepted a cup of tea from the maid. "She mentioned that you have successfully undertaken a similar philanthropic project."

The maid disappeared discreetly, closing the door of the drawing room softly. Ambrose realized that no one was going to offer him any tea so he took out the little notebook and pencil he had brought along and did his best to fade into the floral-print upholstery of his chair.

"Lady Chesterton, I mean *Cynthia,* is aware of my philanthropic efforts?" Mrs. Hoxton could scarcely contain her delight. "I hadn't realized."

"Yes, of course," Concordia said. "She has heard about the good works you are doing at the Winslow Charity School for Girls."

Mrs. Hoxton nodded happily. "I see."

"My late husband left me a rather large sum of money," Concordia explained. "It is my dearest wish to use a portion of it to establish an academy for orphaned girls. But I am not quite certain how one goes about that sort of thing. I hope you can give me some practical guidance in the matter."

Mrs. Hoxton's expression went blank. "What sort of practical guidance?"

"Well, for example, how much of your time must be devoted to managing the charity school?"

"Oh, I see what you mean." Mrs. Hoxton brightened. "No need to concern yourself on that point. I find that being the school's benefactress requires very little time. I give out a few gifts to the girls at Christmas and allow them to express their gratitude to me, but that is the extent of it, I assure you. One extremely dull afternoon a year is all that is required."

"I don't understand," Concordia said. "What about hiring the staff?"

"One leaves that sort of thing in the hands of the headmistress, of course."

"But who hires her?"

Mrs. Hoxton appeared momentarily perplexed. Then her features cleared. "In my case, there was no need to hire anyone. The Winslow Charity School for Girls was already established when I chose to become its benefactress. Miss Pratt was the headmistress at the time and there was no reason to let her go. Every reason to keep her on, in fact. She is an excellent manager. Maintains a very close eye on expenditures. Never a penny wasted."

"What happened to the school's previous benefactor?" Concordia asked.

"He died. Heirs didn't want to be bothered with the school. As it happened, I was looking around for a suitable charity project at the time. It was all quite convenient."

Concordia sipped tea. "How did you discover that the school was available, as it were?"

"That was a simple matter. My very good friend Mr. Trimley learned of the situation and recommended that I consider becoming the benefactress."

Concordia paused, her cup in midair. It was impossible to see her expression through the heavy veil, but Ambrose knew that she was watching Mrs. Hoxton closely.

He was doing the same but making very sure not to reveal his interest.

"I don't believe I am acquainted with Mr. Trimley," Concordia said delicately.

"He is a very charming, very elegant gentleman," Mrs. Hoxton said. "I am entirely dependent on him when it comes to matters of fashion and taste."

"Fascinating," Concordia commented. "How did you meet him?"

"We were introduced at the Dunnington soiree last year." Mrs. Hoxton assumed an air of polite inquiry. "I expect you were there, also, Mrs. Nettleton. I don't recall meeting you, though. But then, it was a dreadful crush, wasn't it?"

Damn, Ambrose thought. He had not prepared Concordia for this sort of question.

"I was not going about much at the time," Concordia said smoothly. "My husband was enduring his last, fatal illness. I felt that it was my place to be at his side night and day."

Ambrose felt a small tingle of admiration. The lady was very fast on her feet.

"Yes, of course," Mrs. Hoxton said quickly. "Forgive me. I did not stop to think. Well, as I was saying, I became acquainted with Mr. Trimley on that occasion. We got along famously."

"You see a great deal of him, then?" Concordia pressed gently.

"Indeed. He will be escorting me to the Gresham ball tomorrow evening, in fact." She smiled proudly. "I assume you received an invitation?"

"Yes, of course. Unfortunately I do not yet feel up to attending that sort of thing."

"I understand."

Concordia placed her cup very carefully on the saucer. "I assume you employ a man of affairs to handle the business aspects of your charity school?"

"Mr. Trimley sees to that side of things for me. I do not pay any attention to those sorts of details. As I told you, I have found that engaging in good works is really no great trouble at all."

"Mr. Trimley sounds extremely helpful," Concordia concluded.

"I do not know what I would do without him," Mrs. Hoxton said.

A SHORT TIME LATER, feeling quite proud of her performance, Concordia allowed Ambrose to take her arm and escort her down the front steps of Mrs. Hoxton's town house.

They turned and walked toward the corner.

"I trust you enjoyed yourself back there in the drawing room," Ambrose said. He sounded wryly amused.

She concentrated on maintaining an air of aloof, fashionable dignity. "Whatever do you mean by that? I thought I did a very creditable job of acting."

"You did. In fact, I got the distinct impression that you rather fancied playing the role of arrogant employer to my humble man of affairs."

"If it is any comfort to you, sir, you were excellent in your part. Indeed, I do not think I have ever seen a man of affairs who looked more like a man of affairs."

"Thank you." He hailed a passing cab. "Over the years I have become quite expert at receding into the wallpaper."

She smiled behind her veil and gave him her hand so that he could assist her into the cab. "You do possess the most astonishing array of skills, Ambrose."

"So do you, Concordia." He closed the door and dropped down

onto the seat across from her. "My admiration for the teaching profession increases every day."

"Well?" She looked at him through the veil. "I assume the next step is to find out more about this mysterious Mr. Trimley?"

"I think so, yes." Ambrose turned his attention to the window. "He seems to be an important figure in this affair. Perhaps he will prove to be Larkin's gentleman partner."

"I think it is safe to say that Mrs. Hoxton is not one of the conspirators. She obviously views the charity school strictly as a means of enhancing her image in the eyes of Society."

"I'm inclined to agree with you," Ambrose said. "I suspect that her very good friend Mr. Trimley is manipulating her. It would certainly not be the first time that a gentleman scoundrel has latched on to a wealthy woman in Society and used her for his own purposes. He appears to have been equally successful convincing Edith Pratt to cooperate in the scheme."

Concordia wrinkled her nose in disgust. "I suspect that obtaining Miss Pratt's assistance would merely require a suitable bribe."

"You have her measure."

"How will you go about finding Trimley?" she asked, very curious now. "Will you keep a watch on Mrs. Hoxton's town house to see if he visits her?"

"That is certainly one way of handling the matter," he said. "But it is very likely that I would waste a considerable amount of time lurking in doorways waiting for him to put in an appearance. I think there is an easier approach."

"What is that?"

"Mrs. Hoxton mentioned that Trimley would be escorting her to the Gresham ball tomorrow night. I will also attend. There will be a great many people around. It should prove relatively easy to observe Trimley in the crowd."

She stared at him, astonished. "You're joking."

He frowned. "Why do you say that?"

"You cannot be serious about attending a fashionable ball."

"Why not?"

"For starters, there is the little matter of an invitation."

"Easy enough to forge, were it necessary," he said. "But in this instance I see no need to go to the trouble. Lady Gresham's affairs are always crushes. No one will take any notice of an extra person."

"I wish I could go with you," she said. "I could help you make observations."

He gave her a long, thoughtful look.

"Hmm," he said.

She shook her head. "Impossible, I'm afraid, but I thank you for considering it."

"I don't see why you cannot come with me. As a woman you might be in a position to learn things that I could not."

"There is the little matter of the proper gown, sir," she reminded him. "The dresses that you had made up for me are quite lovely but none of them is suitable for a ball."

"The gown will not be a problem."

"Are you certain?"

He smiled. "Quite certain."

Excitement spiraled through her. "It sounds very exciting. I've never been to a ball. I shall feel just like Cinderella."

"Nothing like a good fairy tale, I always say." Ambrose stretched out his legs and folded his arms. "On another topic, I have been meaning to tell you that I took a close look at the little book that I found in Cuthbert's desk last night. I thought it might be a journal of accounts, and it is, in a way."

"What sort of accounts? Do they relate to the charity school?"

"No. I think the entries are actually a running tally of his gaming losses." Ambrose paused. "Evidently Cuthbert was not a particularly lucky player. He owed someone a great deal of money at the time of his death."

"Alexander Larkin?"

"I suspect that was the case, yes."

She reflected for a moment. "Do you suppose Larkin and Trimley used the gaming debts as a way of forcing Cuthbert to assist them in their scheme?"

"It seems very probable, yes."

She shivered. "And now Cuthbert is dead."

"People who get involved with Alexander Larkin often end up that way. But in the past most of his victims have been other villains or members of the less respectable classes. It is safe to say that, in general, they were the sort of crimes that did not make sensations in the press. Nor did they inspire the forces of the law to conduct serious, in-depth investigations. But now Larkin and his new partner seem willing to take more risks."

"I see what you mean. The recent murders have included a professional educator, the proprietor of an agency that supplies teachers to girls' schools and a man of affairs."

"None of them moved in Society, of course, but they were all considered to be more or less respectable. Unlike the case of my client's sister, such murders do draw attention."

"But only when they are discovered," Concordia reminded him. "Miss Bartlett simply disappeared. Mrs. Jervis supposedly committed suicide. And Cuthbert's body has yet to turn up."

"True. Nevertheless, it strikes me that Larkin and his associate must consider your four students very valuable, indeed."

32

Concordia grasped the sides of the ladder and looked up at the top of the brick wall that she was about to ascend.

"You will never believe this, Ambrose, but when you told me that we would attend the Gresham ball tonight, I pictured myself in a slightly different style of gown."

He clamped both hands around the rails of the ladder to steady it for her. "Rest assured, you look very fetching as a ladies' maid. The cap and apron suit you."

"At least I am spared the indignity of that flashy footman's costume that you chose to wear."

"I thought I explained the logic behind these disguises. A hostess of Lady Gresham's rank will have taken on extra staff for tonight's affair. No one will notice one additional maid and a spare footman."

She started up the ladder, aware that he had brought it along solely for her convenience. He could have scaled the wall quite easily without one.

"Now I understand why you were not concerned with obtaining an engraved invitation," she said.

"Why bother with trivial details when one can simply climb a garden wall?"

"I suppose that is a very practical way of looking at things."

She reached the last rung on the ladder and paused to hoist the folds of her gray cloak and her skirts out of the way.

Gingerly she swung first one leg and then the other over the top of the wall. The heavy linen drawers she wore beneath the plain servant's dress protected the skin of her thighs from the rough bricks.

When she was safely seated atop the wall, she found herself looking into a vast moonlit garden. The lights of the Gresham mansion glowed in the distance. Music drifted out into the night from the ballroom.

She had a fleeting image of herself, dressed in a fairy-tale gown, waltzing in Ambrose's arms. In her private fantasy her hair was fastened in an elegant chignon studded with jeweled flowers. Ambrose, of course, looked spectacularly handsome in formal black and white.

She smiled to herself.

"What the devil are you thinking?" Ambrose asked from the top of the ladder.

She jumped a little at the sound of his voice right next to her ear. She had not heard him come up beside her.

"Nothing important," she said lightly.

"Try to pay attention. I don't want any mistakes this evening."

"There is no need to lecture me, Ambrose. I am well aware of what I am to do tonight."

"I certainly hope so." He hauled the ladder up and lowered it on the garden side of the wall. "Remember, you are not to take any chances. If you run into any difficulties or feel uneasy for any reason, signal me immediately."

"That makes the tenth time you have given me those instructions since we left the house, Ambrose. Do you know what your problem is?"

"Which one?" He went down the ladder with the agility of a cat. "I seem to have quite a variety lately."

That hurt but she was careful not to let her reaction show in her voice. She moved cautiously onto the ladder and descended with what she feared was considerably less grace than he had exhibited.

He was waiting for her at the bottom. When she was standing in front of him again, she reached up to adjust her spectacles.

"Your problem is that you do not appreciate initiative in a partner," she said.

"Perhaps that is because I am not accustomed to working with one. Haven't had a partner in years."

That piqued her interest. "You once had a partner?"

"Back at the beginning," he said absently. He removed his coat. "How do I look?"

She peered at him closely, but the only aspect of his footman's livery that she could make out in the dark shadows was the pale wig. "I can't say for certain. It is too dark."

"Your cap is askew." He raised his hands to her hair. "Here, I'll adjust it."

"I vow, you have the eyes of a cat, Ambrose."

"That's what Stoner always said." He took her hand. "Come along, my dear, we're off to the ball. After tonight you will not be able to say that I do not take you into elevated social circles."

TWO HOURS LATER, Concordia darted down a darkened hall and opened a narrow door. A shaft of light from the hall revealed a large closet filled with mops, brooms, buckets and brushes.

She slipped inside and closed the door. Alone at last, she thought, slumping wearily against the closet door.

Who would have thought that playing the part of a maid for one evening would prove to be so exhausting? She had not had a moment's respite since she had snuck into the ladies' withdrawing room.

Together with two other equally harried servants, she had assisted an endless series of demanding female guests. Most of the time had been spent on her knees, helping ladies into their dancing slippers and hooking up the elaborate trains of their sumptuous gowns so that they could waltz without tripping over their skirts. In addition there were a number of small disasters involving spilled champagne and torn petticoats. There had also been one or two instances in which she had been called upon to clean some suspicious grass stains on satin skirts.

At least there had been no fear of discovery, she thought ruefully. A maid's white cap and apron had proved to be as good as a weeping veil when it came to a disguise. None of the elegant ladies who had passed through the withdrawing room had taken any notice of the hardworking servants.

The other maids had accepted her presence without question.

Everyone was far too busy to be anything other than grateful for the additional help. Furthermore, no one expected a servant who had been taken on just for the evening to know her way around the mansion.

The only truly unsettling moment had occurred when Mrs. Hoxton, resplendent in a heavily flounced and frilled gown of pink and purple satin, had swept through the door of the withdrawing room.

But the gracious benefactress of the Winslow Charity School for Girls had barely spoken to, let alone glanced at, the maid who had crouched on the carpet to hook up the long, frothy train of the dress.

Reluctantly she raised her hands to her cap to make certain it still sat properly on her head and then opened the door.

She slipped back out into the quiet hall, wondering if Ambrose had spotted the elusive Mr. Trimley in the ballroom.

"Well, well, well, what have we here? Hiding to avoid your duties, I see."

The voice behind her was male and badly slurred from the effects of too much champagne. Concordia pretended not to hear. She hurried on down the hall toward the safety of the ladies' withdrawing room.

Footsteps sounded heavily behind her. She picked up her skirts, preparing to break into a run.

A beefy male hand clamped around her upper arm, halting her in her tracks.

"Now just where do you think you're off to in such a hurry?"

The hand on her arm forced her to turn around. She found herself confronting a large, stout gentleman dressed in expensively tailored black-and-white formal attire. There was enough light in the dim hall to

277

make out his features. She could see that at one time he had probably been quite handsome. But his face had taken on the coarseness that was the hallmark of too much heavy drinking, rich food and a dissolute lifestyle.

He leered at her. "Spectacles, eh? Don't believe I've ever tumbled a maid who wore eyeglasses. A first time for everything, I always say."

The urge to slap his face was almost overwhelming. She reminded herself that she was supposed to be a maid. Servants did not smack gentlemen guests. Neither did teachers, come to that, not if they wished to remain in their posts.

"Excuse me, sir," she said, working very hard to keep her voice cool, calm and ever so respectful. "I am expected back in the ladies' withdrawing room."

He made a wet, chuckling sound. "No need to be concerned about the time. I'll be quick about it."

"Please let me go, sir. They will send someone to look for me if I do not return to my duties immediately."

"Doubt anyone will miss one little maid for a few minutes. Got plenty of them running about the house tonight." He started to haul her back toward the storage closet. "Come along now, let's have some fun. I'll make it worth your while, never fear."

Outrage swept over her. She cast aside her humble maid's accents and launched into her schoolroom voice.

"How dare you, sir?" she snapped. "Is this the way you treat those whose station in life is not equal to your own? Have you no manners? No breeding? No sense of decency?"

The lecherous drunk stopped and stared in astonishment, as though some inanimate object had spoken to him.

"What's this?" he said, somewhat blankly.

"You should be ashamed of yourself. You have no right whatsoever to take advantage of females who are obliged to go into service to make an honest living. Indeed, a true gentleman would see it as his duty to protect such women."

She tried to take advantage of his surprise to free her arm. But his big hand tightened painfully around her. His sickening leer twisted into an expression of righteous indignation.

"And just who in blazes do you think you are to take that tone of voice with your betters?" He used his grip on her arm to give her a violent shake. "I'll teach you your place. Damned, if I won't."

He yanked hard, hauling her toward the closet.

For the first time, Concordia felt a wave of real fear. Matters were escalating out of control. Hoping that there were other servants nearby who might be willing to come to her aid, she opened her mouth to yell for assistance.

The drunken gentleman clamped a massive hand over her lips. "Keep quiet or it will go all the harder for you and that's a promise. You can bloody well forget about a tip, too."

He got the door of the storage closet open and started to pull her into the darkness. His palm covered her nose as well as her mouth. It was all she could do to breathe. Her rising panic was infused with fury.

She reached up and raked her nails across his cheek.

He roared with pain and released her to put a hand to his injured face. "What the devil have you done to me, you stupid bitch?"

She planted both hands against his chest and shoved with all her strength.

The drunken man lost his balance, stumbled backward and went down hard on his rear on the floor of the closet.

She slammed the door closed and turned the key in the lock.

"There you are," Ambrose said from somewhere in the corridor behind her. "I've been looking all over for you."

Just what she needed, she thought, adjusting her spectacles. If Ambrose knew that she had very nearly been assaulted he would no doubt send her straight back to the mansion in a cab.

"I was just taking a little rest," she assured him, straightening her cap and apron. "Being a ladies' maid is really quite exhausting, you know."

There was a furious pounding on the door behind her. An irate, albeit muffled voice boomed through the wood panels.

"Let me out of here, you bitch. How dare you treat your betters in this disrespectful manner! I'll see to it you're turned off without a reference this very night. You'll be on the streets before dawn."

Ambrose contemplated the door.

"Was there a problem?" he asked neutrally.

"No, not at all." She gave him a brilliant smile. "Nothing I could not handle. Why were you looking for me?"

The door behind her shuddered beneath another series of blows.

"Open this door at once."

"Stand aside," Ambrose said to Concordia.

A fresh wave of panic slammed through her. "Ambrose, you must not do anything rash. You cannot afford to engage in a brawl with a gentleman tonight. It will put your entire scheme at risk."

"Hold these." He tossed his topcoat and her cloak into her arms.

"Ambrose, please, we have more serious matters to concern us tonight. This is no time to get distracted."

"This will only take a moment." He unlocked the door, opened it and stepped inside.

"About time," the enraged man began. He broke off, eyes widening, when he saw Ambrose. "What's going on here? What do you think you're—"

The door closed, leaving him alone with Ambrose inside the closet.

Concordia heard a few quiet words followed by a couple of unpleasant, muffled thuds. She winced.

The door opened. Ambrose emerged, righting his footman's wig. Concordia caught a brief glimpse of a crumpled form on the floor of the cupboard before the door closed again.

"Right, then, that's that," Ambrose said. "Let's be on our way. We have lost enough time as it is."

"You didn't kill him, I trust," Concordia said anxiously.

"I didn't kill him," Ambrose agreed, ushering her swiftly along the hall.

"It was not my fault."

"No, it was mine for allowing you to participate in this venture tonight. I should have known better."

"Now, Ambrose, that's not fair. I thought I dealt with the situation very effectively."

"You did. That is not what concerns me."

"What does concern you?" she demanded.

"The fact that he got a close look at your face and could describe you to someone else."

"No need to fret about that," she assured him. "Between the poor lighting and the fact that he was quite drunk, not to mention whatever you just did to him, he will recall very little, if anything, about what took place tonight. I'm certain that he would not be able to describe me. Besides, no one remembers the maid."

"We will discuss the matter later. At the moment there is no time to waste."

He was moving so quickly that she was forced to run every other step in order to keep up with him. "How did you find me?"

"One of the other maids working in the withdrawing room said that you had disappeared down this hall."

They went along a balcony that overlooked the ballroom. She heard brittle, insincere laughter and languid voices raised in inebriated conversation. She glanced down at the glittering scene. The chandeliers glowed on the ladies' jeweled gowns and made the gentlemen look quite elegant in their black-and-white formal attire. It was a glimpse of another world, she thought, a pretty bauble of a world, indeed.

"I regret that you were not able to enjoy your fairy tale," Ambrose said quietly.

"I am quite certain that nothing that is happening down there in that ballroom could be half as exciting as the adventure we are sharing. Your profession is a most interesting one, Ambrose."

He looked startled. Then he gave her a slow smile. "It is rarely dull."

"Why are we rushing like this?" she asked. "What has happened? Did you spot Trimley?"

"Yes. He arrived with Mrs. Hoxton and has been hanging around her all evening."

"Excellent. But why did you come looking for me? I thought your plan was to observe him."

"It was. But a short time ago one of the footmen handed him a note. Whatever news it contained seemed to concern Trimley greatly. He made some excuse to Mrs. Hoxton and the others and exited very quietly out of the ballroom. I followed him and heard him call for his hat, coat and a hansom."

"He is leaving?"

"Yes. But with any luck at all, it will take him a while to get a cab. The street outside is crammed with vehicles because of the crowd here tonight."

"I wonder why he did not request Mrs. Hoxton's carriage."

"I suspect it is because he did not want her coachman to know where he is going," Ambrose said with soft satisfaction.

Excitement sparked inside her. "You believe that he is off to some clandestine rendezvous?"

"Yes. There was an air of urgency about the way he made his excuses and slipped away from the ballroom."

"What are we going to do?"

"My intention was to leave you here while I followed him. There was something in that note that got his full attention. I want to see where he goes in response to it."

"I want to come with you," she said quickly.

"Never fear, you are most certainly leaving with me," he said grimly. "After that unfortunate episode back there in the broom closet, I'm not about to take the chance of leaving you here alone."

"Now, Ambrose, you are making far too much of that small incident."

"*Small incident?* The man tried to rape you."

"It is not the first time I have dealt with his type. In the course of my career as an instructor of young ladies, I have been obliged to put a number of the male relatives of my students in their place. You would be amazed to learn how many so-called gentlemen do not hesitate to take advantage of a woman they perceive to be alone and without resources."

He glanced at her, mouth curving with reluctant admiration. "You have certainly led an adventurous life, Miss Glade."

"As have you, Mr. Wells."

They turned a corner and merged into a river of footmen carrying heavy silver platters to and from the buffet tables.

When they arrived in the hot, smoky kitchens, a cook glowered at them.

"And just where do you two think yer going?" she demanded, wiping sweat from her cheeks with her apron. "There's work to be done around here."

"We'll be right back," Ambrose assured her. "Betsy needs some fresh air."

"Does she now? Well, she can bloody well get her fresh air after madam's guests have all gone home." The cook eyed the coat and cloak that Concordia carried. "Where did you get those? Did you help yourself to some of the guests' things? Is that why you're rushing off so quickly?"

A fearsome crash of silver and china thundered across the kitchens. Everyone, including the annoyed cook, turned to look at the hapless footman who had just dropped his tray.

"Look what you've done, you bloody fool," the pastry cook shouted. "It took hours to prepare those lobster pies. Madam will be furious when she finds out how much food you wasted tonight. You'll be turned off without a reference, I'll wager."

"Come along," Ambrose whispered, pulling Concordia toward the door.

They escaped out into the gardens. Ambrose paused long enough to toss his white wig, hat and elaborately trimmed footman's jacket behind a hedge.

"Give me the coat," he said. "Put on your cloak. I do not want anyone observing a footman and a maid getting into a hansom near this house." He surveyed her briefly and then reached out to pluck the white cap from her head. "Servants do not ride in hansom cabs."

"Respectable ladies do not ride in them, either," she reminded him. "At least not with men who are not their husbands. They are supposed to go about in carriages or omnibuses. The driver will no doubt assume I am very fast if I get into a hansom with you."

"Can't be helped." He turned and led the way through a maze of hedges. "Keep the hood of your cloak pulled up to shield your face. Stay close to me."

They went back through the gardens to the place along the back wall where they had entered two hours earlier. Concordia did not see the ladder lying on the ground until she tripped over it.

"Careful," Ambrose said, catching her easily. He leaned down, picked up the ladder and propped it against the brick wall. "I'll go up first this time."

She followed him, struggling with the folds of her cloak and skirts, intensely aware of his impatience.

A moment later they were both on the ground on the other side of the wall.

"This way." Ambrose caught her wrist and started toward the street. "Quickly. I don't want to lose Trimley."

"What about the ladder?"

"Leave it. We won't be needing it again."

The street in front of the Gresham mansion was thronged with private carriages. A short distance away, lined up in a neat row alongside the park in the center of the square, Concordia could see the lights of several cabs.

She heard a familiar whistle. One of the footmen was summoning a hansom. In response, the first cab in the line started toward the front of the big house.

"That will be Trimley's," Ambrose said. "He is going down the steps now."

He led her quickly through the shadows to the row of waiting cabs and selected the hansom at the end of the line. The driver, seated on the box up behind the covered section where the passengers rode, gave Concordia a cursory glance. But he showed no great interest when she and Ambrose climbed the narrow steps and sat down in the open-fronted cab.

Once seated, Concordia understood why Society frowned upon women riding in hansoms. There was a very dashing air about the small, two-wheeled vehicle. The single seat provided barely enough space for two people sitting quite close together. The close quarters felt extremely intimate.

Ambrose spoke to the driver through the trapdoor. "Follow the cab that is just now leaving the house but do not let the driver notice you."

He shoved some notes through the opening.

"Aye, sir." The driver pocketed the money. "That will be no trouble at all at this hour of the night."

The cab rumbled forward.

Concordia was astonished by the speed and maneuverability of the hansom. "What a wonderful way to travel. One can see everything from this vantage point. And just look at how swiftly we are moving. Very efficient. There is no reason in the world why properly bred ladies should not go about in a hansom."

Ambrose did not take his eyes off the cab in which Trimley was traveling. "Will you teach that notion to the young ladies in your girls' school?"

"Yes, I believe I will."

They passed a gas lamp at that moment. In the dim light Concordia could just make out the slight smile that curved the corners of Ambrose's face.

"Do you find my plans for a girls' school amusing?" she asked quietly.

"No, Concordia. I find them wonderfully bold and admirable in every respect."

"Oh." She did not know what to say to that. No one had ever encouraged her in her dreams since her parents had died. It was very gratifying.

They followed Trimley's cab through a maze of crowded streets. Eventually the other vehicle turned another corner.

"Damn," Ambrose whispered. "So that is where he is going."

Concordia sensed the dangerous energy that was coursing through him.

"What is it?" she asked.

"He is headed toward Doncaster Baths," he said.

"But it is well after midnight," she said. "Surely the baths will be closed to the public at this hour."

"Yes. Which makes Trimley's destination all the more interesting."

A short time later Ambrose spoke to the driver. "Halt here, please."

"Aye, sir."

The cab came to a stop. Concordia looked at Ambrose. "What are you planning to do?"

"It is obvious that Trimley is going into the baths." Ambrose removed his hat and pulled up the collar of his coat. "I suspect that someone, possibly Larkin, has arranged a meeting with him there. I am going to follow him and see what I can learn."

She looked around at the darkened street. Fog was starting to shroud the gas lamps. A shivery sensation sifted through her.

"I think I should come with you," she said.

"Impossible. You will remain here with the driver until I return."

The response was flat, unequivocal. She knew him well enough by now to realize that argument was futile. There were times when she could reason with him and other times when she could not. This was one of those other times.

"I do not like this, Ambrose. Promise me that you will be very, very careful."

He was already on his feet, preparing to step down to the pavement. But he paused to lean over and kiss her once, very briefly, very hard, on her mouth.

"If I am not back here within fifteen minutes or if you grow anxious for any reason, instruct the driver to take you to number seven, Ransomheath Square. Ask for Felix Denver. Do you understand?"

"Who is Felix Denver?"

"An old acquaintance," he said. "Tell him what has happened. He will help you and the girls. Do you comprehend me, Concordia?"

"Yes. But, Ambrose—"

He was already on the pavement.

"Do not allow anyone to approach the lady while I am about my business," he ordered the driver. "Is that clear? Leave immediately if someone comes close. The lady will provide you with an address in the event that I am delayed."

"Aye, sir." The driver secured the reins. "Don't worry about your lady. I'll keep an eye on her. I know this neighborhood. It's safe enough."

"Thank you," Ambrose said.

He moved away very swiftly.

Concordia watched until he vanished into the shadows and fog.

33

Ambrose stood in the dark entranceway of a building across the street from Doncaster Baths and watched Trimley open the front door of the gentlemen's entrance with a key.

A personal key to the establishment was an interesting development, Ambrose thought. Did Trimley own a share of the business? Was he on very good terms with the proprietor? It was possible that the key was stolen, of course, but the familiar manner in which Trimley used it argued for the likelihood that this was not the first time he had let himself into the building after hours.

A short time ago Trimley had abandoned his own cab around the corner in the next street. Evidently he had not wished the driver to see the precise address of his destination.

A very careful man, Ambrose concluded. But then, a gentleman who consorted with a crime lord had to be cautious.

In the few seconds that the door of the baths was open, Ambrose saw a small, weak beam of light. Either an attendant had left a lamp burning inside or someone else had gone into the baths ahead of Trimley. Larkin, perhaps.

The door closed quickly behind Trimley.

Ambrose waited a few more minutes, allowing his quarry time to settle into whatever business he intended to conduct inside the baths. Then he crossed the street and discovered that Trimley had left the door unlocked. The implication was that he did not intend to stay long.

Ambrose slowly opened the door. The small lobby area was mostly in shadow. The dim glow he had noticed earlier came from a half-closed door that opened onto another room.

He moved into the lobby, closed the door very softly behind him and crossed the space to the other door.

He had come here once before in the guise of a customer at the beginning of his investigation into Nellie Taylor's death. That visit had provided him with a good notion of the interior of the baths. The establishment had been designed by an architect who favored the dark, Gothic style. High, vaulted ceilings and deep doorways left a great deal of space for shadows.

He eased the door of the dressing room open a little wider and studied the row of curtained booths. A single wall sconce gave off enough light to reveal the large stack of white toweling sheets on a table.

There was no sign of Trimley, but he could hear rapid footsteps echoing on tiles somewhere deep inside the baths. A gentleman moving swiftly in evening dress shoes, he decided.

He went through the changing room and emerged in the first hot room. The heat had been lowered hours earlier when the baths had been closed for the night, but a residual warmth persisted. A wall sconce with a frosted globe glowed dully on gleaming white tiles.

Weaving a path between the benches and chairs that the patrons used during the day, he made his way to yet another door and eased it open.

The gas jet on the wall in this room had been turned down very low, but he could see the dark shape of the large, square pool in the center of the space.

Somewhere in the shadows water dripped.

He started toward the opening on the far side of the room.

Halfway to his goal, he saw the dark shape floating just beneath the surface of the water in the cold pool.

At first glance it appeared to be a gentleman's overcoat that had been carelessly dropped into the water. Then he saw the pale, lifeless hands extending from the cuffs of the coat.

The dead man's sightless eyes stared up at Ambrose from the depths, oddly accusing.

Alexander Larkin.

A door crashed open in the adjoining pool room. The sudden explosion of sound shattered the eerie silence. Frantic footsteps pounded on tiles.

Not the same footsteps he had heard earlier, Ambrose thought. But most certainly someone bent on escape.

He went through the doorway into the hot plunge room in time to see the figure of a man circle the wide pool and hurtle toward the high, vaulted entrance to a darkened hall.

Ambrose broke into a run. He was closing the distance when the panicked man abruptly skidded to a halt in the opening and flung up his hands.

"Don't shoot." He started to dance backward. "Please, no, I won't tell anyone, I swear it."

Ambrose stopped and then drifted toward the shadows of the curtained booths to his right. He could see the man he had been chasing more clearly now. He was thin and stooped with age and a lifetime of hard work. His cap and heavy, waterproof apron marked him as a bath attendant.

Ambrose recognized him. The man was known in the baths as Old Henry.

"I'm afraid that it is your extraordinarily bad luck to be in the wrong place at the wrong time tonight," Trimley said from the vaulted opening. "I really cannot allow you to tell the police that you saw me at the scene of Larkin's murder, now can I?"

He took a few steps closer to Old Henry. The lamp that marked the entrance to the hall gleamed on the revolver in his hand.

He raised the gun.

"Please, don't kill me, sir," Henry begged.

Ambrose moved deliberately, making a small, soft sound.

Trimley stiffened and swung quickly around, searching the shadows.

"Who's there?" he demanded. "Show yourself."

"Let the attendant go, Trimley," Ambrose said from a veil of darkness. "He has nothing to do with this."

"It's you, isn't it?" Trimley stared hard in the direction of the curtained booths. "You're the one who took the girls away from the castle. Have you finally decided to do business with us? We'll make you a handsome offer for the girls. We'll want the teacher, too, of course. Can't let her live. She knows too much."

"Let the attendant go and we can discuss that subject."

"Why does the damned attendant matter so much to you?" Trimley asked. "Does he know something of importance?"

To a man like Trimley other people had value only if they could help further one's own goals. Money and power were clearly the prime motivators for him.

"Rest assured," Ambrose said meaningfully, "he is more important than you can even begin to guess."

Trimley cast a quick, frowning glance at the trembling attendant. "I find that difficult to believe."

Ambrose thought about the lamps that had been lit throughout the baths that evening and decided to gamble on the logic of the situation.

"Larkin never told you about the attendant, did he?" he said.

"What are you talking about?"

"Use your head, Trimley. Why do you think Larkin trusted him to come here tonight to turn up the lamps?"

"He's just a servant. Turning up the lamps is one of his tasks."

"You didn't know Larkin very well, did you? There were very few people on the face of the earth whom he trusted completely. Evidently you were not one of them."

"That's not true." Trimley seemed offended. "He considered me his partner. He trusted me."

"Partner." Ambrose laughed humorlessly. "Yet he never told you the reason why this attendant was here tonight."

"What in blazes do you mean by that?"

"Larkin and the attendant were old acquaintances," Ambrose said, spinning out the tale in the easy, effortless manner his father and grandfather had taught him. *Throw in a few ounces of detail, lad, and they'll buy the whole pound of smoke.* "They came up out of the stews together. This man saved Larkin's life once, a long time ago. Larkin did not forget that sort of service."

Old Henry whimpered but he seemed to comprehend what was happening. He did not contradict the claim of a longtime association with a master criminal.

"How do you know all this?" Trimley asked sharply.

"I've been watching Larkin for a long time," Ambrose said. "You could say I've made a study of the man."

"Bloody hell," Trimley said. "He told me that someone was out to take over his empire, but I thought he was merely somewhat paranoid."

Ambrose said nothing. Water splashed lightly on tiles somewhere in the darkness. The sound echoed eerily.

"Show yourself," Trimley ordered. "You sound like a gentleman. No reason we can't do business. I'm in the market for a new partner, as you can see."

Ambrose moved forward until he was standing next to a stand that held two large, empty pitchers of the sort used by the hair-washing attendants. He kept the lamp at his back so that his face remained in shadow. The pool separated him from the other two men.

At this distance and in this light, it was highly unlikely that Trimley could use the revolver against him to any useful effect. But the attendant was still in mortal danger.

"What are you proposing?" Ambrose asked softly.

"Stop right there." Trimley sounded calmer. He was obviously feeling more in command of the situation now that he could see Ambrose's silhouette. "Put up your hands. I want to see if you have a gun."

"I'm unarmed." Ambrose held up his palms. "But bear in mind that if you kill me, you'll have an even bigger problem than if you kill the attendant."

"What do you mean?"

"It's true that I was watching Larkin. But someone else is closing in on you, Trimley. I'm the only one who can tell you the name of the police inspector who has concluded that you and Larkin were partners."

"You're lying. No one knows about me. *No one.* I'm a gentleman, damn you, not a member of the criminal class. Why would an inspector take any notice of me?"

"I have news for you, Trimley. The police are not above suspecting members of the upper classes. It is just that they find it more difficult to make arrests in those circles. They require a great deal of proof. But rest assured, in your case, the inspector is well on his way toward acquiring ample evidence against you."

"How do you know all this?"

"Isn't it obvious? I'm the man he paid to obtain the evidence he needed."

Trimley was dumbfounded. "Impossible. You're lying."

"There is no need to be overly concerned. I'm a businessman at heart. As for me, justice is a commodity that can be bought and sold, just like those four girls you and Larkin stole."

"You're willing to tell me the name of the inspector?" Trimley sounded dubious.

"I will sell you his name, assuming we can come to terms on the price," Ambrose replied. "And, for an additional, negotiable fee, I will make the evidence that I have acquired thus far disappear."

34

Ambrose should have returned by now.

Concordia shivered and pulled her cloak more snugly around herself. Something had gone wrong. She was as certain of that as she had ever been of anything in her life.

She leaped to her feet and jumped down from the cab.

"Here now, where are ye going?" the driver demanded. He peered at her, alarmed. "I'm supposed to keep an eye on ye for the gentleman."

"I believe he may be in grave danger somewhere inside the Doncaster Baths. Someone may be trying to murder him. I must go to him. Will you please help me?"

"Murder?" Galvanized by the word, the driver swiftly unhooked the reins. "No one said anything about that sort of trouble."

"Wait, please, I need your assistance."

"The fare was a nice one, but it wasn't enough to make me get involved with murder."

The driver slapped the reins. The horse started forward.

"Will you at least please find a policeman and send him to the Doncaster Baths?" Concordia pleaded.

The driver did not respond. He was too busy wielding his whip, urging his horse into a full gallop.

In a matter of seconds she found herself alone in the street.

She ran toward the entrance of the baths, her cloak swirling out behind her.

35

"You are the man of business who called on that foolish, social-climbing cow, Rowena Hoxton, aren't you?" Trimley said. "Who was the woman who accompanied you? The one who said she wanted to start a charity school?"

"She's not important," Ambrose said. "An actress I employed to play the role."

"That silly bitch Hoxton was the one who put you on to me, wasn't she?" Trimley's voice was laced with disgust. "That's how you learned my name. You must have been at the ball tonight. You followed me when I came here."

"Perhaps," Ambrose allowed.

"I almost had you the other evening when you went to see Cuthbert at his offices, you know."

"Your men were somewhat less than efficient."

"They weren't *my* men." Trimley snorted. "They were Larkin's. When Cuthbert attempted to sell me information about a certain Mr.

Dalrymple who had sought him out to inquire about a girl named Hannah Radburn, I realized at once what had happened."

"You agreed to purchase the information from Cuthbert and then you had him send the message to me at my club. When you had no further use for Cuthbert, you got Larkin to arrange for him to be murdered."

"The plan was to follow you when you left the office that night. I wanted to know who you were and where you had hidden the girls. But things went wrong."

"Just as they did at the castle," Ambrose said. "By the way, were you the one who had the bath attendant, Nellie Taylor, murdered? Or did Larkin give the order?"

"Was that her name?" Trimley asked without much interest.

"Yes."

"Actually, I had nothing to do with her death. She was one of Larkin's little Turkish bath whores. He was very fond of tumbling the female bathing attendants. Nellie Taylor was his favorite of the moment, I believe. I suspect she learned more about his business than was good for her."

"So he got rid of her?"

"Obviously." Trimley's voice sharpened. "Forget Taylor. She wasn't important. I suggest we discuss our business, instead. What is the name of the police inspector you say is watching me?"

"Come now, you don't really believe that I'm going to give you that information as long as you're holding a gun, do you? I'm unarmed. You have nothing to fear from me. Put down your weapon and we will talk this over like gentlemen."

"I can't see you very clearly. Come into the light."

Ambrose moved a little farther into the small circle of light from the nearest wall sconce, closer to the water pitchers.

"Can't you see my empty hands?" he asked, holding them up, palms out.

Trimley peered intently in his direction and finally seemed satisfied. "Very well then, what is your price for the girls? It had better be reasonable, or—"

He broke off abruptly when a faint rumbling sound echoed from the corridor behind him.

"What's that?" he rasped, his earlier agitation returning in full force. "Who's there?"

Damn it to hell, Ambrose thought. Stoner would have been proud of him. The Strategy of Negotiation had been working rather well. But as his father and grandfather had often said, a smart man is always prepared for sudden reversals of fortunes.

"It would seem we have a visitor," Ambrose said. He took advantage of Trimley's distraction to pick up one of the heavy water pitchers.

"One of your men?" Trimley demanded. His head swiveled back and forth between the darkened hall and Ambrose.

"Definitely not one of my men," Ambrose said, keeping the pitcher in the shadows alongside his right leg. "One of Larkin's, perhaps."

The rumbling grew louder. Trimley rounded on the shivering attendant. "Do you recognize that sound?"

"Beggin' your pardon, sir," Old Henry said in a shaky voice. "I think it's one of the linen carts. We use them to move the sheets and towels about the place."

"Damn it to hell and back. Is there *another* attendant here tonight?"

"No, sir. I'm the only one, sir," the man replied. "Least, I thought I was."

A cart heaped with a mountain of linens appeared in the entrance to the corridor. The stack was so high and so wide that it was impossible to see who was on the far side.

"Stop," Trimley ordered.

There was no time to get around the pool, Ambrose realized. He would have to throw the pitcher across the water.

At that moment the cart jolted forward suddenly, picking up speed. Whoever was pushing it had just given it a strong shove.

"Damn you," Trimley shouted, completely unnerved now.

He fired the gun wildly in the directly of the laundry cart.

Ambrose hurled the pitcher. But Trimley was already in motion, scrambling to one side in an effort to avoid being bowled over by the laundry cart.

The pitcher struck him on his shoulder instead of hitting him in the head, as Ambrose had intended.

Trimley howled, but he did not go down. He lost his grip on the revolver, however. It clattered on the tiles.

Frantic, he staggered and then whirled around to search for the gun.

Ambrose broke into a run, circling the pool. He could see the revolver on the floor very near the water's edge.

"Get his gun," he shouted at the dazed attendant.

Old Henry recovered and turned to search for the pistol in the shadows. "I can't see it. Where is it?"

No point calling out instructions for finding the damn gun, Ambrose thought. Trimley could follow them just as well as, if not better than, Old Henry.

A few more strides and he would have Trimley in his grasp.

"I see the gun." Concordia flew from the hallway, her cloak whipping out behind her. She was headed straight for the pool's edge.

Trimley spun around, following her. He, too, finally saw the pistol.

Bloody hell, Ambrose thought. Just what he needed.

Concordia reached the gun a split second ahead of Trimley. She did not even try to pick it up, which would have been a terrible mistake, Ambrose knew, because Trimley would have wrestled it from her.

Instead she used the toe of her shoe to kick it into the pool.

"What do you think you're doing, you stupid creature," Trimley shouted.

He lashed out in fury, knocking Concordia into the pool. She landed with a splash that sent water showering up onto the surrounding tiles.

Then he swung around and charged toward the entrance to the corridor.

Concordia surfaced, gasping for air.

"Are you all right?" Ambrose asked, slowing briefly.

"Yes." She sputtered, coughed and found her footing in the water. "I'm fine. Go on. Don't worry about me."

Taking her at her word, he raced into the heavily shadowed hallway. Trimley had already disappeared, but Ambrose could hear his footsteps pounding toward the alley entrance.

It was dark in this portion of the bathhouse, but Trimley was running with the confidence of a man who knew his way around the building.

At the end of the hall, Trimley yanked open a door and vanished.

Ambrose went through the door a few strides behind him and discovered a narrow spiral staircase. Trimley was headed for the roof.

Ambrose climbed swiftly, listening to Trimley's pounding footsteps on the upper stairs.

A door opened at the top of the stairwell. Damp night air flowed inside.

Ambrose came out of the stairwell in time to see Trimley step up onto the stone parapet that surrounded the rooftop and jump down onto the roof of the neighboring building. He followed swiftly, closing the distance between them.

Little wonder that Felix had been unable to chart Larkin's comings and goings into and out of the baths, he thought. The crime lord had devised a secret route. He wondered if Larkin had ever realized that his gentleman partner had discovered it.

Evidently concluding that he could not outrun his pursuer, Trimley stopped suddenly, bent down and picked up an object that had been lying on the roof. He turned swiftly.

In the fitful moonlight, Ambrose could see the length of pipe in his hand quite clearly.

"I don't know who you are, but you've been a damned nuisance," Trimley said.

He rushed forward, swinging the pipe in a heavy, lethal arc designed to connect with Ambrose's head.

Ambrose threw himself flat onto the hard surface of the roof. The pipe slashed through the air only inches overhead.

He rolled to his feet and went toward Trimley.

"*No, stay away from me.*" Trimley skittered backward. "Stay away, damn you." He raised the pipe for another blow.

Ambrose feinted to the left.

Trimley shifted position again to stay out of reach. Ambrose lashed out with his right foot.

Trimley tried to evade the blow. The back of his leg came up hard against the edge of the stone parapet.

He staggered, lost his balance and toppled over backward.

"*No . . .*"

The scream reverberated through the night. It ended with a shocking suddenness on the pavement of the street below.

36

"A re you certain that you are warm and quite dry?" Ambrose asked from the opposite side of the cab.

"Yes, thank you," Concordia said politely. It was not the first time she had answered the question. "I told you, the water in the pool was still warm and the attendant very kindly supplied me with a number of towels."

Old Henry had also recovered her spectacles for her with the aid of a long hook.

Nevertheless, she knew she looked quite odd, enveloped from neck to ankle as she was in Ambrose's overcoat. The heavy garment had proven useful, however. It had allowed her to pass as a gentleman as far as the cabdriver was concerned.

She did not know what he had made of the large towel wrapped around her wet hair. It certainly added an interesting fashion note, she thought. Perhaps she could single-handedly bring about a return of the turban style that had once been popular in the more exclusive ballrooms.

She was not concerned about her own health. She was certain that she would survive the dunking in the bath quite nicely. It was Ambrose she was worried about. Ever since he had returned from the roof he had been in a dark, shuttered mood.

"You saved that poor old man's life tonight," she said. "If you hadn't arrived on the scene when you did, Trimley would have shot him without a second's hesitation."

"Old Henry is the informant who told me that Nellie had mentioned a conversation with Larkin in which Aldwick Castle was named. He gave me my first solid clue in the case."

"Is Old Henry another one of your former clients?"

"Yes. His bill has been paid in full and then some."

The vehicle came to a halt. Concordia looked out the window and saw a row of handsome town houses.

"This must be Ransomheath Square," she said. "My goodness, what a handsome town house. I am aware that the men who work in the Criminal Investigation Division are paid more than the constables on the street, but I did not realize they earned enough to afford such luxury."

Ambrose opened the door of the cab. "Felix did not pay for this town house out of his income as an inspector."

"Was he born into money?"

"No, but he managed to earn a fair amount of it in another career before he decided to become a policeman. He invested well." He got out of the vehicle. "Wait here. I shall return in a moment."

She sat in the shadows of the cab and watched him go up the steps of number seven. The door opened eventually in response to his knock.

The light of a candle flared. Ambrose spoke briefly to someone Concordia could not see.

The door closed. Ambrose came back down the steps and vaulted up into the cab.

The front door of number seven opened a second time. A man came down the steps with an easy, loping stride. When he passed beneath the gas lamp, she saw that he carried an overcoat. He had taken the time to put on his trousers and shoes but he was still working to fasten his shirt. The ends of a tie flapped around his throat.

"Doncaster Baths," he said to the driver before he hoisted himself up into the unlit carriage. The vehicle set off at a brisk pace.

"Why the devil do you always pay me a visit at two o'clock in the morning, Wells?" he growled. "Can't you learn to come at a more polite hour?" He became aware of Concordia on the opposite seat. "I say, you must be the teacher."

She could not make out his features clearly in the shadows but she liked the sound of his voice.

"Yes, I am," she said.

Ambrose leaned back in the darkness. "Concordia, allow me to present Inspector Felix Denver. Felix, this is Miss Glade."

"Good evening, Miss Glade. Or should I say, good morning?" Felix tied his cravat with a few practiced twists. "No offense, but do you mind telling me what that is on your head? The latest fashion in evening hats, perhaps?"

"It's a towel." Embarrassed, she reached up self-consciously to touch it. "My hair got wet."

"Indeed," Felix said. "I had not noticed that it was raining tonight."

"It is a rather long and complicated tale. I will let Mr. Wells explain."

"An excellent notion." Felix turned slightly in the seat to confront Ambrose. "Explain yourself, Wells."

"The long and the short of it is, Larkin and his mysterious gentleman partner are both dead," Ambrose said.

"*Both* of them?"

"Yes. The unknown partner turned out to be a man named Edward Trimley. He had formed a connection with a wealthy widow named Mrs. Hoxton. It was one of those mutually beneficial arrangements that so often come about in Society. He got the use of her money and connections. She got an elegant escort whenever she required one."

"Mrs. Hoxton is the benefactress of the Winslow Charity School for Girls," Concordia put in helpfully.

"So that was the connection to the school," Felix said, sounding very thoughtful now.

"Yes," Ambrose replied. "Tonight Miss Glade and I followed Trimley from a ball to the Doncaster Baths. It appears that he went there to meet Larkin. Evidently they had a falling-out. By the time I followed Trimley into the building, Larkin was dead. His body is floating in one of the pools."

"Where is Trimley's body?" Felix asked. "Or should I ask?"

"It's in the alley behind the bathhouse," Ambrose said in the flat, emotionless voice he had been employing since his return from the roof.

"Trimley's death was an accident," Concordia explained quickly. "Ambrose pursued him onto the roof. There was a struggle and Trimley fell over the parapet."

There was a short, charged silence. Neither man said a word.

Concordia knew in that moment that whatever had happened on the roof of Doncaster Baths, it had likely not been an accident.

"All in all, a rather neat ending to the affair," Felix said neutrally. "Unfortunately, it leaves me with no one left to question, doesn't it?" He paused. "Unless there happens to be a witness or two left?"

"The only witness is the attendant," Ambrose admitted. "I had a short talk with him earlier, however, and it seems that he did not actually see the murder. He was in another part of the building at the time."

"Trimley intended to kill the attendant to keep him silent," Concordia said. "If Ambrose had not interfered when he did, the poor man would be dead."

"How did the bath attendant come to be involved?" Felix asked.

"He told us that he received a message instructing him to open the baths after hours," Ambrose said. "It was not the first time he has been called upon to perform that task. It seems that Larkin was in the habit of using the baths for secret late-night meetings with his underworld associates, just as you suspected."

"I knew something was going on in those baths," Felix said.

"Larkin used a secret rooftop entrance. That is why you and your men were never able to spot him entering or leaving the baths. Evidently Trimley learned of the route, however. I suspect some of the bath attendants knew about it also, but they, quite wisely, kept their silence and their jobs."

"What of Nellie Taylor?" Felix asked.

"Trimley called Nellie one of Larkin's bathhouse whores and implied that she had learned more than Larkin thought it wise for her to know about his plans for Phoebe, Hannah, Edwina and Theodora."

"So he killed her," Felix concluded. He was quiet for a few seconds. "Bastard," he added with great depth of feeling.

"Yes," Ambrose agreed.

"We believe that Mrs. Jervis, the woman who operated the agency that supplied the teachers to the castle, and Miss Bartlett, the first instructor, were killed for similar reasons," Concordia said. "They concluded that the girls were the first of a number of well-bred young ladies that Larkin intended to transform into high-class courtesans and auction off to the highest bidders. There is no indication that they knew about Larkin's or Trimley's involvement, but they did know how to contact Cuthbert. They made the mistake of trying to blackmail him."

"Cuthbert, of course, immediately informed Trimley of the threat and Larkin arranged to get rid of the two women," Ambrose said. "Later, Trimley and Larkin got rid of Cuthbert, too. I must take the responsibility for that business. They reasoned that if I had found him, the police might also."

"So many deaths," Felix said quietly. "By the way, how was Larkin killed?"

"I didn't pull the body out of the pool," Ambrose said, "but from what I could tell, it appears that he may have been struck on the back of the head, knocked unconscious and left to drown. If it weren't for the circumstances and the identity of the victim, it might have been possible to pass it off as another bathhouse accident."

"As was the case with your client's sister," Felix mused.

"Precisely."

"Well, what's done is done," Felix said. "On balance it is probably for the best. I would have liked very much to question Larkin, especially, about his business enterprises. But, in truth, it would have proved extremely difficult to bring a case of murder against either man. There was no hard evidence against Larkin, and Trimley's status in the social world would have made it very difficult to bring him to justice."

"The most unfortunate aspect of this affair," Ambrose added, "is that it will likely not be long before someone else steps up to take Larkin's place."

"It is the way of things," Felix agreed philosophically. "But on the positive side, it does ensure my continued employment. As long as there are villains, there will be a need for the police." He studied Concordia in the shadows. "May I ask how you came to be soaked to the skin, Miss Glade?"

"Trimley pushed me into one of the pools," she said.

"When I arrived in the baths, Trimley attempted to use the elderly attendant as a hostage," Ambrose explained. "There was something of a stalemate. I did not have a gun. Trimley did."

"I see," Felix said.

"Concordia distracted Trimley by pushing a cart full of linen at him. There were a few moments of confusion and chaos during which Trimley shoved Concordia into a pool."

"Ambrose is being far too polite about the matter," Concordia said. "In point of fact, he had the situation more or less under control when I came along and attempted to rescue him. I fear I upset his plans for the evening to a considerable degree. But I must say, he made adjustments very quickly."

"Yes, Ambrose was always very good at adjusting to changing developments." Felix sounded amused. "The talent came in handy in the old days."

"You two have known each other a long time, I understand?" Concordia said, trying to keep her tone very casual.

The cab halted in the street in front of the Doncaster Baths. Felix opened the door and stepped down onto the pavement. He turned to look at Concordia. In the light of the streetlamp she saw that he was an exceedingly handsome man. She could also see that he was greatly amused.

"Didn't Ambrose tell you, Miss Glade? He and I were business associates once upon a time. We did very well together until John Stoner came along and insisted upon turning us into honest men."

"Stoner also made us his heirs," Ambrose said. "Which rendered the whole point of our earlier careers somewhat moot, to say the least. What's the use of being a thief if one does not need the income? We were both obliged to seek out other professions in which we could make use of our particular talents."

37

"You consult for Scotland Yard?" Concordia watched from the darkened cab as Felix Denver crossed the street and walked toward the gentlemen's door of the Doncaster Baths.

"On an occasional basis." Ambrose rapped on the cab roof to signal the driver to move off. "My path as a private inquiry agent frequently crosses Felix's. That is what happened at the start of this case. When I realized that Nellie Taylor's death might be connected to Larkin, I informed Felix immediately."

"When did the two of you first meet?"

"A few days after the murder of my father. We were both attempting to steal some clothes that had been hung out to dry in a garden. We fought over the prize, a very nice pair of trousers. In the end we decided we could do better working together."

"How did Felix come to be on the street?"

"His parents succumbed to a fever when he was twelve. By the time I met him, he had been on his own for a year. A very hardened criminal, to be sure. I learned a lot from him."

"How did the two of you meet Mr. Stoner?"

"You could say it was in the course of doing business. We broke into his house, employing our customary strategy. Felix kept watch. I went inside. Stoner caught me."

"Good heavens. It's a wonder he didn't summon a constable and have you both arrested."

"Stoner is an unusual man in many ways."

"So are you and Felix Denver." She paused. "When will you inform your client that the men responsible for her sister's death are both dead?"

"Soon."

"The news will no doubt bring her peace of mind."

"Some, perhaps," Ambrose said. "But I suspect it will not give her what she seeks. Justice and revenge make thin gruel. They can provide some basic sustenance but very little in the way of true comfort."

The bleak edge on his words wrenched her heart. "Are you always like this at the conclusion of a case, Ambrose?"

"What the devil are you talking about?"

"Do your spirits always sink for a time after you have found the answers?"

For a moment she feared he would not respond.

"You are a very insightful woman, Concordia," he said at last. "How did you guess?"

"I expect you become depressed at the end of a case because you feel, deep in your heart, that what you have discovered will not truly comfort your clients. You think that, in a way, you have somehow failed them."

"In the end, I cannot give them what they believe they are buying when they do business with me," he said.

"Ambrose, that's not true." She leaned forward and caught one of his hands between her own. "You do not understand what it is that you are in the business of selling. You are not providing your clients justice or vengeance."

"That is why they come to me."

"They may believe that, but justice and vengeance are commodities provided by the law, the police and the courts. Sometimes those institutions give good value. Sometimes they do not. Either way, it has nothing to do with your profession."

His hand tightened abruptly around one of hers. "If that is true, then it would seem that I have little to offer to my clients."

"You are wrong. You provide them with something that they cannot obtain anywhere else."

"What is that?"

"Answers." She realized that his grip had become very fierce. He was holding onto her hand as though she could pull him to safety. "You give your clients answers to some of the questions that keep them awake at night. It is a gift beyond measure. Knowing the truth may not bring justice or a sense of vengeance but it is vitally important to many people."

In the light of a passing lamp she saw that he was looking out the window into the night. His face was starkly etched and shadowed, just as it had been the first time she saw him in the stables at the castle.

After a while he turned back to her.

"I have never thought about my career in the way that you just described it," he said. "You make me see it in a different light. You make me see many things differently. How do you manage that, I wonder?"

"I expect it is the teacher in me. You, sir, are in the business of providing answers. I am not in that line, however."

"What is your line?"

"My task is to teach my students how to ask the right questions."

THE DOGS GREETED THEM joyously when Ambrose opened the garden door of the mansion. The first thing that struck Concordia was that the house was unexpectedly warm and well lit for that hour of the night. The fires should have been banked hours earlier, she thought.

"There you are." Mrs. Oates appeared from the kitchen, a tray of tea in her hands. "About time you two got home." Her eyes widened when she caught sight of Concordia. "What on earth happened to your clothes, Miss Glade?"

"It is a long and somewhat complicated story," Concordia said, patting Dante.

"Pardon my curiosity, but is that a *towel* you've got wrapped around your head?"

"I'm afraid so."

"Miss Glade suffered an unfortunate accident this evening," Ambrose said. "She needs a warm fire and a robe."

"Certainly, sir. The library is quite cozy. She can wait there until Mr. Oates gets the fire going upstairs in her bedroom." Mrs. Oates bustled off down the hall. "Come along. I was just taking some tea in to everyone."

"The girls are still awake?" Concordia asked. "But it is nearly three in the morning. They should have been in their beds hours ago."

"Everyone wanted to wait up for you."

Mrs. Oates went through the door of the library. Bright, cheerful laughter floated through the opening.

Ambrose ushered Concordia into the room. "Brace yourself. I have a feeling it is going to be some time before any of us goes to bed."

"I don't understand." Concordia went briskly into the library. "Why is everyone up and about at this hour? The girls need a proper night's rest. You know very well that I feel quite strongly about such matters."

She stopped short at the sight of Hannah, Phoebe, Edwina and Theodora. The four were seated around a table. Each held a hand of cards. There was a small stack of coins in front of every girl.

The four were not alone at the table. An elegant, silver-haired gentleman sat with them. He had a deck of cards in his long fingers.

"Good heavens," Concordia said in her most carrying voice. "Are you young ladies engaged in *gambling*?"

The giggling halted suddenly. The girls stared at Concordia in open-mouthed shock.

"Oh, no, Miss Glade," Phoebe said quickly. "We were just performing some extremely interesting experiments to test the laws of probability."

"How odd," Concordia said. "It looks exactly like a game of cards, complete with wagers."

"Miss Glade," Edwina burst out. "What happened to your clothes?"

Theodora stared. "He has ravished her again."

"Ruined," Hannah whispered. "Just like Lucinda Rosewood."

The lean, distinguished-looking man at the game table rose with a supple grace that belied his obvious years.

"Home from the ball at last, I see." He surveyed Concordia in her gentleman's topcoat and towel. Then he looked at Ambrose, who still wore his footman's shirt and trousers. "A costume affair, was it?"

"In a manner of speaking." Ambrose walked toward the brandy table with an air of determination. "Concordia, allow me to present John Stoner."

"Mr. Stoner." Concordia adjusted her spectacles. "So you are alive, after all, sir. I must say, this is a pleasant surprise."

Stoner laughed, a rich, hearty sound that warmed the library more effectively than the fire on the hearth.

"I trust you are not too disappointed." He bowed again, this time over Concordia's hand.

The glint in his eye made her smile.

"On the contrary," she murmured. "It is a relief to know that you are not buried in the garden."

"Not yet, at any rate," Stoner said cheerfully. "Come and sit by the fire. You look as if you could do with a glass of brandy."

She had been through too much tonight to waste her energy on what would no doubt be a thoroughly useless lecture concerning the evils of gambling, Concordia decided.

"What a splendid notion," she said.

38

Some time later Concordia sat in front of a cozy fire in her bedroom, bundled in a nightgown, robe and slippers. Hannah and Edwina were curled on the rug at her feet. Phoebe perched on a chair. Theodora drew a brush slowly and methodically through Concordia's hair, holding each long section out to be dried by the flames.

"Both Mr. Trimley and Mr. Larkin are dead?" Phoebe asked.

"Yes." Concordia had answered the question several times in the past twenty minutes. But she was patient in the face of the girls' need to be certain. "You are all safe. Neither of those two men can harm any of you."

Hannah wrapped her arms around her knees and gazed uneasily into the flames. "Now that there is no more danger, are you certain that you want to keep us with you, Miss Glade?"

Concordia did not hesitate. "Absolutely positive. We may not be a real family but we have been through a great deal together. What we have experienced has formed a connection among the five of us that is every bit as strong as the bond of blood that unites those who are related."

Theodora smiled wryly. "It certainly feels stronger than the bond Edwina and I share with Aunt Agnes and Uncle Roger. They could not wait to get rid of us after our parents died."

Phoebe pushed her spectacles more firmly onto her nose. "What of Mr. Wells?"

"What about him?" Concordia asked.

"He has been very nice to us but he may not want to take us on permanently."

Hannah nodded somberly. "That is true. Why would he want to keep the four of us around after the two of you are married?"

"That is quite enough of that sort of chatter," Concordia said coolly. "Let me make something clear. There has been no talk of marriage between Mr. Wells and myself."

The door opened quietly. Ambrose looked at the group gathered around the fire. "Did I hear my name mentioned?"

Hannah turned quickly toward him. "Miss Glade says that there has been no talk of marriage between the two of you."

The girls all looked at him for confirmation of that accusation.

Ambrose folded his arms and leaned against the door frame. "Now that is a bold-faced falsehood. I distinctly recall a conversation on the subject. It took place in a cab on our way to interview Mrs. Hoxton." He met Concordia's eyes. "Don't you recollect it, Miss Glade?"

"It was a rather murky discussion, as I recall," she said weakly.

"There you have it," Ambrose said to the girls. "Murky or otherwise, there has been a conversation."

"Thank goodness," Theodora said, looking greatly relieved.

"Excellent news," Phoebe declared happily.

"That settles it, then," Edwina said.

Hannah smiled. "For a while there, I confess I was concerned that there might be a problem in that direction."

"If you are all quite satisfied," Ambrose said, "I think it is past time that everyone went to bed. No need to rise early. Breakfast will be served late tomorrow. *Very* late."

He stood to one side to allow Phoebe, Hannah, Edwina and Theodora to file through the doorway. When their footsteps sounded on the stairs, he looked at Concordia.

"Are you all right?" he asked. He remained firmly lodged in the doorway, making no move to enter the bedroom.

"Yes," she said automatically. Then she wrinkled her nose. "No, actually, I'm not. I feel very much the same way I did the night we all escaped from the castle. Uneasy. Restless. I don't know how to explain it."

"Perfectly normal," he said. "I believe I explained that night that the sensations are a result of the danger and excitement you experienced. I am not immune to them, either."

"But you are obviously far more adept at dealing with such feelings."

His mouth curved faintly. "Merely a little more skilled at concealing them."

She looked at him. A tide of passion and a deep sensual hunger rose up inside, closing her throat so that she could not speak. She realized that she wanted him to kiss her more than she had ever wanted anything in her life.

Control yourself, she thought. You cannot throw yourself at him. Not

here in your bedroom, at any rate. The entire household would be aware
of what was happening.

She clutched her hands very tightly together in her lap. "Yes, well, I
expect we both need a good night's sleep."

"Very true." He moved out of the doorway and into the hall. "But,
like you, I do not think that I will be able to get much rest until my anxious sensibilities have been calmed."

"And just what do you intend to take to soothe your sensibilities, sir?
Another glass of brandy?"

"No," he said, looking thoughtful. "I believe I will take a stroll."

"You're going for a *walk*? At this hour?"

"I will not be going far. I thought I would take my relaxing stroll in
the conservatory. I find it a very soothing environment."

"I see."

He smiled slowly. "The conservatory is not only good for the nerves,
it is extremely private. If two people were to meet there by chance at this
hour of the night, for example, no one else in the household would be
aware of the encounter."

He walked off down the hall.

Concordia contemplated the open door of her bedroom.

Someone, Mrs. Oates, no doubt, turned down the lamps in the library and the halls. The faint patter of the girls' footsteps ceased on the
floor above.

The house gradually fell silent around her. She could not take her
eyes off the empty doorway.

39

He waited for her in the shadows of a cluster of palms, not knowing if she would come to him, uncertain what he would do if she did not appear.

The conservatory was pleasantly warm from the effects of the heating pipes that had been installed in the floor. Moonlight poured down through the glass panes of the high, curved ceiling and splashed on the leaves of the enclosed jungle. The scent of the rich earth and lush greenery filled his senses.

It took far more willpower than it should have to stand quietly in the darkness. There had been times in the past when he had wanted a woman after a night of violence. But until he met Concordia he had not *needed* one, not with this desperate longing, at any rate. He was Vanza— master of his passions.

But with Concordia everything was different. She threatened his self-mastery in ways that no one else ever had, and he did not give a damn.

The moonlight shifted subtly. The last of the house lights went out. A bleak, melancholy sense of loss ghosted through him.

She was not coming, after all.

What had he expected? She had been through a harrowing experience tonight. She was exhausted.

He heard the door of the greenhouse open.

The despair of a moment ago was instantly drowned beneath the rising tide of exultant anticipation.

He watched her come toward him, an ethereal figure in her pale dressing gown. When she moved through a swath of silver light, he saw that she had not put up her dark hair. It fell around her shoulders in lustrous waves, creating mysterious shadows that partially veiled her face.

He could have sworn in that moment that he was caught in a spell cast by a sorceress.

She moved cautiously down an aisle of thick greenery, pushing broad leaves aside with one hand.

"Ambrose?" she called softly.

It dawned on him that she could not see him. He broke through the shimmering trance she had created and walked out of the shadows of the palms.

"Over here," he said.

He went toward her with the same sense of certainty that he had felt all those years ago when he cast his lot with John Stoner and the way of Vanza.

When she saw him, she ran toward him without a word.

He opened his arms and caught her close, glorying in the soft warmth and weight of her body against his own. Her arms went around him. She clung to him as though she would never release him and raised her face for his kiss.

When their mouths came together, he knew that tonight her need was equal to his own. The realization that she wanted him with the same intense desire that he felt for her swept away the remnants of his self-control. There were things he had planned to say to her tonight if she came to him, but he could no longer think clearly enough to recall the words. Not that it mattered, he thought. Talking was no longer important.

He stripped the robe from her shoulders and dropped it on a bench. When he undid the fastenings of her nightgown, her small, elegantly curved breasts fit perfectly in his hands. He could feel the tight, hard buds of her nipples against his palms.

She tore at the fastenings of his shirt with trembling fingers. When she got the garment apart, she flattened her palms across his chest, covering the Vanza tattoo. The heat of her hands on his skin caused everything inside him to clench with need and desire.

Out of the corner of his eye he saw a folded tarp on a nearby table. He seized the sheet of canvas and flung it full length on top of a large patch of young, green ferns.

Concordia made no protest when he pulled her down onto the makeshift bed. She kissed his throat and sank her nails into his shoulders. He pushed the nightgown up around her waist and found the full, wet, voluptuous place between her legs. The scent of her created a fever in his brain.

She pushed herself against his hand, shivering and urgent. He had to concentrate hard in order to open his trousers. She encircled him with her fingers and drew the tip of her thumb across the head of his erection, exploring and testing.

The raging demands of his body overwhelmed him. He had to sink himself into her or he would not be able to breathe. Shaking with the effort required to control his entrance, he pushed into her tight, supple heat. She tensed, drew a deep breath and then raised her knees to take him deeper.

When her release came upon her, he stopped fighting his own. Together they plunged into the whirlpool of sensation.

His last coherent thought before he was lost in the waves of satisfaction was that, whether or not Concordia was right when she told him that he was in the business of finding answers, one thing was certain. She was the answer to the questions that had awakened him in the middle of the night for most of his life.

40

The household did not sit down to breakfast until eleven o'clock the next day.

"Mr. Oates says that someone must have left the door of the conservatory open last night," Mrs. Oates announced. She plunked a heavy pot of tea down on the breakfast table. "The dogs got in and trampled a bed of young ferns. Smashed the whole lot, he says."

Concordia's fork stilled in midair. Heat warmed her cheeks. She hoped she was not turning an unbecoming shade of pink. She looked down the length of the table at Ambrose, who was calmly eating eggs.

"It's the nature of dogs to dig in the earth if they get an opportunity," he observed with a philosophical air. "Phoebe, would you please pass the jam pot?"

"Yes, sir." Phoebe picked up the dish and handed it to him. "You must not blame Dante for the damage to the ferns, though. He was in the library with us all evening until you and Miss Glade returned. He spent the rest of the night in the bedroom that Hannah and I are using. Isn't that right, Hannah?"

Hannah looked up. Her face crunched into a perplexed expression, as though she had been distracted from other, more pressing thoughts. "Yes, he did."

"Must have been Beatrice," Mrs. Oates said.

"She was in the room with Theodora and me last night," Edwina said helpfully.

John Stoner used a small knife to spread butter on a slice of toast. "So much for blaming the dogs. I wonder what happened to those poor ferns?"

Concordia saw the amused gleam in his eye and knew that he had a very good notion of the dire fate that had overtaken the ferns. She beetled her brows at Ambrose in a warning frown but he paid no attention. It was clear that he did not appear overly concerned with the unfortunate direction of the conversation.

Anticipating a disaster, she pulled herself together and took over the task of changing the subject.

"A stray must have somehow got into the garden and found its way into the conservatory," she said crisply. "Now then, I think that is quite enough on that topic. Hannah, are you feeling ill? Did you have one of your bad dreams last night?"

"No, Miss Glade." Hannah straightened quickly in her chair. "I was just thinking about something else, that's all."

Concordia did not entirely trust that response but she let it go. The breakfast table was not the place to question the girl.

"Now that the danger is past, it is time that I take the girls out for some fresh air and exercise," she said. "They have been confined indoors far too long. The garden is very pleasant but it is not large enough to provide room for an invigorating walk."

Edwina brightened. "Can we go shopping, Miss Glade? That would provide excellent exercise."

"I want to go to the museum," Phoebe announced. "One can get a great deal of healthy exercise walking around a museum."

"I would rather go to an art exhibition," Theodora chimed in.

Hannah stirred her scrambled eggs with the tines of her fork, saying nothing.

Ambrose picked up his teacup. "I think the park is far enough for today." He looked at Concordia. "You will take the dogs, of course. They need the exercise."

It was an order, not a suggestion, Concordia realized with a start. A trickle of dread went through her. She wanted to ask him why he insisted that they have the protection of the dogs, but she dared not do so in front of the girls.

"May I wear my trousers for our walk, Miss Glade?" Phoebe asked eagerly.

"Only if you are willing to go to the trouble of putting up your hair under a cap and masquerading as a boy," Concordia said. "A girl dressed in boys' clothes would draw attention. We do not want to do that."

Phoebe beamed. "I don't mind, so long as I can wear my trousers outside."

"I am going to wear my new blue walking gown," Edwina announced with an air of anticipation.

"I must remember to take my sketchbook and a pencil," Theodora added. "It has been a long time since I have had an opportunity to do some landscape work."

Hannah set down her fork. "Would you mind very much if I went up to my bedroom? I do not feel like going for a walk."

Concordia frowned. "What is wrong, dear? Do you have the headache?"

"No. I'm just tired, that's all. I did not sleep well last night."

"ALLOW ME to congratulate you, Ambrose." Stoner settled his long frame into an armchair, put his fingertips together and regarded Ambrose with an expression of pleased satisfaction. "The young ladies informed me that you and Miss Glade are to be wed soon."

"The matter is not entirely settled." Ambrose walked to the far end of the library and stood looking out into the garden. "I am still waiting for Miss Glade to ask for my hand."

"I beg your pardon?"

"Miss Glade is an unconventional lady. She holds modern views on the relationship between the sexes."

Stoner cleared his throat. "I beg your pardon, but I understood from my conversation with the girls that there was a matter of ravishment involved." He paused a beat. "To say nothing of the unfortunate disaster that overtook the ferns late last night."

Ambrose turned abruptly and went toward the desk. "Miss Glade certainly has a lot to answer for in this affair. I can only hope that she will eventually come to feel the weight of her responsibilities in the matter and do the honorable thing."

Stoner raised his brows. "The weight of *her* responsibilities?"

"Precisely."

Stoner watched him steadily for a long moment. "Damn it to blazes, you're afraid to ask her, aren't you? You think she might turn you down."

Ambrose gripped the back of his chair very tightly. John Stoner knew him very well, he thought. "Let's just say that I do not want to make her feel that she must marry me for the sake of her own reputation."

"Ah, yes, I comprehend now." Stoner smiled and inclined his head. "You are employing the Strategy of Indirection."

"More like the Strategy of Desperation."

"But what if Miss Glade remains true to her unconventional modern principles and never asks you to marry her? Surely you do not intend to carry on a clandestine affair with a professional teacher? Not indefinitely at any rate."

"I will take Miss Glade any way I can get her. And that is enough on that topic." Ambrose removed a sheet of paper from the center drawer. "The subject of my forthcoming nuptials or lack thereof is not what I wished to discuss with you this morning. I would like your advice on another matter."

Stoner looked as if he wanted to argue the point, but in the end he merely shrugged. "Very well. How can I assist you?"

Ambrose studied the notes he had made on the paper. "There is something that feels . . ." He hesitated, searching for the right word. "Unfinished about this case."

"A question or two not yet answered?"

"Yes. And it may prove impossible to obtain answers because Larkin and Trimley are both dead. Nevertheless, I mean to try."

Stoner settled himself more comfortably in his chair. "What is it that still bothers you?"

Ambrose looked up from his notes. "The question I find myself asking over and over again is, what, exactly, did Larkin and Trimley plan to do with Hannah, Phoebe, Edwina and Theodora?"

Stoner's silver brows bunched together. "Thought you said they planned to auction off the girls as exclusive courtesans."

"That is the conclusion that Concordia and her predecessor, Miss Bartlett, came to, and there is a certain logic to it. But what disturbs me is that Larkin already had financial interests in several brothels, one or two of which catered to an exclusive clientele. As far as Felix can determine, he had not bothered to concern himself with the day-to-day operations of those businesses for the past several years. So long as they made money for him, he remained in the background. He considered himself an investor, not a pimp."

"Your point?"

Ambrose lounged back in his chair. "My point is that he appears to have taken an exceedingly personal interest in the scheme involving the four girls. I find myself wondering why he did so when, from all accounts, it was not his customary manner of dealing with his criminal affairs."

"Perhaps he considered the potential profits justified his personal involvement in the plan."

"Perhaps," Ambrose allowed. "But there are other aspects of the case that make me curious, as well. One of them is the rather high number of murders committed in the course of this affair. While it is true that Larkin was quite ruthless and certainly did not hesitate to get rid of anyone he believed was a threat to his empire, he did not climb to his position by leaving a lot of dead bodies around for people like Felix to find. At least not the bodies of people who were considered to be members of the more respectable classes."

"I see what you mean." Stoner looked very thoughtful now. "He would have been well aware that it would be quite simple to get away with the murder of a woman like Nellie Taylor. But he would have been considerably more reluctant to murder people such as Miss Bartlett, Mrs. Jervis and Cuthbert because their deaths might eventually attract the attention of Scotland Yard."

"Granted, he and Trimley do seem to have been on the verge of getting away with the murders. Nevertheless, the sheer number of them does not fit with what Felix has told me over the years concerning Larkin's usual methods."

"Perhaps the murders were the result of Trimley's influence." Stoner's mouth twisted in disgust. "He was new to the business of violent crime and may have enjoyed wielding that sort of power."

Ambrose sat forward again. "As it happens, Trimley's presence in the affair is the third question that remains unanswered. Why did Larkin take on a partner? It would seem to be the last thing he needed. He had everything a man of his nature could desire—a handsome fortune, a fine mansion, servants, elegant carriages, beautiful women. What more could he want?"

"There is an old Vanza saying. 'Greed is a ravenous beast that can never be satiated.'"

Ambrose drummed his fingers on the desktop. "And as my father and grandfather were fond of repeating, 'When you discover what a man desires most in the world, you can sell him anything.'"

"I thought it was Felix's opinion that Larkin acquired a gentleman partner because he wanted to extend the reach of his business enterprises into the upper classes."

"That has certainly been the working hypothesis to date," Ambrose said. "But I have some doubts. Larkin was not the type to trust anyone, let alone a gentleman who moved in much higher social circles. He would have formed a partnership with a man from that world only if he believed it would help him obtain something he wanted very badly, indeed. Money, alone, could not have been the goal. He knew how to get that on his own."

"What are you thinking?"

"I am thinking," Ambrose said, getting to his feet, "that Felix and I may have badly underestimated Larkin's ambitions. But there is someone who may be able to shed some light on the subject."

"Who?"

"Rowena Hoxton."

Stoner grimaced. "Good lord, not that silly, brainless social climber."

Ambrose was halfway to the door. "I see you are acquainted with her. Would you care to accompany me while I pay her a visit?"

41

The day was warm. A brisk breeze had dissipated the customary haze. The outing in the park would have been quite pleasant, Concordia thought, if only the girls had not taken the opportunity to press the subject of her relationship with Ambrose.

"When will you ask Mr. Wells to marry you?" Phoebe demanded on the way home to the mansion. She tugged at Dante's lead, urging him away from a tree that had caught his interest. "If I were you, I would not wait too long. Someone else might come along and sweep him off his feet."

"I'm not so sure about that," Concordia said. "As you and Hannah pointed out that first night at the inn, Mr. Wells is getting on in years. You will observe that no other woman has yet come along to whisk him off to the altar. Presumably there is no great threat from that quarter."

"You're teasing us, Miss Glade," Theodora said. "You know very well that Mr. Wells is just the right age for you."

"Do you think so?" she asked. "A younger man might be less set in his ways."

"But you are hardly likely to find a younger man," Edwina said. "Not at your age."

"Thank you for pointing that out, Edwina."

"Perhaps you should give Mr. Wells some flowers, Miss Glade," Theodora suggested. "That would be a very romantic gesture."

Edwina adjusted Beatrice's lead. "Women do not give gentlemen flowers."

"Not in the usual way of things," Theodora conceded. "But Mr. Wells is not like other gentlemen."

"No," Concordia said, going up the steps of the mansion. "He is not at all like other men."

He is the man I love. That makes him utterly unique in the entire world. And what in blazes am I going to do about that?

Mrs. Oates opened the door and gave the small group an approving smile. "I do believe that bit of exercise did you good. I expect you'll be wanting a nice cup of tea and some cakes."

"Thank you, Mrs. Oates." Concordia removed her gloves. "Has Hannah come downstairs?"

"She's still resting." Mrs. Oates closed the door behind the girls and the dogs.

"Is Mr. Stoner home?" Phoebe asked. "He promised to tell us about some of the antiquities that he collected in his travels."

"Mr. Stoner and Mr. Wells both went out right after you did," Mrs. Oates said. "They said they would be gone for some time. Something about tying up a few loose ends. Now, why don't you go into the library? I'll have Nan bring in a tray."

Concordia walked toward the stairs. "I'm going to check on Hannah first. It is not like her to take to her bed during the day. I'll join you in the library in a few minutes."

She hurried up the staircase, her sense of anxiety growing with each step. Hannah was an anxious girl but her health was generally excellent. Perhaps the strain of the last few days had proved too much for her nerves.

The door of Hannah's room was closed. Concordia knocked softly.

"Hannah? Are you all right, dear?"

There was no response. Deeply uneasy, Concordia turned the knob and opened the door.

Hannah was gone. A folded sheet of paper lay on top of the neatly made bed.

Dear Miss Glade:

Please do not worry about me. I will be home in time for tea. I know that you and Mr. Wells will not approve, but I have gone to the Winslow Charity School for Girls.

The students are allowed outside to take their exercise on the grounds for twenty minutes three times a week. Today is one of those days. There is a small opening in the wall that is concealed by a hedge. I hope to use it to catch the attention of my friend Joan. I must let her know that all is well with me. She will be very concerned.

Yrs. Vry. Truly,

Hannah

Concordia lowered the note and looked at Mrs. Oates, Phoebe, Edwina and Theodora, who had all come upstairs on Concordia's heels, and now stood crowding the doorway worriedly. "This is dreadful. She did not have any money. She must have walked. It will be a wonder if she has not gotten lost."

Phoebe bit her lip and exchanged a look with Edwina and Theodora before she turned back to Concordia.

"I think she may have had enough money for a cab, Miss Glade," she said.

"What do you mean?" Concordia asked.

"Last night Mr. Stoner showed us how to open some of the secret drawers in the old chest in the library," Edwina explained. "We found some bank notes and coins in one of them. Mr. Stoner said that we could keep them. We divided them up among us."

"That was the money that we used to place our wagers when Mr. Stoner demonstrated the theory of probability to us," Theodora said. "Hannah had just won a rather nice sum when you and Mr. Wells walked through the door."

Edwina looked stricken. "If Miss Pratt discovers Hannah trying to speak with Joan, she will put her into the cellar."

"I suppose the only thing we can do is wait and hope that Hannah returns quickly," Phoebe said, looking miserable.

Concordia rose. "I cannot leave this to chance. I am going to the school. When Mr. Wells and Mr. Stoner return, tell them what has happened."

T he shock of hearing of Mr. Trimley's death has, of course, completely shattered my nerves." Rowena Hoxton put a hand to her
ample bosom and gave Stoner a wan smile. "And now there is talk that
he may have consorted with a man who is rumored to have had criminal
connections. I simply cannot believe that I was so utterly deceived."

"I understand." Stoner accepted a cup and saucer from the maid.
"That is why I came at once this morning after I heard the gossip. I did
not want you to think that you had been abandoned by your acquaintances in Society merely because of your extremely unfortunate association with Edward Trimley."

Hoxton's eyes widened in horror. "But I knew nothing about his
connections to the criminal class."

"Of course you didn't." Stoner made a *tut-tutting* sound with his
tongue and teeth. "You know how it is in Polite Circles, however. Perception is all."

"Oh, dear." Mrs. Hoxton looked stricken. "Surely no one will believe that I was aware of Mr. Trimley's activities in the underworld?"

"I'm quite certain that the damage from this affair can be contained," Stoner assured her.

Ambrose stood quietly, his back to the window, and cloaked himself in the unobtrusive aura of the role he was playing, that of Stoner's assistant.

He could not help but admire Stoner's deft handling of Mrs. Hoxton. After all these years, he thought, he could still learn a thing or two from his mentor.

Mrs. Hoxton fixed her attention on Stoner. "What do you mean?"

Stoner winked knowingly. "As it happens, I am in a position to, shall we say, correct some false impressions that may or may not have been formed by certain members of Society."

Mrs. Hoxton went pale. "Oh, dear," she said again.

"Now then, if you will supply me with a few details concerning your association with Trimley, I will see to it that the proper version of events is put about in certain quarters."

"I am very grateful to you, sir. What do you wish me to tell you?"

Mrs. Hoxton's relief was pathetic to behold, Ambrose thought. The woman was absolutely terrified of the possibility of being embroiled in a scandal.

Stoner leaned back in his chair, hitched up his trousers and crossed his legs in an elegant fashion. "Did Trimley ever discuss two young ladies named Edwina and Theodora Cooper with you?"

"The Cooper twins?" Mrs. Hoxton frowned, baffled. "What do they have to do with this matter? I heard they both perished quite tragically several months ago."

"Indeed. Did you ever have a conversation about them with Trimley?"

"Well, yes, as it happens, I believe I did mention them to him." Mrs. Hoxton waved an impatient hand. "But only in the most casual manner."

"Can you recall why the subject arose?"

"I don't see what this has to do with nipping a scandal in the bud."

"Bear with me, Mrs. Hoxton," Stoner said. "I assure you that I know what I am doing."

"Yes, of course. Forgive me. It is just that I am so rattled this morning." She took a fortifying swallow of tea and put down her cup. "The subject of the Cooper twins came up in the course of a silly little game that Trimley wanted to play."

"What sort of game?"

"He challenged my detailed knowledge of persons who move in Society by asking me to name several young ladies of good families who rarely came to London. All of the girls had to fit a certain list of requirements that he set down."

Ambrose did not move. He knew that Stoner had gone equally still.

"What were the requirements?" Stoner asked.

"They had to reside in the country, have very little in the way of close family and they all had to be heiresses." Mrs. Hoxton snorted softly. "I must say, it was not much of a challenge for me. I came up with the Cooper twins and two other names almost immediately."

43

The Winslow Charity School for Girls appeared every bit as bleak and forbidding upon second viewing as it had the last time she had come here, Concordia thought, going up the front steps. The warmth of the afternoon did not appear to have made any impression upon the dark windows of the old mansion.

She had chosen the most severely tailored of the gowns that Ambrose had commissioned for her, a dark blue dress with a discreet bustle, high neck and long, tight sleeves. A pair of high-button boots, kid gloves and a straw hat trimmed with a single velvet bow completed the effect. There would be no weeping veil to conceal her face today.

She had given the question of how to approach the matter of re-covering Hannah a great deal of close consideration during the cab ride to the school. It did not seem likely that she could simply knock on the door and inquire as to whether or not Hannah was on the premises. Edith Pratt had, after all, been involved in an illegal scheme involving the girl. She was unlikely to admit that she now had her in the mansion.

If, indeed, Hannah was here and not already halfway back to John Stoner's mansion.

That was the most difficult aspect of this thing, Concordia concluded. She had no way of knowing if Hannah had been discovered or if she was safely on her way home.

She banged the knocker with great force three times.

The door was opened by the same faded-looking Miss Burke, who had ushered Concordia into Miss Pratt's office on the previous occasion.

No trace of recognition appeared in the woman's face. "May I help you?"

Concordia brandished the notebook she held in one hand. "Kindly inform Miss Pratt that Miss Shelton is here to see her. You may tell her that Mrs. Hoxton sent me."

The name of the school's benefactress had a very motivating effect upon Miss Burke.

"Please follow me, Miss Shelton. I will show you to Miss Pratt's office. She is discussing the week's menus with Cook at the moment. She feels there is far too much food going to waste and that the quantities of vegetables and meats that are ordered must be further reduced. But I will let her know that you are here. I'm sure she will be with you shortly."

Miss Burke led her quickly down the hall and opened a door.

"Thank you."

Concordia swept into the office. Miss Burke closed the door quite smartly and hurried away in search of her employer.

Concordia surveyed the room. Little had changed since her last visit. Edith Pratt's expensive-looking gray cloak hung from a hook near the door. The plaque with the list of Golden Rules for Grateful Girls was still positioned squarely behind the desk. Mrs. Hoxton and the Queen still gazed regally down from their framed photographs.

Concordia studied the desk and considered the wisdom of searching it again. Perhaps she would discover some reference to Hannah.

A muffled voice echoed in the distance from the far end of the hall.

"I've never heard of a Miss Shelton." Edith sounded thoroughly irritated. "Can't imagine why Mrs. Hoxton would send her here."

That settled the matter, Concordia thought. There would be no time to go through the desk drawers.

She composed herself for the part she intended to play and turned to face the door.

The cloak hanging next to the door caught her eye. It did not look quite right. There were large, dark patches around the hem.

Concordia moved closer and quickly shook out the heavy folds. There were more damp patches on the front. It appeared the headmistress had been caught in a spring shower.

But it had not rained recently.

Concordia's pulse, already beating uncomfortably fast, lurched into a pounding staccato. A shuddering thrill of comprehension seared her nerves.

A cloak might well have gotten soaked in such a manner if the person wearing it had been standing too close to a large pool of water when a body happened to topple into the depths. The resulting splash would have carried for some distance.

Calm yourself. Think carefully. Don't leap to conclusions.

There were many ways in which the cloak might have been accidentally dampened, she thought. She was tempted to speculate along the lines of a body falling into a deep pool merely because of recent experience.

Nevertheless, Edith Pratt had been connected to this affair from the beginning. The assumption was that she had been a minor actor in the deadly play, that her only role had been to conceal the girls on the grounds of the charity school.

But what if everyone had misjudged Pratt's part in the drama?

Concordia touched one of the darkened sections of the garment. The folds were most certainly damp, but not soaking wet. Once thoroughly saturated, a heavy woolen cloak such as this one would take a long time to dry completely indoors, she reflected.

"I shall have to make it clear to Mrs. Hoxton that I cannot be interrupted on a whim." Edith's voice was much closer now.

Miss Burke's mumbled response was too low for Concordia to make out the words.

She could scarcely breathe. She had to get Hannah out of this place. The dark cellar was the least of the possible terrors here. If Pratt was as deeply enmeshed in the affair as the wet cloak indicated, she might well murder the girl to conceal her secrets.

Dear God, what if the worst had already happened?

The door opened with some force. Edith strode into the room, her handsome face pinched with a mix of impatience and irritation.

"Miss Shelton? I am Miss Pratt. What is all this about having been sent by Mrs. Hoxton? I was not told to expect anyone."

"Of course you were not informed," Concordia said, instinctively sliding into her most authoritative tones. "I am the founder and director of the Society for the Protection of Female Orphans. It is our mission to make certain that young girls in orphanages and charity schools are properly cared for. Perhaps you have heard of my group?"

Edith stiffened. "No."

Concordia smiled thinly. "That is unfortunate. As it happens, Mrs. Hoxton has commissioned me to conduct a surprise inspection of this school."

Edith's jaw dropped. "What are you talking about? Mrs. Hoxton has never before seen fit to inspect the school."

"Your kindly benefactress recently read a piece in the papers regarding the deplorable conditions at a certain orphanage. It seems that young girls were being sold to brothel keepers. You may have noticed the report?"

"Yes, yes, I saw that scandalous tale in the sensation press. But I assure you, Winslow is a respectable institution that only accepts orphans from respectable backgrounds. Our girls become governesses and teachers, not prostitutes."

"I do not doubt you, Miss Pratt. Nevertheless, for the sake of her own peace of mind, Mrs. Hoxton has requested the inspection. She is quite anxious."

"Anxious about what?" Edith demanded, reddening with anger.

"She wishes to assure herself that no scandal could possibly develop here at the school. I'm certain you understand her position. Mrs. Hoxton moves in Society. A lurid sensation involving her charity would be extremely embarrassing."

Edith drew herself up and squared her shoulders. "I assure you that there is nothing going on here that need concern Mrs. Hoxton."

"Nevertheless, I have been given my instructions and I intend to carry them out. Mrs. Hoxton insisted that I inspect the school from top to bottom."

"But—"

"Top to bottom, Miss Pratt." Concordia took out a pencil and flipped open her notebook. "I was told that if you refuse to cooperate, a new headmistress will be found immediately."

Shock flashed across Edith's features. "That is outrageous. I have managed Winslow for well over a year. There has never been a hint of scandal."

"If you wish to continue in your post, I suggest you follow the orders of the school's benefactress." Concordia whisked past her into the hall. "Come along, Miss Pratt, the sooner we begin, the sooner we will be finished. I shall start with the cellar and the kitchens."

"Hold on here." Edith hurried after her. "If you will give me a few minutes to notify the staff and make arrangements, I'm certain this can all be handled in a convenient manner."

Concordia was already halfway down the hall. "Please summon all of the girls to the dining hall. I wish to ascertain that they appear well nourished and in good health. Call the staff together, too. I shall want to inspect them as well."

Edith came to a halt in the corridor behind her. "Miss Burke, summon the girls and the staff to the dining hall immediately."

"Yes, Miss Pratt." Miss Burke's footsteps retreated back toward the front hall of the mansion.

The unappetizing aroma of spoiled food, curdled milk and rancid cooking fat guided Concordia to the kitchen. She went through the entrance at a brisk pace . . .

. . . And very nearly fell flat on her elegant bustle when the heel of her shoe skidded across some of the old, greasy residue that had collected on the linoleum floor.

"Good heavens." She grabbed hold of the edge of the heavy planked table that dominated the center of the room to steady herself. "When was the last time this floor was properly washed down with soap and vinegar?"

Two women dressed in badly stained aprons and caps stared at her, openmouthed. One of them stirred the contents of a large iron pot. The smell was not what anyone would have called mouthwatering.

"Never mind." Concordia straightened and gave one of the two kitchen servants her full attention. "I am conducting an inspection on behalf of the benefactress of this institution. I intend to start with the cellar. Kindly point out the door."

"Uh, on the other side of the hearth, ma'am," the first woman said uncertainly.

"Thank you." Concordia hurried toward the narrow door.

"But it's locked, ma'am," the cook added.

Concordia's heart sank. "Where is the key?"

"Miss Pratt keeps it," the second cook offered hesitantly. "She don't abide anyone goin' down into the cellar without permission."

"Miss Shelton?" Edith's voice rang out loudly from the hallway. "Wait for me, if you please. I will guide you through the school."

"Watch yerself," the first cook said in low tones to her companion. "She's been in a foul temper all day."

Edith entered the kitchen. She stopped and glared at the cooks. "Go into the dining hall and wait with the others. Miss Shelton and I will be along shortly."

"But the soup will burn," the first cook protested.

"Never mind the soup."

"Yes, Miss Pratt."

The two women hurried out of the room.

"The key to the cellar, if you please, Miss Pratt," Concordia said in her most commanding voice.

"Yes, of course." Edith unhooked an iron key from the chatelaine that hung from her waist.

She tossed the key directly at Concordia, who managed to catch it somewhat awkwardly in her gloved hands.

"Go on." Edith made an urgent motion. "Open the door. I cannot imagine why you are so keen on inspecting the cellar, but that is your business. I trust you will find everything quite satisfactory."

Concordia turned cautiously toward the door and slid the key into the old lock.

"Be quick about it," Edith snapped, closing the distance between them. "We do not have all day."

Concordia had to use both hands to pull the heavy door toward her. As the opening widened, the light from the kitchen slanted down into the depths, illuminating a flight of narrow steps. The rest of the cellar was drenched in Stygian darkness.

She opened her mouth to call out to Hannah.

Running footsteps sounded behind her.

She looked back over her shoulder and saw that Edith was bearing down on her, teeth clenched, eyes fierce and wild.

Edith had seized a heavy iron frying pan from the long table. She clutched it in both hands as though it were a club.

The woman was intent on murder, Concordia realized. Edith was planning to crush her skull with the pan.

Concordia tried frantically and somewhat awkwardly to get out of the path of the lethal iron pan. Her shoes skidded on the slippery floor. She fell hard onto the linoleum.

The accident saved her life. Edith's savage blow missed her head by inches.

Edith staggered to an awkward halt, adjusted her aim and brought the pot downward in a crushing arc.

Knowing that her skirts would hamper her, Concordia did not even try to get to her feet. Instead, she lurched to her knees and crawled quickly under the planked table.

She made it just in time. The frying pan struck the table with such force that the pots and platters on top rattled and clanged. A couple of lids bounced off and fell to the floor.

Edith hissed in fury and frustration. She hurled the pan against the nearest wall.

Concordia scrambled out on the far side of the table, hoisted her skirts and managed to get to her feet.

"You've ruined everything." Edith's face was a mask of rage. "You're going to pay for what you've done."

She yanked a massive carving knife from the knife board.

Concordia stared at the blade, mesmerized with horror. She was trapped between the long table and the wall. Edith advanced on her.

"Not so bold now, are you, Concordia Glade?"

"You know who I am?" Concordia swiftly assessed the clutter of pots and skillets on the table. She grabbed the only object that looked as though it might function as a defense against the knife: the large, heavy lid of a roasting pan.

"Oh, yes, Concordia Glade. When Hannah showed up here earlier today she mentioned you." Edith's smile could have been carved in ice. "When I put her into the cellar she kept saying that you would come for her. I never doubted her for a moment. You found out how valuable she and the others are, didn't you?"

"You killed Alexander Larkin last night, didn't you?"

"I had to kill him. He betrayed me."

"How on earth did he do that?"

"I discovered that he intended to marry one of the girls." Anguish and rage twisted through the words. "After all I'd done for him, he was planning to take one of them as his wife. He didn't even care which of the girls he got so long as she was a respectable virgin with good social connections. He wanted the same sort of well-bred lady a *real* gentleman of means would take for a wife, you see. He didn't care that I loved him."

Concordia edged around the end of the table. For some reason she was suddenly aware of the unwholesome smell of the soup. It was starting to burn.

"Why would Larkin want to marry a penniless orphan, even if she was well bred?" she asked, desperate to stall Edith as long as possible. Surely someone would eventually return to the kitchen to see about the delay.

"But they're not penniless." Edith's voice was thick with disgust. "They're *heiresses.* All four of them. Worth a fortune each. It was my plan, right from the start, you know."

"*Your* plan?"

"We were going to auction them off to the highest bidders, you see. There's any number of fortune-hunting, social-climbing gentlemen who would jump at the chance to move up in Society. Nothing like marrying an heiress from a good family with a pristine reputation to help a man better his station in life, now is there? And the beauty of it was that they could pay for their wives out of the young ladies' inheritances."

Understanding jolted through Concordia. "I thought the girls were going to be sold off as courtesans."

"Bah. There's whores aplenty in the world. Respectable heiresses, on the other hand, are always in short supply. The plan was simple enough. The girls were made to disappear temporarily. They were presumed dead by their greedy relatives, who rushed to claim their money and properties."

"But after the auction each of the missing heiresses was to miraculously reappear, respectably married to a gentleman who would be in a position to claim the lady's inheritance."

"Precisely," Edith hissed.

"It sounds like something out of a sensation novel, one of those stories about secret marriages and missing heirs."

Edith snorted. "There certainly would have been a great sensation when the girls were found, safe and sound and respectably wed. But the press and the public would have loved it, and the girls' positions in Society would have been secure because they had not been ruined."

"That was why you went to all the trouble of creating a proper boarding school when you were forced to remove the girls from Winslow. You had to protect them from scandal at all costs."

"Ruined heiresses would have been valuable, of course, but not nearly as valuable as those who were still respectable."

"Did you kill Mrs. Jervis?" Concordia asked.

"That stupid woman and her friend Bartlett figured out that the girls were intended to turn a profit. The fools tried to blackmail Cuthbert. Alex had his men take care of both of them."

"But you needed someone to take Bartlett's place at the castle, didn't you?"

Edith's mouth twisted. "Alex insisted that the girls' reputations be protected at all costs. I thought it was because they would be worth more that way. But later I found out that it was because he wanted to be certain that *his* bride was unsullied."

"You went through Jervis's files and you found me."

"Jervis had made some notes about you. Did you know that she knew your great secret? Oh, yes. She was well aware that you were the daughter of the founders of the Crystal Springs Community."

"Jervis knew about my past?"

"She no doubt planned to use the information to blackmail you at some future date. But thanks to me she never got the opportunity."

"You used the information instead, though, didn't you? That was how the headmistress at my former school discovered my real identity. You informed her of my past and made certain that I lost my post. Then you sent me the offer of a position at the castle knowing I would be desperate."

"I made the mistake of assuming that because of your situation you would have the good sense not to give us any trouble. But it seems that I was wrong on that count. *Damn you.*"

Edith hurled the carving knife across the table. The distance was so short, she could not miss.

Instinctively Concordia flung up the hand in which she held the roasting pan lid.

The blade struck the iron lid with a bone-jarring clang and clattered to the floor.

Edith whirled and rushed back to the knife board.

Concordia clutched her skirts in one hand, hauling them up above her knees, dashed around the end of the table and ran toward the stove.

Dropping her skirts, she grabbed a thick dishtowel. She used it to protect her palms when she grasped the handles of the soup pot. It required all of her strength, more than she realized she possessed, to lift the heavy iron pot.

When she turned back she discovered that Edith was almost upon her, the point of a carving knife aimed at her heart.

She swung the pot off the stove, dashing the contents straight at Edith.

Too late, Pratt understood the danger.

"No . . ."

With a howling shriek, she dropped the knife and raised her arms in front of her face to protect herself from the cascade of scalding soup.

She managed to turn partially away before the steaming liquid struck, but she screamed when the soup splashed across her hands and arms and spattered her face.

She groaned and sank to her knees. Sobbing with pain and fury, she frantically used her skirts to wipe the soup off her hands and face.

Footsteps pounded in the hall. Concordia heard Ambrose's voice, hard with urgency and command.

"Where are they?" he demanded.

"In the kitchen," Miss Burke said. "But Miss Pratt gave very strict orders. No one is to disturb her conversation with Miss Shelton."

Ambrose slammed through the doorway into the kitchen. Stoner, Felix and a uniformed constable followed close behind.

"Mind the slippery floor," Concordia warned.

Everyone except Ambrose halted and looked at Pratt.

"Bloody hell," the constable muttered. "Will you look at the size of that knife."

Ambrose reached Concordia and pulled her into his arms. "Tell me you're all right."

"I'm unhurt. We must find Hannah."

Ambrose looked past her toward the entrance to the cellar. "I don't think that will be a problem."

She turned quickly and saw Hannah standing in the opening to the cellar. Her face and hands were smudged with coal dust and her new gown was filthy, but she appeared unharmed. She stared at Concordia with solemn eyes.

"Hannah." Concordia went to her and gathered her into her arms. "My dear girl, I was so worried about you. You must have been terrified."

Hannah hugged her tightly and started to cry.

"I knew you'd come, Miss Glade. That's what I kept telling myself all the time I was down there. And I was right."

The constable dug out a little notebook and pencil. He looked at Concordia and cleared his throat. "Who might you be, ma'am?"

Stoner watched Ambrose tuck Hannah under one arm and wrap Concordia close with the other.

"Allow me to introduce Miss Glade," he said. "She's the teacher."

44

They gathered together in the library later that evening. Ambrose poured brandy for Felix, Stoner and himself. Concordia accepted a glass of sherry. Hannah, Phoebe, Edwina and Theodora got tea. Dante and Beatrice settled down in their customary position in front of the hearth.

Ambrose took his glass and went to stand behind his desk. He took a healthy swallow of the brandy. He needed a restorative more than anyone else in the room, he thought. He had come so close to losing Concordia, he could not bear to contemplate it.

Felix looked at Concordia. "Pratt's plan was to bash you on the back of the head while you concentrated on getting the cellar door open, Miss Glade. You would have fallen down the steps and wound up dead from a tragic household accident. If necessary, Pratt would have followed and given you a few more blows to finish you off. She really did not anticipate any great difficulty in disposing of you."

"The school was her realm," Concordia said quietly. "She ruled it without question. The students and the staff were terrified of her. No one would have dared to suggest that my death had been anything other than an accident. In any event, there would have been no witnesses except Hannah because Pratt sent everyone else into the dining hall at the far end of the building."

"If you don't mind," Ambrose said, swirling the brandy in his glass, "I would prefer to change the subject from what might have been to what actually happened. I am still trying to recover from the shock of the day's events. Not all of us are endowed with a teacher's strong, resilient nerves, you know."

Stoner chuckled. "Quite true."

Felix smiled ruefully, sat back in his armchair and extended his legs. "Pratt's plan to get rid of you, Miss Glade, was, of necessity, concocted in an extremely hasty, last-minute manner. She knew that she could not allow you to discover Hannah in the cellar so she had to do something immediately. It was risky, but given her previous success with similar tactics on at least two prior occasions, she had no reason to think that they would not suffice a third time."

Phoebe looked up from her tea, eyes widening behind the lenses of her spectacles. "Miss Pratt killed *two* people?"

"My client's sister was the first victim," Ambrose said. "She was one of Larkin's—" He caught Stoner's warning frown and hastily altered what he had intended to say. "She was an attendant at the baths who happened to be a, uh, rather close friend of Alexander Larkin's."

"Is that why Miss Pratt killed her?" Hannah asked.

"Well . . ." Ambrose stopped again and looked at Concordia for direction. He was not certain how many of the sordid details of the case she wanted the girls to know.

Concordia took over. "After what these young ladies have been through, I think they can tolerate some straightforward talk." She turned to the girls. "Miss Pratt was in love with Alexander Larkin. They were in the habit of conducting their trysts in a secluded room in one of Larkin's many properties. But she began to suspect that he had plans of his own for the auction. Distraught, she went to the Doncaster Baths to confront him one night. That was when he informed her, quite carelessly, that he intended to marry one of you four."

The girls wrinkled their noses in disgust.

"He was so *old,*" Phoebe said.

"And he was a murderous criminal," Hannah added, shuddering. "None of us would have married him or any of those dreadful fortune hunters he intended to invite to his auction."

For a moment no one said a word. Ambrose looked at Felix and Stoner. He knew that they were thinking the same thing he was thinking. The girls would have been raped and ruined by the vile men who had purchased them. There would have been no choice left for any of them except marriage. Society would have accepted the husbands readily enough. Gentlemen fortune hunters were common in Polite Circles. Trimley was a case in point. The state of a man's finances was not nearly as important as whether or not he had been born into the proper social class.

"Quite right," Concordia said, smiling proudly. "I am sure that none of you would have allowed yourselves to be forced into marriage, regardless of the scandal or the threats involved. But Edith Pratt and Larkin and Trimley had no way of knowing that you are all such modern, free thinking young ladies."

Hannah, Phoebe, Edwina and Theodora glowed. Ambrose hid a smile. Concordia's influence on them grew stronger with each passing day.

"As I was saying," Concordia continued, "Edith Pratt was enamored of Alexander Larkin. So when he told her that he was going to marry one of the young ladies she had found for him, there was a terrible quarrel in the baths. Edith was in a great rage when she left the private room where she had met with him. She had only taken a few steps when Larkin put his head around the door and summoned Nellie Taylor for a private session."

"It was too much for Edith," Felix said. "Until that point she had been able to tell herself that Larkin considered her better than his bathhouse girls. But that night she realized that he had no more respect for her than he did for the Nellie Taylors of the world."

"Pratt hid in a private room and waited until Larkin had left and the baths had closed for the night," Ambrose added. "When Nellie began her nightly scrubbing tasks, Edith crept up behind her and struck her with the poker. It was a murder committed out of frustration and rage but it served another purpose. It made certain that Nellie could never tell anyone that she had seen Edith Pratt meeting with a suspected crime lord."

Concordia looked at Felix. "How did Larkin and Trimley come to form a partnership?"

"We can give Edith Pratt credit for that, too," he said. "Pratt and

Larkin had a long-standing connection. It was formed several years ago when she was in charge of another orphanage for girls. Larkin was still doing a lot of his own dirty work in those days. He approached her about the possibility of purchasing some of the orphans for his brothels. She agreed and both a business arrangement and a personal connection was formed between them."

Concordia shuddered. "Dreadful woman."

"Indeed." Felix glanced at the girls and shifted somewhat uncomfortably in his chair. "Pratt was well aware that Larkin was a womanizer, but she consoled herself with the knowledge that she occupied a special place in his affections. She was *respectable,* after all. It was true that she was impoverished and forced to make her living as a teacher, but she was, nevertheless, the daughter of country gentry. She knew that status mattered to Larkin. It convinced her that their association was based on more than mere passion and convenience."

"She also considered herself his business associate," Concordia said softly. "A partner of sorts."

"Yes." Ambrose went to stand at the window looking out into the garden. "Larkin never considered her to be anything other than useful, however. Nevertheless, he did her a few favors and she prospered. Eventually she decided to get out of the business of selling orphans to brothels. She believed it to be too risky. One major scandal in the press linking her name to such transactions and she would lose everything. In addition, she wanted to become the headmistress of a more respectable institution. Larkin helped her obtain the position at the Winslow Charity School for Girls."

"Miss Pratt immediately realized that the best way to turn a profit at the school was to find a generous benefactor or benefactress who would supply an unlimited amount of funds but who would not take an active role in the operation of the school," Concordia said. "She did some research and came up with Mrs. Hoxton's name."

Stoner nodded. "And with Mrs. Hoxton, she got the added bonus of the lady's new friend, Edward Trimley. Pratt took one look at him, recognized Trimley for the ruthless social parasite that he was and realized that he could be useful."

"That was when she began to put together the grand plan to acquire some young heiresses and auction them off to ambitious gentlemen eager to advance themselves in Society," Ambrose said. "She realized at once there was a fortune to be made. She presented the scheme to Larkin and he was delighted with it. To obtain Trimley's cooperation they all agreed to split the profits three ways."

"She understood Trimley very well," Felix said. "He was delighted to form an alliance with a genuine crime lord. I think he had visions of wielding great power. It is safe to say that he underestimated Pratt, however. He likely never saw her as anything other than Larkin's mistress."

Concordia sighed. "As for Edith Pratt, she did not understand until too late that Larkin planned to take advantage of her scheme to obtain a respectable heiress of his own. When she did discover what he intended to do, she felt utterly betrayed. After she murdered Nellie Taylor, she immediately began to plot Larkin's death."

"She arranged for the murder to take place the night of the Gresham ball," Ambrose said. "She sent word to Old Henry to open the baths as usual for one of Larkin's late-night meetings there. Then she sent urgent messages to Larkin and Trimley informing each that a critical problem had come up and that they had to meet immediately. She hoped Trimley would eventually be arrested for the murder."

"She confronted Larkin in the baths before Trimley arrived," Felix said. "When he realized that she had tricked him into the rendezvous, he was annoyed. She found it remarkably easy to kill him, however, because, in spite of his obsession with his own security, he never dreamed that she would turn on him. She struck him from behind with a poker. He fell into the water, unconscious and probably dying. He quickly drowned."

"Pratt then fled the premises," Ambrose said. "A short time later Trimley arrived. He found the body, panicked and tried to escape the baths through one of the rear doors. But he stumbled into the attendant and immediately realized the man was a threat because he could place him at the scene. He concluded that he had to kill him."

"But at that moment you arrived," Concordia said.

Ambrose nodded. "And shortly thereafter, so did you."

"Trimley never stood a chance against the pair of you," Stoner said with an air of satisfaction. He looked at Felix and the girls for confirmation. "They make an excellent team, don't they?"

"They do, indeed," Felix agreed with a suspiciously benign grin.

"That is very true," Edwina said, face glowing with enthusiasm.

Theodora nodded. "Perfect."

"It is quite amazing how well they seem to work together," Phoebe offered in a very emphatic manner. "It is a very *modern* sort of relationship, isn't it, Hannah?"

"Yes, but nevertheless a very *romantic* relationship," Hannah insisted.

"Pratt's scheme really was quite clever," Ambrose said before anyone else could comment on the subject of his relationship with Concordia. "Trimley mined Hoxton's detailed knowledge of Society to select the first batch of heiresses. They wanted girls descended of solid, respectable country gentry families that were not well known in fashionable circles."

"The ideal candidate was a young lady who was alone in the world and who, because of her status as an heiress, was inconvenient to someone," Felix added.

"In other words, if the young lady was removed, her money would go to another heir," Stoner said.

"Precisely." Felix drank some more brandy. "An heiress is always inconvenient to someone, of course. It is merely a question of identifying that person. Trimley was very good at doing just that. He located the one individual in each situation who might be willing to pay to have the heiress vanish, no questions asked."

"And then he made the girl disappear in some sort of tragic disaster that left no body for identification," Stoner said.

"But instead of murdering the girls in those so-called accidents, Trimley brought them to Winslow," Ambrose said. "The plan was to keep them there until the news of their deaths had faded and an auction could be arranged. But Phoebe's aunt started to make inquiries. Pratt became alarmed and decided that the girls had to be sent somewhere else. She could not afford to have them discovered at the school."

"Trimley and Larkin forced Cuthbert to make the arrangements to send the girls to the castle," Concordia said. "The girls' reputations were an important part of their value, however, and that meant that Edwina, Theodora, Hannah and Phoebe had to be properly chaperoned. Hence, the creation of the so-called academy for young ladies at the castle."

Ambrose looked at her, aware of the pride and admiration flooding through him.

"Miss Bartlett didn't work out for obvious reasons," he said. "So Pratt used the agency files to find a replacement. That was where she made her most serious mistake. When she hired you, she got someone who truly cared about her students. She got a real teacher."

45

That night Concordia waited in bed until the household fell silent. When she was certain that everyone was asleep, she pushed aside the bedding, rose and reached for her robe and slippers.

Enough was enough.

She found her eyeglasses and pushed them on her nose. Taking a deep breath, she lit a candle, opened the door and went out into the hall.

The door of Ambrose's bedroom was firmly closed. She knocked once, quite softly.

Ambrose opened the door immediately, as if he had been expecting her. He wore his black dressing gown. For some reason she noticed that his feet were bare. He had very nice toes, she thought.

"Have you come here to compromise me yet again?" he asked.

She raised her head quickly. The flame of the candle wavered. She realized that her fingers were trembling.

"No," she said.

"Pity."

Irritation steadied her nerves. "Ambrose, that is quite enough of your strange sense of humor. We must talk."

"About what?"

"Us."

"I see." He folded his arms and propped one shoulder against the door frame. "And just where did you intend to have this conversation?"

"The library?"

"I seem to recall that the last time we were together alone late at night in the library, I got ravished."

"Ambrose, I swear, if you do not cease teasing me—"

"And don't even think of suggesting the conservatory." He held up one hand. "It would be too cruel to let Dante and Beatrice take the blame for another floral disaster."

"That is quite enough." She straightened her shoulders. "Follow me, sir."

"Yes, Miss Glade." Obediently, he moved out into the hall and closed the door of the bedroom very quietly. "Where are we going?"

"A place that not even you will be able to view as a suitable location for a passionate tryst."

"I would not depend upon that if I were you."

Pretending that she had not heard the remark, she led the way downstairs and along the hall to Mrs. Oates's immaculate kitchen. Setting the candle down on one of the worktables, she faced Ambrose from the opposite side.

"Sir, I realize that you find the little jokes and quips about marriage amusing, but they must cease."

"I assure you, I am quite serious about the subject."

She squeezed her eyes shut to force back the threat of tears. When she had recovered her composure she looked at him very steadily.

"I am aware that your sense of honor has convinced you that you must give me the option of marriage. I appreciate it more than I can say. But it is unnecessary."

"Speak for yourself." He looked around the kitchen. "I wonder if there is any of the salmon pie left?"

She glared. "Try to pay attention here, Ambrose."

"Sorry." He sat down, folded his hands on the table and regarded her with the air of a well-behaved schoolboy. "What was it you were saying?"

"We both know that, in spite of your attempt to make light of the matter, your reputation is not in grave danger here. And neither is mine, for that matter."

"Huh." He rubbed his chin. "Are you quite certain of that?"

"Yes." She drew herself up and attempted a brave smile. "I can deal with any problems that might develop from this affair. Do not forget that I have spent many years concealing my past. I will be able to forge a new identity again. Sooner or later I will obtain another position in a girls' school."

"I see. You do not need me to protect your reputation, is that it?"

"My reputation is my responsibility, Ambrose, not yours. It is very kind of you to assume such a gallant attitude, but I assure you, it is not necessary."

"What about the girls? I got the impression that they rather enjoyed

living here. I know that Phoebe has written to her aunt and is quite looking forward to being reunited with her. But surely you do not intend to
send the others back to the very same relatives who were only too happy
to pay Trimley and Larkin to dispose of them."

"Of course not." She stiffened, shocked by the notion. "I gave the
girls my word that they would have a home with me as long as they
wished. I would not dream of going back on such a promise."

"No," he said. "You would never do that."

"They may be wealthy young ladies now, but they still need protection and stability until they are mature enough to go out into the world,"
she continued. "They must also learn to manage their inheritances and
to be cautious of men who might try to wed them for their money."

"I agree."

"But the girls are my responsibility, Ambrose, not yours," she said
earnestly. "Now that the danger is past, you must not feel that you have
any further obligations toward them. Or to me."

He got to his feet, leaned forward and planted both hands on the
table. "In other words, I am free to go back to the life that I have created
for myself. Is that what you are saying?"

"Well, yes. Yes, I suppose that is what I am trying to say."

"But what if that life no longer appeals to me?" he said.

"I beg your pardon?"

"What if I have discovered that I rather like having a partner again?"

"Ambrose—"

"Before you offer any more excuses for your failure to make an honest man of me, will you answer one question?"

She could hardly breathe. "What is that?"

"Do you love me, Concordia?"

The tears that she had been struggling to hold back leaked from the corners of her eyes. She removed her eyeglasses and dabbed furiously at the moisture with the sleeve of her robe.

"You must know that I do," she whispered.

"No, I did not know. I admit that I had hopes in that regard, but I could not be sure and the uncertainty has been damn near intolerable. Concordia, look at me."

She blinked hard to clear her eyes and replaced her glasses. "What is it?"

"I love you," he said.

"Oh, Ambrose." More tears welled up and spilled down her cheeks. "You must see that it is impossible."

"Why?"

She flung her arms wide. "You are a wealthy gentleman, one of the heirs to Stoner's estate. If you truly wish to marry, you can look much higher than an impoverished teacher with a disreputable past."

"How many times do I have to tell you I am no gentleman. I am merely a somewhat reformed thief who is still addicted to the dark thrill of crawling through other people's windows late at night, opening locked drawers and digging up secrets that are none of my business."

She frowned. "You know very well that is not an accurate description of yourself. You are a noble, dedicated knight who is committed to righting wrongs."

"No, my love, I'm a professional thief who is descended from a long line of rogues and scoundrels. You are the noble, dedicated person in this kitchen, not me. It is clear that I desperately need your strong moral guidance and influence if I am to resist the temptation to fall back into my old habits."

"Ambrose." She did not know whether to laugh or cry. "I do not know what to say."

"Ask me to marry you." He straightened and moved around the end of the table to take her into his arms. "That is the best way to ensure that I stay on the right path. It will also settle your account."

"I beg your pardon?"

"I take my fees in the form of favors, if you will recall. The favor I wish from you is an offer of marriage."

She put her hands on his shoulders. She could see the warmth and the promise in his eyes. Ambrose would not lie to her, she thought. She had trusted him with her life and the lives of her students. He had said that he loved her. She could trust him with her heart.

Something inside her that had been very cold and alone for a long time blossomed as though struck by sunlight. She had found someone to love. She would not reject this extraordinary gift.

"I love you with all my heart," she whispered. "Will you marry me, Ambrose?"

"Yes," he said against her mouth. "Yes, please. As soon as possible."

Joy sang through her. She wrapped her arms around his neck and returned his kiss with all of the passion and love she had been storing up for the right man.

He moved his mouth to her throat.

"You were wrong about one thing," he said.

"What was that?"

"My imagination is more wide-ranging than you think. I am, for example, quite capable of viewing this kitchen table as a suitable location for a passionate tryst."

"Ambrose."

"Not in front of the dogs, I trust," Stoner said from the doorway.

Dante and Beatrice bounded into the room.

"Or the young ladies," Stoner added.

Hannah, Phoebe, Edwina and Theodora arrived in the doorway behind Stoner.

"Did she ask him yet?" Hannah demanded.

Stoner smiled benevolently at Ambrose and Concordia. "Yes, I believe she did."

"What did Mr. Wells say?" Edwina asked eagerly.

From the circle of Ambrose's arms, Concordia looked at the enthusiastic crowd in the doorway. They were all linked together, she thought. She could feel the invisible bonds that connected her not only to Ambrose, but to John Stoner and the four girls. Felix Denver was a part of this circle, too.

She recognized this feeling. It had been a very long time since she had last experienced it, but some things one never forgot.

This was how it felt to have a family.

She smiled. "I am delighted to inform you that Mr. Wells said yes."

46

Annie Petrie made her way through the old cemetery shortly after midnight. Fog shrouded the headstones and monuments, much as it had the first time she met him here. She clutched the edges of her cloak with one hand and held the lantern aloft with the other.

"Are you here, sir?" she whispered into the shadows.

"Please turn the lantern down, Mrs. Petrie."

The voice came from the entrance of a nearby crypt. She swung around with a start and then hastily turned down the lantern.

"I got your message," she said. "And I saw the reports in the newspaper this morning. All about how that Edith Pratt killed Nellie. I don't know how to thank you, sir."

"You are satisfied with the results of my inquiries?" he asked.

"Yes, sir."

"Sometimes answers do not bring us the solace that we would wish."

"That's as may be," she said, surprising herself with the strength of her own voice. "But I can tell you for certain that my mind is more settled now that I know that the person who murdered my sister will pay for her crime."

"I am pleased to have been of service."

She hesitated. "About your fee, sir. I hope you haven't changed your mind about taking it out in trade? I have a little money, but not a great deal."

"I told you when you hired me that I might someday require a quantity of your wares. That day has arrived somewhat sooner than I anticipated."

"I beg your pardon, sir?"

"I wish to purchase thirty-eight parasols."

She was thunderstruck. "But whatever will you do with so many, sir?"

"I have a plan."

"Yes, sir." She reminded herself that the rumors concerning this man had always made it clear that he was an odd one. Sensible people, after all, did not engage in the sort of work that he did. "You can have as many parasols as you like. There's no need to pay for them. I will give them to you. After what you've done for me, it is the least I can do."

"We will consider one of the parasols as payment in full for my services," he said. "You will receive a fair price for the rest."

"If you insist, sir."

"I would like the one that will settle your account to have a very special design. Can you manage that?"

"Yes, sir. My assistant is very good at that sort of thing. What sort of design did you wish for the special parasol?"

"I will see to it that you receive a sketch."

"Very good, sir."

"Thank you, Mrs. Petrie."

There was an almost imperceptible movement in the deep shadows of the crypt. Had he just bowed to her as though she were a proper lady instead of a shopkeeper?

"Will that be all, sir?"

"Yes, Mrs. Petrie. I hope you will recommend my services to others who might be interested in hiring me."

He could not possibly be teasing her, she told herself. A man with his reputation was unlikely to possess a sense of humor.

"Good night, sir."

She hoisted the lantern and went quickly toward the cemetery gates.

She knew she would sleep a little more soundly tonight.

47

A hushed silence descended when Concordia walked into the dining hall. Thirty-seven anxious young girls rose respectfully. Thirty-seven pairs of eyes turned toward her. Miss Burke and the handful of other staff members who had been retained stood in a small cluster against the wall. They looked just as uncertain and as uneasy as the students. Hannah, Phoebe, Edwina and Theodora stood on the opposite side of the hall. Phoebe's aunt Winifred was with them, smiling happily.

Concordia went briskly down the aisle between the assembled students. She came to a halt at the front of the room and turned to face her audience. She saw Hannah's friend Joan sitting in the first row. She looked hopeful and expectant.

Ambrose watched from the doorway. Love and a fierce pride radiated from him in waves that she could feel across the distance that separated them. Felix stood next to him, lounging elegantly against the side of the door. John Stoner was directly behind the two men. His face was alight with satisfaction.

She turned her attention back to the girls in front of her and felt a glorious sense of exhilaration. No one looked into the future in the same way that a teacher did, she thought. That was because a teacher looked into the eyes of her students.

"You may be seated," she said.

There was a soft rustle of skirts and petticoats as the students dutifully took their seats.

"Good morning," she said. "My name is Miss Glade. I am the new headmistress of your school. I am to be married soon, and then you will call me Mrs. Wells. But that will not change my position here at Winslow."

A soft, audible intake of breath rippled across the room. Several of the girls exchanged baffled glances. Ladies never worked outside the home after they were married.

"As you will soon discover, I have some very modern, some would say unconventional, theories concerning the education of young women," Concordia continued. "There will be a number of changes taking place here at Winslow. Among other things there will be a new cook and a new menu. There will also be new uniforms and more fires lit on cold days. The sheets will be changed more frequently. In addition, this school will accept girls who are alone in the world from all walks of life, whether or not their backgrounds are deemed respectable."

A murmur swept through the room.

"I shall be your primary instructor, but I will have the assistance of four former students who have decided to train to become teachers. Their names are Edwina and Theodora Cooper, Hannah Radburn and Phoebe Leyland."

At the back of the room the four beamed.

"We shall also enjoy the attention of a new benefactor," Concordia continued. "His name is Mr. Stoner. In addition to providing for the financial needs of the school, he will immediately begin instructing a new class in which you will all be taught an ancient philosophy and a series of physical and meditative exercises. You will be the first females ever to be trained in the arts of Vanza."

Curiosity sparked in the faces of the girls.

"My goal," Concordia continued, "is to provide you with an education and the accomplishments that will allow each of you to make choices regarding your own futures after you leave Winslow. The world is changing with great speed. The young ladies who graduate from Winslow will be prepared to take advantage of those changes. Indeed, I have every expectation that some of you will *lead* them."

The students were staring at her, openmouthed and wide-eyed now.

She smiled. "We have a lot of adventures in front of us. But at this moment the sun is shining and for once the air is clean outside. I understand that most of you have not been allowed beyond the boundaries of the grounds of this school since the day you arrived. I am a strong believer in the importance of daily exercise. I intend that we shall institute the habit immediately. Please follow me."

She swept back down the aisle between the rows of chairs. There was a short, startled silence followed by a great deal of scurrying behind her.

The girls jumped to their feet and hurried in her wake.

She paused briefly at the door and turned back to face them again. "One more thing. In the front hall there are a number of pretty new parasols. You will each take one. They are yours to keep."

Ambrose winked at her as she led the excited students toward the door. She smiled at him with all the love that was in her heart.

Stoner and Felix handed out the parasols in the front hall. Then Ambrose opened the door with a gallant air.

"Where are we going, Miss Glade?"

Concordia looked down at a small, freckle-faced girl. She could not have been more than eight years old and already there was an adult's wariness and hesitation in her eyes.

But beneath the caution and anxiety there was also the glimmer of a child's hope and resilience.

"What is your name?" Concordia asked gently.

"Jennifer, ma'am."

"There is a fair in the park today, Jennifer," Concordia said. "I thought it would be instructive to attend. Fairs are very educational events."

Jennifer and the other girls stared in stunned delight.

"We're going to a fair," someone whispered.

Ambrose winked at Concordia. "I shall look forward to hearing about your day when you return home this evening, Miss Glade. Have fun with your new students."

"I will," she promised.

She stepped out onto the steps and unfurled the beautiful green parasol that he had given her. The flower of Vanza worked into the design in gold thread caught the light and glowed as bright as the day.

"Follow me, ladies," she said to the girls hovering in the front hall.

She led her students outside into the sunshine and into the future.